The

Redemption

Also by this author

The Lancefield Mysteries

Salvation Hall

Hemlock Row

The Rose Bennett Mysteries

Dead on Account

Dead Ringer

Death Duties

Death Benefit

Dead & Buried

The Redemption

A Lancefield Mystery

MARIAH KINGDOM

~ Perceda Press ~

This novel is entirely a work of fiction. Any resemblance to actual persons, living or dead, or to events, locations or premises is purely coincidental. Salvation Hall, the Lancefield family, the Woodlands Plantation and the village of Penwithen do not and have not ever existed, except in the author's imagination.

First published in digital form 2022 by WL Fowler

Copyright © Mariah Kingdom 2022

This paperback edition Perceda Press 2023

Mariah Kingdom asserts the moral right to be identified as the author of this work.

A catalogue record for this publication is
available from the British Library

All rights reserved. No part of this publication may be reproduced, stored in a retrieval system or transmitted in any form or by any means, electronic, mechanical, photocopying, recording or otherwise, without the written permission of the author and/or publisher.

ISBN 978-1-8380834-6-5

Cover design by www.ebooklaunch.com

'I have not come here to be insulted by a set of wretches, every brick in whose infernal town was cemented with an African's blood'

George Frederick Cooke, tragedian, 1756-1812

1

Liverpool Lime Street.

He'd arrived at the station far too early, an uncharacteristic display of punctuality that he could only ascribe to anxiety. Now, standing on the concourse, an inanimate obstacle for the noisy throng of impatient early-morning commuters weaving their way to work, he was beginning to question why he was there at all.

He cast reluctant eyes up to the departure board and squinted at the illuminated times and destinations, and then nodded to himself. Fate was reluctant to intervene. There was to be no shortage of rolling stock this morning, no signal failure on the line, no possibility that the driver had overslept and failed to arrive on time. It wouldn't matter how many times he looked at the board, the train for Bristol Temple Meads would still be departing from platform eight at 7.47 am.

He licked his lips and closed his eyes for a moment, thinking. It was still only 7.18 and there was almost another half an hour to kill. Twenty-nine minutes of thinking time, every one of them an opportunity to change his mind and walk away; to catch the 7.57 back to Huyton and forget all about it.

He put a hand up to his chest and patted at the outside of his navy woollen overcoat. The letters were still there. He could feel the gentle crackle of paper as two monogrammed envelopes concealed within the inner pocket of his coat pressed against each other under the gentle pressure of his fingers. The letters weren't going anywhere and neither was he, however difficult the task which lay ahead. He'd made a commitment to travel to

Bristol, and he wasn't going to back out now. There had been enough secrets in the past. Enough secrets and enough lies to bury them. There was only one way to deal with those letters and that was to bring out the truth.

He drew in a deep, deliberate breath, sucking in unwelcome smoky fumes of dirt and diesel, and blew them out again through chilled, thinned lips. He was resigned to going through with the task, but he needed to clear his head before he boarded the train. He needed to get cold, fresh, sustaining Liverpool air into his lungs before making the journey.

He turned up the collar of his coat and thrust his hands deep into its outer pockets, and then strode purposefully towards the station exit to his left. Outside in Lord Nelson Street, the air was freezing and he shivered involuntarily against the cold. He turned his head and looked up the hill to his right, where a line of taxis waited patiently for the chance of an early-morning fare, and then turned again to look down to his left. At the foot of the street, the dual carriageway was busy with fast-flowing traffic, and behind the moving stream of vehicles St George's Hall loomed silently in the half-light.

A walk around the block would only take a matter of minutes. One circuit, he thought – one quick turn down the hill, around the corner, along the front of the station and back in through the main entrance. Coupled with the purchase of a morning paper, a takeaway coffee and a sandwich for the journey it would keep him busy, keep his mind occupied and distract him from the possibility that – even now – he might be making an irrevocable mistake.

He took a hand out of a pocket and used it to tug on his scarf, pulling the soft grey lambswool up to cover his chin and his mouth, and then began to make his way carefully down the slippery street towards the main road. The pavement was icy, treacherous under foot, and he picked his way carefully with a cautious step. A taxi slithered down the hill beside him as he walked, and turned left at the bottom to join the stream of flowing traffic. Somewhere behind him, he could hear the engine of another, drawing parallel as they reached the corner of the street in tandem. He paused as the taxi made its turn, a little too close to the kerb, and then turned on his heel slowly, to continue his walk.

He didn't hear what came behind him as he turned, didn't see *who* came behind him, and the push – when it came – was so unexpected that it didn't really register. He heard a sickening screech of brakes and felt an exquisite rush of pain as his cheek scraped across the tarmac of the road. And if he heard the dull thud and crunch as the wheels of the bus rolled over his body he was already too shocked, too traumatised, too close to death to realise that the bones he could hear disintegrating were his own.

*

'So, Dennis Speed is my seventh cousin, once removed?' David Lancefield frowned, an uncertain fold of his gentle face. 'And we share a common ancestor on my father's side?' He spoke with deliberation, as if learning a speech, worried perhaps that he may soon be called upon to explain the relationship, and fearing that he would be found wanting.

Kathryn Clifton smiled at him across the table. 'That's right. Your common ancestors are Thomas Lancefield and Lysbeth Quintard, of St Felix. You are descended from their eldest son Benedict, and Dennis is descended from their younger son Richard. Both sons were born in St Felix and sent back to England to be educated, but in later years Benedict divided his time between Salvation Hall and the Woodlands Estate, while Richard moved his family to Liverpool.'

'And there was a rift. Something happened to drive a wedge between the two brothers?'

'Not quite. Benedict and Richard remained friends. I

think the problem was with Richard's son.' Kathryn studied David's face and saw eager anticipation. 'Of course, I haven't fully examined all of the relevant documents yet.' She managed the small lie skilfully. 'But I have certainly seen a letter from Richard to his brother Benedict, advising that his son had made an unsuitable marriage against his family's wishes.'

'Well, good for him.' David looked pleased by the notion. 'You know, of course, that my father has never approved of my marriage to Stella. But I wouldn't let that stop me.' He leaned forward towards Kathryn. 'Do we know what the problem was?'

'I'm still trying to put the full picture together from letters between the brothers.' A bigger lie this time. Kathryn was still trying to come to terms with the story herself.

She turned her face away for a moment, to gaze out through the train's window at the passing winter scenery. Barely two weeks had passed since David's father, the latest in a long and distinguished line of Richard Lancefields, had reached out to a distant cousin in Liverpool in the hope of healing the long-standing family rift. It was a desperate sort of act, to reach out so candidly to a complete stranger, but Richard wouldn't be dissuaded. Not that Kathryn considered it any of her business what the Lancefield family chose to do or not do with their distant, just-discovered cousin. Her remit had been to establish whether such a cousin existed, not to stand in judgement of the outcome.

She turned back to look at David. He was staring down at the simple family tree she had drawn for him, his grey eyes narrowed, sad anxiety drawing down the corners of his mouth. The last of the Lancefield line, he was already struggling with the weight of a bequest that he would rather not receive. The Lancefield fortunes, and the legacy of dark heritage that surrounded them, would be a bitter-sweet inheritance for any beneficiary. They were the reason that David had lived most of his life at odds with his father. Now, in his middle years and without any immediate family to carry the burden with him, there was no doubt that he would benefit from the support of an extra relative or two.

But was Dennis Speed the answer?

She felt a sudden pang of sympathy and put out a reassuring hand, resting it gently on David's arm. 'You do still want to go through with the meeting? Because if you don't, it's not too late to back out. I'm sure that your father will understand if you want to let it go.'

The corners of David's mouth twitched and his lips rearranged themselves into a smile. 'Kathryn, you always seem to find the right thing to say.' He spoke quietly, his voice barely audible against the rattle of the train. 'I know that my father doesn't want me to carry the estates alone. And I know that he's gone to a great deal of trouble to find Dennis Speed. But you are right to think that I'm nervous. You only have to look at the relationship between myself and my father to see that sharing a blood line is no guarantee that two individuals will share the same values. I'm not worried about meeting Dennis, I'm only concerned that we will have nothing in common – that our views of the world may be too far apart to find any common ground.' David raised an eyebrow. 'And is it not possible that Dennis himself might be of the same opinion?'

'Why would you think that?'

'You saw the letter that my father sent to him. Dennis was invited to Salvation Hall to meet with us, and he was asked to extend the invitation to his cousin Barbara and his son Jason. They were all invited to be our guests. But Dennis insisted on meeting us in Bristol, and on coming alone.'

'Do you think he might be ashamed of his family in some way?'

'Good heavens, no.' David banished the suggestion

with a smile. 'I think it's more likely to be the other way around. I can't help wondering whether he already knows of the Lancefield family and is ashamed of the connection. What if he's aware of how our family made its fortune and wants nothing to do with us? Perhaps he is coming to tell us to stay away.'

'And what if he had never heard of the Lancefield family until he received your father's letter and is simply coming as an envoy, to build an early bridge between the two families? It must have come as a shock to discover that he had distant family who were looking for him. Perhaps he just wants to take things one step at a time and move at his own pace. He might even think that the letter was some sort of hoax.' Kathryn took back her hand and settled deeper into her seat. 'I don't think he could be blamed for adopting a little caution before accepting an unexpected invitation from a very distant cousin. Wouldn't you have done the same if the invitation had been extended to you?'

David closed his eyes and gave a gentle shake of the head. 'If I were Dennis Speed, Kathryn, and the invitation had been extended to me, I would have taken steps of my own to make enquiries into the Lancefield family. And had I done so, everything I turned up would have led me to tear that letter into pieces and throw it on the fire without another thought.'

*

Richard Lancefield lowered his gaunt frame awkwardly into the chair with a wry smile. The chair, a long-abandoned affair of solid mahogany, had lain unused in the attic for so many years that he had almost forgotten its existence. His father had called it "the captain's chair", so when Kathryn's latest line of research into the Lancefield family's heritage had turned up a ship-owning Lancefield, its restoration became a temptation that Richard could not resist.

Now, in the library at Salvation Hall, he found himself wondering why such a beautiful piece of craftsmanship had been consigned to the attic in the first place. The lustrous, dark-green leather that swathed both the seat and the low, curved backrest had required nothing more than a generous application of saddle soap, and the delicately carved spindles which ran between the two had revealed barely a scratch. Even the brass castors, dulled by a century or more of neglect, had responded magnificently to a couple of hours of diligent polishing. Richard ran a gnarled finger along the armrest to his left and purred with satisfaction. The restoration had been a success. The chair suited him well. And he felt – he hoped – that Kathryn herself, the most regular user of the library these days, had been pleased with the result.

And God knows, he thought, Kathryn Clifton deserved to be pleased. It was a lucky wind that had blown her in the Lancefields' direction; a quiet introduction by his old friend Hugh Ferguson that he didn't think could ever be satisfactorily repaid. She had arrived at Salvation Hall with a simple mission in mind – in return for a fee and unlimited access to the family's private papers, she had agreed to curate several centuries-worth of diaries, letters, accounts and photographs. The items would be indexed and documented, a family tree constructed, and the family's achievements would be written up and preserved for posterity.

If only it had been so simple.

Richard drew in a breath and banished an unwanted memory. When unexpected tragedy had visited the Lancefield family, and the rules of the game had changed, Kathryn might so easily have moved on. But when his desire to document the family's history was supplanted by the need to track down any distant part of the family who might still be alive, when he found himself not in need of a genealogist or archivist, but of a friend and ally, she had proven to be both. She had stood with him. And he knew that such people were rare.

Such people were to be treasured.

He let out a sigh and gently rolled the captain's chair forward until it was close to the desk. The leather covering which protected the top had been cleared of Kathryn's working papers, but a small collection of framed photographs – a reminder, she said, of why her work for the Lancefield family was so important – hung on the wall above it.

He scanned the pictures with rheumy eyes: an image of himself as a young man on the sun-drenched island of St Felix; one of his son David and granddaughter Lucy relaxing on a family holiday in the Mediterranean; yet another of Lucy, taken in the drawing room at Salvation Hall, her arms wrapped tightly around her fiancé, Marcus Drake; and a small but striking portrait of Richard's secretary, Nancy Woodlands, her youthful energy bursting forth from the picture in the carefree tilt of her head and the spirit in her eyes.

The old man's sigh deepened. It was lonely in the house without them. Not just David and Kathryn – their absence was only for the day. But Nancy, Lucy and Marcus… all had lived with him at Salvation Hall and he had become accustomed to the sounds of young people filling the house. Now Nancy was in St Felix, visiting her family, and Marcus was up in Edinburgh, safe in the care of his mother. And Lucy…

Lucy was gone.

He muttered to himself under his breath. 'Come along now, Richard. Buck up.' He tapped on the desk with an impatient finger, suddenly irked by his own mawkishness, and lifted a hand to pull a small gold watch from the pocket of his woollen waistcoat. 'Not long now until David and Kathryn will arrive in Bristol.' His plan to extend the Lancefield family was well under way, under Kathryn's watchful eye. Now was the time to turn his attention to more pressing matters.

He pushed the watch back into his pocket and glanced down at the desk. A large manila envelope franked with the name Mayhew and Mayhew was lying unopened in front of him. It hadn't taken long for his solicitors to churn out a new draft of his will. He chuckled softly to himself. Perhaps old Mayhew knew that time was running out.

He picked up the envelope and slid a fingertip along under the flap, and then pulled out the contents. His eyes ran slowly over the covering letter and then he set it aside with a nod, before examining each page of the accompanying document in turn.

The future of the Lancefield family's Cornish estates, his plans for the Woodlands Plantation, the care of Salvation Hall and the covenants to ensure that his wishes would be carried out – all of the salient points appeared to be documented firmly in place. He ran a finger down the list of personal bequests and turned the page to examine Mayhew's interpretation of his wishes should any beneficiary fail to comply with the conditions attached to their inheritance. Everything appeared to be in order.

There was one more page to inspect and he hesitated before turning the paper to read it. Hugh Ferguson, he knew, could be counted upon, as could Douglas and Robert, Hugh's sons. But his fourth choice of executor, the one that he needed the most?

What if the answer was *no*?

2

'An accident?' Jason Speed uttered the words in a slow, hoarse whisper and he coughed to clear his throat. 'Near Lime Street station?' He sank slowly onto the small hessian-covered sofa beside the wall and cast bewildered eyes up towards the police officer. 'What was he doing near the station?'

Detective Constable Kate Jenkins inhaled a silent breath to steady her voice. 'We believe your father was planning to travel to Bristol. There were train tickets in his wallet – an outward journey on the seven forty-eight this morning to Bristol Temple Meads and a return ticket for the four o'clock train back to Liverpool.' She turned her eyes from Jason to the blonde girl standing beside the sofa. There were questions to be asked, and experience had taught her that sometimes it was best to direct those questions away from the immediate next of kin. 'You didn't know that Dennis was planning to make the journey?'

'No.' The young woman's voice was hollow, her face blank, the shock of unexpected death still taking its time to fully register. 'We thought he was driving to Salford today, to spend the day with a friend.' She flicked her eyes down to look at her partner and her face crumpled. 'Jason, I'm so sorry.' She swallowed down a sob. 'I'm so very sorry.' She lowered herself onto the sofa beside him and took his hand in her own.

Kate watched them for a moment, sizing up the depth of their closeness with a practised eye. 'We're still trying to build a picture of exactly what happened. But we think that Dennis slipped and fell into the road. It was very icy outside the station. The pavements were slippery and we think he may have lost his balance.' She knew the explanation sounded lame, but for the time being it was all she could offer them. 'There wasn't anything the bus driver could have done to avoid him.' She turned her head to the left and exchanged a meaningful glance with a colleague, a sandy-haired young constable with an ill-fitting uniform and worried eyes. 'Danny, I think we could all do with a cup of tea. If you wouldn't mind?'

Danny looked only too happy to oblige. As he closed the door of the small kitchen behind him, Kate turned back to Jason Speed. His broad forehead was creased beneath a bristle of cropped auburn hair, his eyes tightly closed under pale, translucent brows, the freckled cheeks below them drawn and bloodless behind a mask of rough-shaven stubble. 'As I say, we are assuming that it was an accident, but we do have to investigate the circumstances of your father's death to be sure. Can I ask when you last spoke to him?'

'Yesterday evening.' Jason's voice was barely audible. 'We work together as painters and decorators.' He opened his eyes and nodded vaguely through the living room window, in the direction of a blue transit van parked on the driveway beside the house. 'We finished a big job yesterday, over in Huyton. A hall, stairs and landing.' He blinked and then looked up at the police officer through pale lashes. 'How did you know where to find me?'

'His driving licence was in his pocket so we began with his home address. We thought we might find a next of kin there, but there was no one in. A neighbour told us where to find you.' DC Jenkins paused, and then asked, 'When did he tell you he was going to Salford?'

'Last week. He said he was going to take a day off to visit a mate, Lenny Dawson. Lenny lost his wife this time last year. Dad said he was going to spend the day with him. He said Lenny needed cheering up.' Jason turned to the young woman beside him. 'Why would he lie about that?'

Emma squeezed his hand. 'He must have had a good reason. Dennis wouldn't have lied to you unless he thought it was necessary.' She turned mournful eyes towards Jenkins. 'Dennis was old-school. He wouldn't take a day off work, or lie to Jason like that, unless he had a good reason.'

'I'm sure you're right.' The policewoman kept her eyes on Jason's face. 'We found some letters in your father's pocket, Jason. They suggest that he was going to Bristol to meet someone called David Lancefield. Does that name mean anything to you?'

Jason's colourless brows beetled forward and he shook his head. 'Lancefield? No, I've never heard of any Lancefields.' His eyes took on a wary look. 'What were the letters about?'

Jenkins reached into the inside pocket of her coat and pulled out two slim envelopes. She held them out towards him and watched his frown deepen as he took them. 'They're quite self-explanatory. I can't see that they have any bearing on his accident, but they might help you to understand why he was going to Bristol.'

'Are you saying that Dennis had some reason to lie to Jason about going to Bristol?' Emma's cheeks were pink now, the pale wash of grief suddenly obliterated by an indignant flush.

Jenkins smiled. 'That's not for me to say, Emma. I'm just asking if Jason knew about the Lancefields or the letters, and it would appear that he didn't.' Her voice was still kind. 'I think I should let you know that we have contacted David Lancefield to let him know about your father's accident so that he knew not to hang around in Bristol.' She hesitated, momentarily unsure of her ground, and then said, 'The letters mention you, Jason, and someone called Barbara. Can I ask who Barbara is?'

'She's Dennis's cousin, on his mother's side. They are – I mean, they were – very close.' Emma's face contorted again and she turned towards Jason. 'Oh, Jase, I can't bear it. How on earth are we going to tell your Auntie Barb about Dennis? She'll be heartbroken.'

A disaffected scowl settled unexpectedly across Jason's brow. 'Why would she be heartbroken, Em? Because he's died?' He dismissed the suggestion with a sullen shake of the head. 'Or because it turns out that he's been keeping something from us?'

*

Barbara Gee pulled the thick cable-knit cardigan a little tighter around her shoulders and huddled into it with a shiver. It was warm in the Picton Reading Room, but her journey into Liverpool earlier that morning had left her chilled to the bone.

She had been suitably dressed against the icy blast that had blown unforgivingly across the station platform at Newton-le-Willows as she waited for the train, and the heat from a takeaway cappuccino had warmed her hands on the short, uneventful journey into town. But the sight of a police cordon at the front of Lime Street station, the mutterings amongst her fellow travellers of an accidental fatality, the unexpected clots of blood congealing slowly on the road… no amount of warm clothing could insulate against the kind of disquieting inner chill that an unforeseen tragedy could induce.

Now, in the warmth of the reading room, she was unable to shake off the thought that some poor fellow creature had lost their life that fateful November morning. Some traveller on their way to a new day, their future unexpectedly sacrificed by a wrong step or a misjudged dash in front of the busy morning traffic. A family soon to learn that a loved one wouldn't be coming home.

She lifted her head and glanced at the studious souls around her. At the desk to her left a tired-looking girl with sallow skin and untidy hair was clicking furiously into the keyboard of a neat, silver laptop. To her right, an elderly man in a moth-eaten jumper was poring over a large, dog-eared book, his sunken eyes close to the print, his thin lips pursed in dogged concentration. Life goes on, she thought. At least for some.

The thought produced a second involuntary shiver and she pulled her attention back to the hand-drawn family tree laid out on the table in front of her. *Barbara Gee* – she mouthed her own name silently as she placed a plump, beringed finger on a box drawn at the bottom of the paper – *only daughter of teachers George Gee and Annie Cook*. She traced up the line with the finger. George was the elder son of tobacconist William Gee and his wife Felicity Marsh. William was the eldest child of shopkeeper Robert Gee and his first wife, Alice Watkins, and grandson to his namesake William Watkins, a merchant seaman, and his wife Sarah.

Sarah, the daughter of one Alice Banks and her husband, Thomas Moses Lancefield, who married in 1830, the details of their marriage confirmed in Liverpool's parish records.

Barbara tapped the paper gently where Thomas's name was neatly written in a hand-drawn box, and then lifted the corner of the document and pulled out another sheet of paper from beneath; a copy of Alice and Thomas's marriage entry showing the names and occupations of their fathers. Alice was the daughter of a master mariner and Thomas's father was listed as a ship owner and merchant. It was possible, Barbara supposed, that Digory Banks had some maritime connection with the ship-owning Richard Lancefield. But it wasn't the link between the fathers that Barbara had come to investigate today – it was Thomas Moses Lancefield.

She put the marriage entry to one side and picked up her pen from the desk. For a moment the pen hovered tentatively over the paper. And then she lowered her hand and in small, neat letters added the words "West Africa Squadron" next to Thomas Moses Lancefield's name.

The simple act brought a smile to her lips. She had been proud to discover her ancestor's distinguished naval record and she was looking forward to the act of digging deeper, of delving into her family's history in search of something more exotic than primary school blackboards and corner shop tobacconists. Genealogy had proven to be an enjoyable pastime since taking early retirement. It was a pity that Dennis and Jason didn't share in her enthusiasm.

The thought of Dennis made her shiver again, a subconscious and unexpected tremor of unease, and she glanced again at her watch. He would be close to Temple Meads by now and he'd promised to let her know when he arrived. Whatever the outcome of his journey today, she couldn't help thinking that a little more interest in his family's history might have been of use.

She dropped her pen back onto the desk and reached down under her chair to fish in her handbag. Her mobile phone vibrated between her fingers as she pulled it out of the bag, the familiar intermittent buzz that signalled an unopened text in the inbox. The train must have arrived a little early. She nodded to herself with satisfaction as she flicked at the screen with her thumb, and then squinted at the display through her reading glasses. It took a moment for the contents of the screen to register – seven missed calls from Emma and just one unopened text.

Barbara's mouth felt suddenly dry and she swiped again at the screen, her fingers shaking now. The text was from Emma too.

Please call me as soon as you get this, Barb. Something terrible has happened. We need you to come home.

A swell of panic rose in the pit of Barbara Gee's stomach and an unstifled sob made its way up to her lips, fracturing the reading room's fragile silence. Somewhere behind her a woman coughed and clicked her teeth at the disturbance. But Barbara paid no heed. She was already on her feet and making her way to the door, her documents and notebooks and Thomas Moses Lancefield now forgotten and abandoned behind her.

*

'Are we cursed, Kathryn?' David stirred absently at the coffee in front of him with a plastic teaspoon, folding scattered grains of golden sugar into the froth. 'We didn't even get to meet Dennis Speed, and he was gone. What on earth does it mean?'

If only she had the answer. 'It was an accident.' Kathryn watched as her companion sipped carefully on the drink, his lips pursed to the cup to catch the waves of coffee as they flowed and eddied in sympathy with the gentle motion of the train. 'No one could have foreseen this.'

'Yes, but he was on his way to meet with us, wasn't he? To meet with *me*. If we hadn't arranged to meet with him in Bristol, he would have been safe at home in Liverpool.' They had barely arrived in Bristol when the call from DC Jenkins had come through to David's mobile phone. It was hard to believe that a cruel twist of fate could send them both ricocheting back to Cornwall on the next available train.

Kathryn leaned across the table towards him and rested her chin on an upturned hand. 'There's nothing to stop you from extending your respects to the family, is there? To Jason and Barbara. There's no need to intrude upon their grief, but I'm sure a message of sympathy at the appropriate time would be appreciated.'

'Would it? Has it occurred to you that they might not even know who I am? That Dennis might not have told them that he was coming to meet us?'

'But didn't the police officer say that Dennis was carrying your father's letters in his pocket? That was how she knew to contact you. At some point, she will return those letters to the family.' If she hadn't done so already.

'You are right, of course. We're probably yesterday's

secret.' David scratched thoughtfully at his ear. 'Do you think we should call my father to tell him or keep it to ourselves until we return to Salvation Hall? He will take this very badly, I'm sure.'

'I think he should be told in person when you get back to Penwithen. If nothing else, it will give you time to come to terms with the situation yourself before you have to discuss it with him. It has come as a bit of a shock, hasn't it?'

'I'm afraid it has.' The hint of a blush suffused David's cheek. 'I'd be grateful if you would come with me to break the news. You seem to be able to handle my father better than anyone else I know.'

It was a valiant attempt at persuasion and Kathryn tried — and failed — to suppress a smile. 'I can't help thinking that you all expect too much of me, David. I only came to Penwithen to document the family's history.'

'Ah, but we had no idea when my father engaged you just how far your talents would spread.' David's mood was beginning to lift. He placed the mobile phone gently down on the table. 'I don't know what we would have done without you. I really don't.'

If pushed on the point Kathryn would have to admit that she didn't know either. It was barely six weeks since she had arrived at Salvation Hall to curate the Lancefield family's history. Just six short weeks since she had found herself drawn irresistibly into the enigmatic family's fold. Enchanted by their history, witness to their losses and even frustrated by the dysfunction of their relationships, she knew that in that short span of time she had grown from a stranger into a trusted family friend. It wasn't a path that she had expected to walk, and yet it was a path that almost seemed to be made for her.

Unless it was just a convenient way of blotting out her own discomfiting past.

She brushed the thought aside. 'I'm sure you would have managed just fine without me, David.' She lifted her head from her hand and settled back into her seat. 'We have another few hours to travel yet. Would it help to pass the time if we spoke a little more about the Liverpool branch of the family?' There was a soft leather briefcase on the seat beside her and she reached into it to pull out a thin sheaf of handwritten documents. 'In the event that Jason and Barbara do wish to forge a connection with yourself and Richard, it might be useful to know a little more about their family, and how they came to be so deeply embedded in Liverpool.'

'That sounds to me like an excellent idea. I would be delighted to hear more about it.' A wry smile tugged at David's lips. 'Especially if it has anything at all to do with the rift within the family.'

3

Emma leaned against the door frame and wrapped her long, thin arms around her body. In the small, neat kitchen behind her, a kettle rumbled to boiling point and switched itself off with a click that she barely registered. Putting the kettle on again after DC Jenkins and her colleague had departed was nothing more than a reflex action, something resembling normality for Emma to hold on to, but it wasn't going to help Jason. Jason didn't want more tea.

Jason wanted answers.

He was sitting just a few feet away from her, at the square oak table to the rear of their lounge, Dennis's wallet, the train tickets to Bristol, and the Lancefield letters spread out in front of him. He looked numb, the only sign of emotion showing in the angry red blotches that mottled his cheeks and streaked across the pale flesh of his throat. She'd seen those blotches so many times in the two years that they had lived together. They were the telltale sign of a temper under tight control, of seething emotions suppressed but not yet quite successfully buried. She'd often wondered whether those feelings would ever make their way to the surface. And sometimes hoped that she wouldn't be there to witness it if they did.

Jason was deep.

Her sister Jayne had said that he was moody and that she'd be better off with someone who was calmer to live with and easier to read. But Dennis, himself so placid and so easy-going in his ways, always said that it wasn't really Jason's fault. That he'd been a happy sort of child until the untimely loss of his mother had robbed him of his confidence in the world.

And now he'd lost his father too. And that wasn't Jason's fault either.

Emma stepped forward from the doorway and sat down at the table. 'So what do the letters say?' She was almost afraid to ask.

'This one' – he tapped a stubby finger on the paper without looking at her – 'is from a solicitor's firm called Mayhew and Mayhew in Penzance. They say that they're acting on behalf of a client, Richard Lancefield, who they believe to be a distant relative of ours. They say they've enclosed a letter from their client and that any response should be sent directly to them, to be forwarded to him.' Jason slid the paper to one side to reveal another beneath. 'This is the letter from Richard Lancefield.' He pushed it across the table towards her. 'Here, read it for yourself. I can't read it aloud.'

Emma took the letter from him and looked down at the strong, scrawling script that filled the page. 'So these Lancefields are distantly related to you, many generations back? An old man and his son? And they don't have any other family.' She lowered her head a little closer to the page and swept her eyes quickly over the words. 'He's invited you all to… does that say "Salvation Hall"?' She glanced up at Jason. 'What's that?'

'I suppose it's where they live.'

'But I don't understand why Dennis didn't tell you.'

'No?' Jason's lips twisted inwards. 'Maybe he was ashamed of me.'

'Your father was never ashamed of you.' She put out a hand in reassurance and rested it gently on his arm. 'He didn't tell Barbara either, did he? Do you think he was ashamed of her too?' Emma gave the arm a squeeze. 'He loved you both, Jason. There has to be a reasonable explanation.' If only she could think of one. 'Perhaps he was looking out for you. Maybe he didn't trust these Lancefields and wanted to meet them on his own, to make sure that everything was okay.'

'Why wouldn't they be trustworthy? They sound wealthy.'

'Wealthy?' Emma winced. 'What's that go to do with anything?'

'Well, think about it. We're just tradesmen, aren't we? Painters and decorators. Maybe he thought we weren't good enough.' Jason turned to look at her through bitter eyes. 'How could our family be related to people like this?' He flicked at the letter with his fingers. 'Look at the fancy, embossed writing paper. And who can afford to pay a solicitor just to write a few letters and act as a go-between?'

'Of course Dennis didn't think you weren't good enough.' It could only be the grief talking. 'Look, why don't you put the letters away until your Auntie Barb gets here? Let her read them. She might be able to work out what the Lancefields wanted.'

'I know what they wanted. They wanted family. They're dying out. There's only the old man and his son left. There are no heirs to the family. It's the end of the line. It says so in the letter.' He nodded towards it. 'But my dad kept it to himself.' Jason's mouth twisted, a contortion of pain. 'He was my dad, Emma, and he didn't tell me about this. He didn't tell me that we were related to these people, or that he was going to meet them. I just feel like I didn't know him at all.'

'Is there anything in the letters that might explain why he was going to Bristol? If the Lancefields invited you all to their home in Cornwall, why didn't he just visit them there?'

'I'm not really sure. But there's something in this one.' Jason slid a third letter towards her. 'It's from the solicitor and it says something about David Lancefield agreeing to meet up in Bristol, *as requested*. As if it was my dad who asked for the meeting to be held there.' He looked up from the table now, and into her face. 'They were meeting for lunch at the Regency Hotel, wherever that is. David

Lancefield's mobile number is on the letter.' Jason drew in an angry breath and hissed out his frustration. 'So why the hell did he tell me he was going to Salford to spend the day with Lenny?'

Emma had no answer to the question, but it did give her an idea. 'Why don't you just call Lenny and ask him? If Dennis said he was going to Salford today, then maybe Lenny knows what was really going on.' It was the flimsiest of possibilities and she didn't hold out much hope. But it might be enough to keep Jason's mind occupied, at least until Barbara arrived to take control of the situation.

*

'It doesn't take a detective constable to investigate a road traffic accident.' Detective Chief Inspector Andy Drummond turned a cynical eye towards Kate Jenkins, but there was a hint of amusement in his voice. 'The guy slipped on the pavement. Or else he lost his footing. Or he wasn't concentrating. The bus was too close to the kerb to miss him when he stumbled. The driver was pulling in towards the stop outside the station.' The greying eyebrow above the cynical eye arched into an inquisitive curve. 'What's to investigate?'

Kate rested a curvaceous hip on the edge of his desk and folded her arms across her chest. 'His son didn't know that he was going to Bristol. There were letters in his pocket from someone claiming to be a distant relative. The son didn't know anything about that either.'

Drummond arched the other eyebrow. 'I'm still not hearing why it needs a detective.'

'Dennis Speed and his son worked together as painters and decorators. They're close. They live in each other's pockets, together at work day in and day out. They would have been working together today but he told his son that he was taking the day off to spend time in Salford with a mate. So why lie about it?' She leaned in a little towards the senior officer. 'It's not the accident that I'm bothered about, sir. It's what might happen next.' She lowered her voice. 'The son was angry. Angry that he hadn't been told about this distant family or the meeting. The first of those letters landed almost two weeks ago and Dennis Speed had kept it to himself.'

Drummond's eyebrows returned to base and he lowered his voice to a teasing whisper. 'And that's a minor domestic. You know that we don't have time to get involved with minor domestics. Let the family sort it out for themselves.'

Kate narrowed her eyes and pouted. 'When I came here to work with you, you told me that intuition was a precious thing.'

He leaned forward to meet her gaze. 'And so it is when it's applied to something that deserves your time and attention. I've had four cases land on my desk already this morning. Two assaults in the city centre, a break-in at a car dealership on the Manchester Road, and a suspicious death at the docks.' He tapped a finger on a page of scribbled notes on the desk. 'Take your pick. In fact, take two if you've got so much time to spare.' He settled back in his seat. 'How the hell did you get drawn into this Speed business anyway?'

The constable shrugged. 'My sister had a meeting in Manchester this morning, so I gave her a lift to Lime Street on my way in to work. The accident had just happened and there was a patrol car there, so I stopped by to see if there was anything I could do to help. One of the lads asked me to witness him going through the deceased's pockets.' She sniffed. 'They were looking for ID so they could contact his family, and the letters were in his coat pocket.' She thought for a moment and then pointed to the computer on the desk. 'I know that this isn't a case in our workload, but I think you should take a look at the family that Dennis Speed was going to meet. I think you should try putting their name into a search engine, and see what comes up.'

'Hell's teeth.' Drummond stared at her for a moment. 'Is that what it's going to take to get you off my desk and back to work?' He swivelled gently in his chair to face the computer screen and then clicked on the keyboard to bring up a search engine. 'Go on, then. What's the name?'

'Put in "Lancefield", "Salvation Hall" and "Cornish Enquirer".'

He turned his head slowly and sent a quizzical gaze in Kate's direction. 'I thought you said that Dennis Speed was going to Bristol?'

'He was, but the family live in Cornwall. The Enquirer is a local paper, sir, a rag. I couldn't find anything in the mainstream press.' Her cheeks warmed under his gaze. It was a look she had seen before. 'I promise you, you'll understand when you read about it.'

He turned back to the screen and muttered under his breath as he punched the words into the keyboard with reluctant fingers. It took a moment for him to scan through the matches that filled the screen, and when he turned to look at her again it was with a more enquiring eye. 'Did you give the letters back to the family?'

'Yes, but I took copies first. They're on my desk if you want to see them.'

'Who's taking this forward?'

'I was going to volunteer myself, sir. As you say, it might not be anything important. But I thought I'd pop back this afternoon to give them an update. Jason Speed was too shocked this morning to take in much of what I was saying to him. And we still need someone to identify his father's body, and instructions for where to take it after the post-mortem.'

'And what about the Lancefields? Has anyone told them why Dennis Speed didn't turn up to meet them?'

'Yes, sir. I called David Lancefield to let him know what had happened. I didn't make any other enquiries at this stage.'

Drummond surrendered with a sigh. 'Okay, here's the deal. You pick up the break-in at the car dealership, that's your official focus for the day. But keep an eye on Jason Speed until he's given us a formal identification and we have a post-mortem report. And let me take a look at the letters. It's probably nothing to worry about but I have a contact in Penzance. I'll give him a call and see if he has anything to say about these Lancefields. If there's anything to worry about, he'll give us a steer.'

Kate Jenkins slid quietly off Drummond's desk with a nod and a solemn smile, and tried not to look too pleased with herself as she made her way back to her own distant corner of the open-plan office. It was good to know, she thought, that Andy Drummond could still be a pushover when the occasion called for it. For one nerve-wracking moment then, she'd thought she was losing her touch.

*

Richard placed the small spray of hot-house orchids gently down on top of the grave. In weather like this, he knew, the blooms would barely last a few brief hours before surrendering to the cold and damp. But it was the thought that mattered – for the tribute to be appropriate and for his friend to know that he hadn't been forgotten.

The old man straightened his back and bowed his head, and leaned heavily on his stick. It was six weeks now since Philip McKeith had been taken, and still he was missed beyond measure. Six weeks since they had laid the young man to rest here under the horse chestnut in this most sheltered corner of the churchyard. There would be no more talk now of orchid growing, no more prizes to be won together at the village show, no more coffees shared in the potting shed as Philip worked and Richard talked. Salvation Hall hadn't just lost a gardener. Richard Lancefield had lost a kindred spirit.

He turned his rheumy eyes towards the church, to the spot beside the porch where Lucy rested in a plot beside her mother. At least she was sheltered from the unforgiving winds that often blew across the village. What a damned mess the whole affair had been. It should never have got out of hand. He should have put a stop to it, he could see that now. If he'd thought for one moment that Philip and Lucy's flirtations, their assignations, would lead to this, to both of them lying cold and buried in the shadow of St Felicity's…

His frail body shook with a tremor of remorse. He'd known about their passions and he'd turned a blind eye. He'd believed those passions to be nothing more than a harmless distraction, perhaps even something of a rite of passage, but he'd been wrong.

He'd been wrong and the damage was done. Lucy dead by Philip's hand and Philip murdered by her fiancé Marcus in revenge. Or perhaps in anger. Or even in despair. And therein, Richard knew, lay the biggest mistake of all.

He had completely underestimated Marcus Drake.

Richard still wasn't sure that he believed the young man's story. As Marcus had told the tale, he had stumbled across a murder scene in the garden – Lucy lying prone and lifeless beside the ornamental lake and Philip leaning over her as if responsible for the death. Marcus claimed that he had lashed out in anger at the man he believed had murdered the girl he was going to marry. But the thought was more than Richard Lancefield could bear. Philip was too gentle a soul to take a life – any life – and he would never have taken Lucy's.

Still, this was the only story they had, and they might never know the truth. In fact in some respects, Richard mused, it would probably be better if they didn't. He cast his eyes back down to Philip's grave. 'I am so very sorry, old chap.' He muttered the words under his breath. 'You'll never know how sorry, that it had to be like this.'

He hesitated for a moment and then turned on his heel,

picking his way carefully between the gravestones to where Lucy lay cold beneath a marble slab. Samson, his ever-faithful terrier, had reached the spot before him and was sitting patiently next to the headstone, his wiry head tilted as if trying to hear Lucy's voice. Richard drove his stick into the soft, yielding ground beside the grave and leaned down to rub at the dog's neck with a bony finger. 'She's gone, old boy. But we can still come and see her when we like. We can still talk to her, even if she can't answer us.' He straightened his back and leaned heavily on the stick.

'Well, Lucy, I heard from Marcus today.' He addressed the words to the marble slab. 'He misses you but, otherwise, he seems to be bearing up, all things considered. And his legal team are hopeful that the case against him will go as well as we could hope for. That's the good news, my pet. I'm afraid the not-so-good news is that I can't give you an update on our attempts to find some family for your father. No news yet from Bristol. But my hopes are high.' If only that were true. 'Your father and I are getting on quite well these days. We're still not quite on the same page when it comes to the estate, but I think we're at least reading from the same chapter now. And we have Kathryn to thank for that. Kathryn and Nancy.' The thought brought a smile to his face. 'Nancy sends her love. She sent me a splendid letter from St Felix at the end of last week, full of all the goings on.'

He straightened his back and shivered against the insidious cold of the churchyard. 'Well, my dear, I think we'll have to be heading off for home now. I'm running out of things to say and my old bones are feeling the chill. But we'll come and see you again tomorrow, you and Philip.' He pulled up his stick and turned to click his teeth at Samson. 'Come on then, dog, we'd better make for home.'

He took a step back from the grave and cast his eyes once more to the pristine marble slab. 'I hope you know that you're missed, my pet. I didn't bring you flowers today, I'm waiting until some of these have gone over.' He lifted his stick and gently nudged at a bouquet of fading lilies. 'The ones I brought you on Sunday are beginning to show their age, but the ones from your father are still almost as good as new.' Beside the lilies, a swathe of orange roses glowed almost luminously against the blue-black hue of Lucy's headstone. And beside the roses…

'Now where on earth have these come from?' For the first time, Richard noticed that beside the orange roses, someone had placed a modest bunch of dusky pink chrysanthemums. He peered down at the flowers through wary eyes and then stretched down a hand to tug at a small white card that was tucked between the stems. He lifted the card to his eyes and stared at it for a moment, and then bit angrily on his lip.

Dear God, was this nightmare *never* going to end?

4

Barbara followed Emma down the short, narrow hallway from the front door to the lounge, slipping off her coat as she went. She dropped the coat onto the back of an armchair and then turned to take a long appraising look at Jason's girlfriend. Emma's blonde hair was untidy, the normally-sleek tresses lying coarse and wispy around a face that was unusually pale and drawn. 'Sweetheart, you look exhausted.'

Emma offered the older woman a desperate smile and then her face contorted as the morning's grief finally burst through its weakening banks. 'Oh, Barb, I don't know what to do. Jase has taken Dennis's death really badly. Like he's shutting down. And I don't know how to help him.'

Barbara stepped forward and enveloped the girl in a hug. 'Let it out, honey'. She closed her eyes and rested her head against Emma's, squeezing the girl a little tighter. 'Let it out, and then you can tell me all about it.' She waited for Emma's sobs to subside and then gently released her grip. 'Where is he now?'

'He's upstairs, resting.' Emma pulled a tissue from the pocket of her dress and dabbed at her eyes. 'He got really angry after the police had been here. It took me ages to calm him down.'

Barbara stroked the girl's cheek with warm, plump fingers. 'It's the shock, honey.' At least she hoped it was the shock. 'What was he angry about?'

'Dennis told us that he was going to Salford today, but he was on his way to Bristol. That's what he was doing at the station.'

'Bristol? But I thought he was going to visit Lenny

today. Weren't they supposed to be going fishing?' Funny how easily one could lie, when the situation called for it. 'Have you tried calling Lenny?'

'Jase has tried calling him more than once, but there's no answer. He's left a message.' Emma looked up at the ceiling and blinked away a tear. 'What does it mean, Barb? There were letters in Dennis's pocket from a family called Lancefield. A family who wanted to meet with him.' She lowered her eyes back to Barbara's face. 'Who are they, Barbara? Have you heard of them?'

'I've certainly heard the name Lancefield connected to our family in the research I've been doing for our family tree.' At least she didn't have to lie about that. 'It's a long way back, at the beginning of the nineteenth century. I found an ancestor called Thomas Moses Lancefield, and his father was a ship owner called Richard.'

'That's the name in the letter. It talks about a common ancestor called Richard Lancefield who came from the island of St Felix. I've never heard of it.'

'It's in the Leeward Islands, near Barbados.' Barbara hesitated, and then asked, 'Will you show me the letters?'

'Of course.' Emma turned on her heel and made for the small oak table at the back of the room. She sank onto a chair and waited for Barbara to take a seat opposite. 'There are three letters – two from a solicitor, and one from Richard Lancefield.' She slid them across the table towards Barbara. 'What do these people want, Barb?'

Barbara cast her eyes down to the letters and skimmed through the contents, one after another, pretending to read them. 'Well, if we take it at face value, it seems to be a genuine invitation to meet and get to know them. It's about family. They must be lonely if there are only the two of them left.'

'But why you and Jase? Why don't they have anyone else?'

'I suppose it's the way of the world.' Barbara kept her eyes on the letters. 'You have a large family, but this

Richard Lancefield and his son, they only have each other.' The thought brought a lump to her throat. 'I only had Dennis and Jason, and now I only have Jason.' Tears were beginning to sting at the back of her eyes and she wrestled to hold them back. 'Jason and I only have each other now, in terms of family.' She turned to Emma with a gentle smile. 'Blood relatives, that is. You know that you will always be a part of our family.'

Emma pushed out her lip. 'So why do you think Dennis kept these letters to himself? It says quite clearly that all three of you were invited to meet with the Lancefields.'

'I wish I could answer that, Emma, but I can't.' The lies were flowing too easily now. 'And in any case, I don't think that now is the time to think about it. There is too much to do. There's the funeral to arrange and Dennis's affairs to sort out. There will be time after all that's been done to wonder about these Lancefields.' Barbara straightened in her seat. 'We have to be strong now. The best thing to do is to think about Dennis and how we're going to say goodbye. Not about where he was when this happened, or where he was going.' She lifted a hand and rubbed at her eyes with the cuff of her cardigan, brushing away unwanted tears. 'Have the police said what will happen next? Do we know where they've taken Dennis's body?'

'To the hospital mortuary. We've been told to wait for further instructions, but they've suggested that we take steps to arrange for a funeral director, for when the body is released. They'll be in touch again later today.' Emma lowered her voice. 'And they will need someone to identify the body.'

'I'll go with Jason to do that when the time comes. And I can contact a funeral director, if you and Jason are happy for me to deal with it.'

'I don't think Jase is in any state to make decisions, let alone to deal with anything. And they had a full order book of work for the next eight weeks. I'll have to start calling around to let customers know that the work will be delayed.' A solitary tear of frustration made its way down Emma's cheek. 'Is it the grief, Barb? He doesn't want to talk about it or face up to what needs to be done.'

Barbara placed a hand on top of Emma's. 'It's still too soon for grief. He's had a terrible shock. We all have. And we all deal with things like that in our own way. My way is to keep busy. When my mother died, someone told me that all the things you have to do when someone passes are nature's way of keeping you occupied while you come to terms with the loss. So' – she patted the hand beneath her own – 'while Jason rests, let's you and me keep as busy as we can. You make us a brew while I get the number for a funeral director. Then you can start contacting the customers while I make a list of all the things we need to do to get Dennis's affairs in order.'

'And what about the Lancefields?'

'Just forget about the Lancefields. There will be plenty of time to think about them when Dennis has been buried.'

*

'Bulldog Drummond? Where the hell have you been hiding?' Detective Chief Inspector Ennor Price laughed into the handset of his phone. 'It must be at least three years?'

At the other end of the line, Drummond gave a good-humoured snort. 'And the rest. How are things down there in sunny Cornwall?'

'Not so sunny.' Price swivelled on his chair to look out of the office window. 'Cold for the time of year. And wet.' So wet that he could barely see through the glass. 'How are things with you?'

'Probably the same as they are with you – too many cases and not enough manpower to deal with them.'

Drummond paused and then said, 'Talking of cases, I'm sorry to call out of the blue like this, but I'm looking for a favour. I need information about a family that lives in the Penzance area. They're fairly high profile. I thought you might be able to help me out.'

'Of course, if I can. What's the name?'

'Lancefield. Richard and David Lancefield.'

As if Price couldn't have guessed. He blew out a sigh and closed his eyes. 'Are you still based up in Liverpool?'

'Sure.'

'And does this enquiry have anything to do with a family called Speed?'

'How the hell did you know that?'

'It's a long story.' Price opened his eyes and rubbed at his forehead. 'What do you want to know?'

'I've read a report in the Cornish Enquirer about the murder of David Lancefield's daughter, Lucy.'

Price laughed softly. 'You should have just referred to the internal case files, Andy. The case is still open and you've just found your way to the senior investigating officer.' He tucked the phone's receiver into the crook of his neck and relaxed back into his chair. 'If you've read about the case you'll know that Lucy was murdered at the family home in September. We suspected the estate's gardener, a bloke called Philip McKeith. He disappeared the day her body was found. Then a day or so later his body turned up at the bottom of the family's ornamental lake. We finally nailed both murders on Lucy Lancefield's fiancé, Marcus Drake, although he still refutes that he murdered Lucy. He's blaming McKeith for that. He's claiming involuntary manslaughter, on the grounds that he thought Lucy was still alive and he could stop McKeith from killing her.'

'Are you confident of a conviction?'

'Not as confident as I would like to be. The Lancefields are sparing no expense when it comes to building a defence.'

'The Lancefields? But I thought you said that Marcus Drake had been charged with Lucy Lancefield's murder?'

Price swivelled on his chair and gazed out of the window. 'Where do I start?' He let out a low, self-deprecating chuckle. 'Richard Lancefield was Lucy's grandfather and David was her father. David's wife is Stella Drake Lancefield, and Marcus Drake is her son from a previous marriage.'

'I thought you said that Marcus was Lucy's fiancé?'

'I did. He was Lucy's fiancé and he is Stella's son. Which makes him David Lancefield's stepson. Lucy was planning to marry her stepbrother. And before you say anything, I'm told that's not illegal.' Price chewed on his lip. 'Incredible though it sounds, the Lancefields don't blame Marcus for Lucy's death. They believe his story – that he was trying to save her from McKeith. Initially, they didn't even believe that I had grounds to make a case against him, but they got that one wrong. And when I charged him with murder, Richard Lancefield offered to bankroll his defence.'

Drummond let out a long, low whistle. 'Do you have a trial date yet?'

'No. And we're not expecting it to come to trial until the beginning of next year, due to the complexity of the case. In the meantime, Marcus is out on bail and up in Edinburgh with his mother.'

'That's a hell of a long way from Cornwall. Are you okay with that?'

'I have reason to be. McKeith lived on the Salvation Hall estate with his partner, Becca Smith, and their little girl Frankie. Since the murders, the Smith family have turned nasty. They blame the Lancefields for Philip's death and for leaving Frankie without a father. There have been verbal threats against the family and a war of petty crimes to go with them – graffiti on the property, damage to their gardens and their cars, that sort of thing. We're sure that the Smith family are behind it and I don't want it to escalate. I have no issue with Marcus Drake staying out of the way in Edinburgh as long as he sticks to his bail conditions. The murders were a domestic, and I don't believe he's a threat to anyone else. If he was down here he would need protection from the Smith family, and that would be more work and expense for me.'

'So where do the Speeds fit into all this?'

'Lucy was an only child and her death has left the family without an heir. David Lancefield stands to inherit a significant estate, but he's without any other family apart from his wife Stella and stepson Marcus. The old man, Richard, doesn't like the idea of his son being left without any family connections, and he doesn't want to see his estates sold off to outsiders, so he's decided to trace distant family members in the hope of finding some ready-made relatives for David. He's engaged a genealogist to help him; her name's Kathryn Clifton. She's been working to curate the family's history for the last six weeks or so and she's come up with a branch of the family that leads to your Dennis Speed. In fact, she's gone up to Bristol today with David to meet with...' The implication of Andy Drummond's call hit Ennor Price like a brick, and he fell silent.

'You were going to say that she's gone up to Bristol to meet with Dennis Speed.'

'What's happened, Andy?' Price could feel his anxiety rising. 'Is Kathryn alright?'

'Kathryn? You're on first name terms then?' Drummond gave a low chuckle. 'There's no need to worry, pal. As far as I know, she and Lancefield are absolutely fine and probably half way back to Penzance by now.' He sucked in a breath. 'No, it's Dennis Speed. He found his way under a bus this morning, outside Lime Street station. I'm afraid there was nothing anyone could do.' Drummond paused and then said, 'We found some letters in his pocket relating to the Lancefield family, and train tickets for a day return to Bristol. It looks to me like a straightforward road traffic accident but I have a DC on my team with an itchy nose. When she broke the news of the death to his family, his son claimed to know nothing about the Lancefields or the trip to Bristol. I think it's just a family squabble but Kate Jenkins – that's the DC – she took a look at the letters and decided to dig a bit deeper. That's how she found the report of Lucy Lancefield's murder in the local rag. We thought we ought to just check out the connection.' He paused, and then asked, 'By the way, how did you manage to keep a juicy case like this out of the tabloids?'

Price raised his eyes to the ceiling. 'I didn't – Richard Lancefield did. These people have influence. I'm surprised you managed to turn up anything about it at all.' He tapped his fingers on the desk. 'They're usually pretty thorough when it comes to burying their family's dirty linen. They've had plenty of practice at it over the centuries.'

*

Kate Jenkins perched on the edge of an uncomfortable armchair in Emma and Jason's lounge, rested her hands on her knees, and tried to work out what was different.

She could only conclude that the brittle atmosphere in the house had been mellowed by the arrival of the plump, middle-aged woman sitting opposite on the sofa. Barbara Gee exuded that sort of secure, warm feeling that arose when a safe pair of hands arrived to take control in a crisis, and she had certainly worked some kind of magic on Emma. Seated quietly on the sofa beside Barbara, the girl looked calmer this afternoon and the shock of sudden death appeared to have receded, making way for sadness and a pall of weary acceptance.

'Would it be possible for Jason to join us?' Kate threw the question into the air and waited to see who would catch it.

'Jason is asleep upstairs. Unless it's absolutely necessary, I would rather he slept on.' Barbara's voice was gentle, slightly lilting. 'He's finding his father's death very difficult to cope with. He's asked me to deal with things today on his behalf. If that's okay with you?'

Kate gave a nod of understanding and couldn't help wondering if Jason was avoiding her. 'Of course it's okay. Sudden death takes people in different ways. And it's early days.' She ventured a smile. 'Can I give you this?' She leaned across the small coffee table that separated them and handed a business card to Barbara. 'It has my contact details on it. We won't be assigning a family liaison officer to you, because Dennis's death was the result of an accident, but we understand that this is a difficult time for the family. So' – she gave a gentle shrug of the shoulders – 'I volunteered to keep in touch with you over the next few days. I thought I could help you to navigate the identification of the body and the findings of the post-mortem. If you think it would be useful?'

Barbara looked at the card and then lifted her head. 'It's very good of you. I'm sure we'd appreciate any help you can give us, wouldn't we, Emma?'

'Yes, of course.' Emma's words were barely audible. 'We don't know what to expect.' She cleared her throat with a cough. 'Have you any information for us yet?'

'Well, I can tell you that we've interviewed the driver of the bus. He wasn't injured himself in the accident but he's very upset, as you can imagine. He doesn't remember anything clearly other than the moment of impact. He has a vague recollection of a person moving towards the bus as he pulled across the road towards the bus stop, and he thinks he pulled instinctively on the steering wheel to swerve away, but that's about it.' Kate paused for a breath. 'We've also interviewed the four passengers who were on the bus, but none of them saw what happened. We haven't found anyone yet who actually witnessed Dennis slipping on the pavement, but that's not unusual. At that time of the morning, people are on their way to work, they have their heads down, hands in their pockets. We've put an enquiry board up where the accident happened, asking for witnesses. It's a pretty basic way of trying to get information, but it can generate more feedback than you would expect.'

'And when can we see Dennis?' Emma sounded unsure, almost afraid to ask the question.

'Tomorrow, after the post-mortem. I'm sorry that it can't be before then. After that, we'd like a member of the family to formally identify him. I'd be pleased to take you to the mortuary tomorrow, to do the identification, if that would help.'

Barbara's forehead creased gently into a frown. 'I'm sorry, but why is there to be a post-mortem?'

'It's standard procedure for an unexpected death.' Kate looked from Barbara to Emma, and back again. 'We think the most likely explanation for the accident is that Dennis slipped into the path of the bus, but we can't discount the possibility that he had an underlying health problem. A heart condition, perhaps, or a stroke – something that might have led him to collapse rather than just slip on the ice.' There was a more difficult point to make. She might as well make it now. 'I think you should prepare yourselves for the possibility of an inquest. Because a third party was involved – the bus driver and his employers – their insurers will expect an inquest verdict to make clear where the responsibility for the accident lies.' She saw Barbara flinch and momentarily lose her composure. 'Please try to understand that this isn't to blame Dennis in any way. But a verdict of accidental death would absolve the bus company of any liability.'

'Whereas a verdict of driving without due care and attention on the part of the bus driver, for example, might lead to a civil claim against the company for compensation?' Barbara snuffled a quiet laugh under her breath. 'I don't suppose they can be blamed for not wanting that.'

'If there has to be an inquest, how soon will that take place?' Still seated beside Barbara, Emma was becoming agitated. 'Jason isn't going to like this.'

Kate didn't suppose that he would. 'It may not be for several months. I know it's a distressing thought but I'll do my best to support you through the process if I can.' Assuming that Andy Drummond would let her. 'If I can just go back to the identification, will it be Jason who does that for us?'

Barbara's amiable face clouded. 'I hope so. I will try to persuade him because I think it will help him to come to terms with the loss. But either way, I will be there.' She looked down at her fingers. 'It's all come so unexpectedly.' For a moment her lip trembled. And then she lifted her eyes back to Kate. 'Is there anything else we need to know?'

'I don't think so. If you can let me have a number where I can reach you, Barbara, I'll call you in the morning to arrange a time for the identification. It will probably be in the afternoon. And if you could let me know at the same time which funeral director you've engaged, that would be a real help. Apart from that…' Kate paused, the important question lingering reluctantly on her lips. But there was no going back now. It was the whole point of her refusing to let go of the case. 'There was one other thing, although it isn't really anything to do with the accident. Emma and Jason didn't have any idea that Dennis had been in communication with the Lancefield family, or that he was planning to make the trip to Bristol. I just wondered, Barbara, whether he had shared that information with you?'

5

'We thought it best for me to break the news to you in person.' David hovered by the large wing-backed chair to the left of the drawing room fireplace. Divested of his overcoat he looked dishevelled from his journey back to Salvation Hall, his silk tie adrift from his collar, the once-crisp sleeves of his Egyptian cotton shirt now crumpled from too many hours spent sitting on a train. 'It would have been difficult to explain to you over the phone, there was so much background noise in the carriage.' He lowered himself wearily into the chair.

Richard stared at his son with unseeing eyes and then cast a glance down to the floor, where Samson lay dozing by his feet, impervious to the looming disappointment. He dropped a hand down to the dog's neck and ruffled his coat. 'The police are certain, I suppose, that it was an accident?'

'I believe so. They have no reason to suspect any sort of crime. The most likely explanation is that he was dashing for the train and slipped on an icy pavement.' David looked down at his hands. 'I can't stop thinking that we might be responsible for his death. That if we hadn't set up the meeting in Bristol, he might still be alive.'

Richard baulked. 'Come now, that won't do. I might just as easily say to you that had Dennis accepted my invitation to visit us here at Salvation Hall, he might have travelled by car and been nowhere near the station.' The old man narrowed his eyes. 'This is an unexpected blow to our plans but it's also a tragedy for the Speed family.' He exhaled his regret and then looked up to frown at his son. 'Where's Kathryn?'

'She's gone back to Penzance. She did offer to come home with me, to help break the news. But it's been a long day and I didn't think it made sense for her to travel all the way out here just for a few minutes of conversation.' He leaned forward towards his father. 'I hope you don't mind. She sends her very best regards and her condolences, and I'm to tell you that if you wish to speak to her this evening she will take your call at any time, however late the hour.'

David's words hung in the air for a moment and suddenly Richard was aware of the tension in his son's shoulders, and the anxiety etched across his brow. Dear God, after all these years of disagreement and discord, was he actually looking for his father's approval? The old man smiled to himself and nodded. 'You were quite right to send her back to the hotel, David. I'm sure it's been a very long and tiring day for both of you. When she returns to Salvation Hall in the morning, we can discuss how best to proceed. I think it may be a little too soon to approach what's left of the family, even to pay our respects. They will need time and space to grieve their loss. And it is possible that Jason and Barbara still don't know of our existence.'

'They will know of us by now. Dennis was carrying your letters in his pocket; that's how the police knew where to contact me. Those letters will have been handed back to the family.'

'In which case they will know where to contact us again, either directly or indirectly through Mayhew and Mayhew.' Richard clicked his teeth. 'This is a terrible thing to have happened but it can't be helped, you know. It's an unfortunate twist of fate. I suppose that just because a seed is sown, there is no guarantee that it will grow and bear fruit. In the morning I'll let old Mayhew know what's happened so that he will be ready if Jason or Barbara makes an approach.' Richard paused and thought for a moment. 'Of course, the one thing we might never know is why Dennis didn't want to come to Salvation Hall. He may not have shared that with his son or his cousin. It's a mystery that may never be solved.' Richard leaned back in his chair and steepled his fingers. 'I think we should turn our attention away from the tragedy towards things within our control. The draft of my revised will arrived in the morning post. Perhaps we could discuss that over supper this evening? It all seems to be in order, but before I sign it I would like you to satisfy yourself that it covers everything we have agreed.'

'As you wish.' David looked relieved at the change of subject. 'Did Kathryn agree to take on the role as fourth executor?'

'I'm pleased to say that she did.' Pleased beyond words, Richard thought, and not only because Kathryn knew the importance of keeping the Lancefield estates together. Pleased because her agreement to be an executor to the will also signalled her agreement to remain in David's life, perhaps to stand by his son in administering the estates for as long as she was needed.

'Well, that's the best piece of news that we've received today. Dare I hope for another?' David rested his head wearily against the wing of the chair. 'Dare I hope that there has been no more unpleasantness at Salvation Hall during my absence? No more harassment for us during the day?'

Richard pursed his lips. 'At Salvation Hall? No.' He spoke slowly. 'But I went to the churchyard this afternoon, to visit Philip and Lucy.'

'All the way there on your own? Was that wise, on such a cold day?'

'Not so much wise, as necessary. Samson and I might be growing old but we still need our daily dose of fresh air, and at least the day was a dry one.' The old man twisted in his seat and pushed a hand into the pocket of his trousers, pulling out a small white card. 'There were flowers on Lucy's grave this afternoon, a bunch of garden chrysanthemums that I didn't recognise. This card was with them.' He stretched out an unsteady hand to pass the card to David. 'I threw the flowers in the bin beside the lychgate.'

David took the card and studied it through narrowed eyes. It was a commonplace thing, white and unremarkable, and it bore a single word written in dark blue ink, the letters carefully scripted in a small, neat, inoffensive hand.

Whore.

*

It was quiet in the police station's canteen.

Kate Jenkins sat down on the hard plastic chair opposite Drummond and ripped open a sachet of sugar. 'Emma introduced Barbara Gee as Jason's aunt, but it turns out that she's Dennis Speed's cousin, not his sister. I asked her if she knew anything about the Lancefields, or about Dennis's plan to travel to Bristol.' Kate poured the sugar clumsily into the plastic cup on the table and set about opening another sachet. 'She said no.'

'Did you believe her?'

'I don't know. She looked away when she answered me, as if she couldn't look me in the eye.' Kate picked up the cup and gently swilled the contents around. 'I don't know why I drink this muck out of the machine. It doesn't matter how much sugar you put in, it never tastes any better.'

Drummond observed her with a wry smile. 'The Lancefields have connections to sugar. They own a sugar plantation.'

'You're kidding me?' Kate paused, the plastic cup halfway to her lips. 'A sugar plantation, like… somewhere hot? Like the Caribbean?'

'Exactly like the Caribbean. That place referred to in Richard Lancefield's letter – St Felix – that's in the Leeward Islands, though the family have lived in Cornwall, in a house called Salvation Hall, for hundreds of years. They're significant land and property owners, not just in Cornwall but overseas. Their ancestors were amongst the original settlers on the island of St Felix and most of their money came from sugar and rum production in the eighteenth century.'

Kate's eyes widened. 'Sugar and rum? But then they must have owned…'

'Slaves.' Drummond grinned at her reaction. 'Now that might be a reason why Dennis didn't want to have too much to do with them. There's no question that they're wealthy, but the way they came by their money? You can see how that could put some people off.' He put a hand up to his mouth and chewed on his thumbnail. 'You know how they feel about that sort of thing up here. Liverpool's like the rest of the country when it comes to the subject of slavery – always trying to find a way to atone for its sins, and never quite managing to get there.'

'How did you find this out?'

'I spoke to Ennor Price this afternoon. I did my SIO training with him and we were both stationed in Bristol for a while. He's based in Penzance now. I knew a call would be useful, but I didn't expect him to be the senior officer on the Lancefield murder case.' Drummond laughed softly. 'He's tying himself in knots, trying to put a case together against Lucy Lancefield's fiancé. We had a long chat about it, but I can't see any reason there why Dennis might want to keep those letters from his family.' Drummond frowned. 'Would it disturb you, Kate, if you discovered that you were related to a family like the Lancefields?'

'What, filthy rich and with their own Caribbean property?' A mischievous smile lit Kate's face. 'Not bloody likely. I'd be looking for a free holiday to St Felix so that I could commune with my family's roots. Preferably during the winter months, when the weather's at its best.' She risked a sip of her coffee. 'All that stuff happened hundreds of years ago. There's no point in being touchy about things that we can't change, is there?' She thought about it for a moment and then turned teasing eyes towards her senior officer. 'Would it bother you?'

'I don't know, it's not something that I've ever had to think about.' He folded his arms on the table. 'I asked Ennor what the Lancefields were like and he said they were old-school country gents who kept pretty much to themselves. Richard is obsessed with his family's heritage and has engaged someone to document the family tree and build some sort of archive. David would rather not be inheriting his family's fortune and the stigma that goes with it, but he's bowing to pressure to take it on when the old man dies.'

'So how did they find the connection with Dennis Speed?'

'Through the diligent work of their consultant genealogist, Kathryn Clifton. Ennor seems to be on pretty friendly terms with her.' Drummond permitted himself a sly grin. 'I suppose that could be another hook in, if we need it.' He folded his arms and bounced back in his chair. 'I suppose the burning question is, did it bother Dennis Speed? Did he find out about the Lancefields' origins and decide that he didn't want to know?' Drummond turned towards his colleague. 'I suppose when you searched the internet this morning, you searched for "Lancefield" and "Penwithen"? And when you saw the references to Lucy Lancefield's murder you jumped to the conclusion that Dennis might have seen them too?'

A faint flush lit up in Kate's cheeks. 'And I suppose that you're going to say I should have dug a bit deeper, instead of latching on to the obvious?'

Drummond laughed out loud. 'After I spoke to Ennor, I searched for "Lancefield" and "St Felix". It's all there, on the web. Lots of "sunny Caribbean" stuff about the Woodlands Plantation and the long and illustrious history of the Lancefield family. It looks idyllic. And valuable. But the way it was acquired?' He blew out his doubts in a sigh.

'Maybe Dennis did the same internet search and didn't like what he saw. Maybe he asked for the meeting in Bristol so that he could tell David Lancefield to his face that he didn't want to be associated with them. Either way, I don't really see that it has any bearing on what happened to him this morning.'

Kate pouted and ran a disconsolate finger around the edge of the plastic coffee cup. 'I guess now you're going to tell me that there's nothing else to investigate.'

'You see, there you go again, jumping to the wrong conclusion.' He delivered the rebuke gently. 'I'm not going to tell you that until I'm certain. Ennor's having supper with Kathryn Clifton this evening and he's promised to sound her out about the Speed family. Let's give this thing another twenty-four hours to see if anything falls out of the tree. He's going to call me in the morning. If Kathryn can come up with a theory that we've missed, I'll give you the nod to dig a bit deeper. If she doesn't, then I'll ask you to support Barbara and Jason until the body is identified, and then leave Dennis Speed's family in peace to bury their dead.'

6

Ennor Price took a good, long look at Kathryn Clifton. Seated at the other side of the table, she was perusing The Zoological Hotel's evening menu with the weary eye of someone who knew that food was essential but who, at that moment, could barely be bothered to eat. It was a good thing, he mused, that they'd set up the dinner date before she had made the trip to Bristol. He knew that the day's events would have disappointed her and he could only hope that she was still prepared to discuss them with him.

He lifted his copy of the menu from the table and ran his eyes quickly down the limited list of choices. 'The sardines sound good. And then maybe the roasted lamb rump.'

She glanced up at him, her brow creased above the clear, hazel eyes. 'Don't make it sound too easy, will you?' At least her tone was teasing. 'I'll go for the dressed crab, and then the pork loin.' She put down the menu. 'So did you insist on keeping this supper date because you wanted to make sure that I ate this evening? Or because you have some ulterior motive?'

Ennor tried to suppress a self-conscious smile. 'I could have just wanted the pleasure of your company. Isn't that usually why we meet for supper?'

'I would hope so. But given the day's events, and the fact that you've already confessed to knowing about Dennis Speed's accident thanks to your colleague in Liverpool, you can't blame me for wondering.' She put out a hand and playfully nudged at his arm. 'Come on, Ennor, spit it out. Then we can forget about what's happened today and get on with enjoying our supper.'

He leaned across the table, his forearms resting on the edge, his face as close to hers as the span of the table would allow. 'Why do you think that Dennis didn't tell his family about Richard's letters? Do you think that he was ashamed of the connection?'

Kathryn raised an eyebrow. 'I didn't know for certain until now that he *hadn't* told them, only that he preferred to meet with David in Bristol and that he was planning to come alone.' The thought seemed to trouble her. 'Was his death definitely an accident?'

'Can you ever say that something was definitely an accident? All I can say is that Andy Drummond was adamant there was no evidence of anything criminal to be reported.'

'So why did he call you to ask about the family?'

'Touché.' It was good to see that, however tired she might be, Kathryn had lost none of her spark. 'You know what policemen are like. We see the prospect of trouble where none ever existed. It's in the DNA. We're just permanently terrified that we'll miss something.' He leaned back in his seat. 'Dennis had Richard's letters in his pocket, and Drummond's team searched on the internet for "Lancefield" and "Salvation Hall", and came up with details of Lucy's murder. It's standard practice to follow any lead, Kathryn, as much to eliminate it as anything else.' He leaned forward again. 'You didn't answer my question.'

'That's because I know what you want me to say. This has nothing to do with Lucy's murder. You want me to say that Dennis didn't want to connect with the family because of their heritage.'

'If I had a distant relative reach out to me and I discovered that they made their fortune from slavery, then I'd think twice about whether I wanted anything to do with them.'

Kathryn's cheeks dimpled. 'And what about your own heritage?'

Ennor flinched. 'What's *my* heritage got to do with it?'

'Well, I can easily think of more than one Caribbean slave owner who bore the surname "Price". Some of them even had connections to Cornwall. How do you know that you don't have slave-owning ancestors? How do any of us?' She lowered her voice. 'And as to Dennis Speed… think about it, Ennor. He was related to the Lancefields by a connection that dates back to the late eighteenth century. He could be as sniffy as he liked about how the Lancefields made their money but, at the end of the day, he was a part of it too. The common ancestors that bind them were all involved in the same business. In fact, at one point, one of Dennis's direct ancestors had a much bigger crime to answer than anything the rest of the family did.'

'And how do you come to that conclusion?'

'You've never asked me how there comes to be a branch of the Lancefield family up in Liverpool. Haven't you ever wondered?'

'I can't say that I have. It's not unusual for families to be scattered across the country. People move to find work, to make marriages, to buy property. What's unusual in that?'

'Nothing, when you put it in such general terms, but when it comes to the Lancefields?' Kathryn lowered her voice further. 'The link between Dennis and Richard traces back to brothers who were born in St Felix but were educated in England. Richard's ancestor Benedict was the eldest son and he returned to St Felix to run the Woodlands Plantation. His brother Richard, Dennis's ancestor, had a different role to play.' She looked momentarily troubled. 'Some time ago, I told you that the Lancefield family used slaves on their plantation, but they didn't trade in them. I told you that they bought the labour that they needed to run the plantation, but they didn't make money from buying and selling slaves.'

'As if that makes a difference.'

Kathryn hissed through her teeth. 'Making a difference

or not, I was wrong.'

Ennor let out a spontaneous laugh. 'Wrong? You? About the Lancefield's heritage?'

'It's not funny, Ennor.' She stretched out a hand and gently wrapped her fingers around his wrist. 'Ever since I began investigating this Liverpool branch of the family, I've come to realise that I couldn't have been more wrong. For a number of years, Liverpool was the beating heart of the slave trade in Britain and, for a very short time in their history, the Lancefield family not only bought and sold slaves, they shipped them from Africa to the West Indies.' She looked suddenly crestfallen. 'They owned their own slave ship, Ennor. It ran from Liverpool to St Felix, via the west coast of Africa.

'And it was called "The Redemption".'

*

Barbara placed a large gin and tonic down on the side table and sank into the plush green armchair beside it. There was a slim white envelope in her right hand and she let it fall softly into her lap as she relaxed her shoulders into the folds of the armchair's generous padding. She closed her eyes and drew in a breath, and then blew out the pain of the day with a languorous, audible hiss.

So much unbearable loss. So much insufferable grief. So much unnecessary regret.

So much misery to endure, and not just for herself, but for Jason, too. And Emma. There would be a time, soon, when holding back her own grief would be out of the question. But for now, she would have to stay strong. Strong for Jason, strong for Emma.

And strong for Dennis.

She opened her eyes and glanced across the room to the mantelpiece and the framed photograph which took pride of place in the centre. She could still remember the day that it was taken, the beginning of a week-long family holiday. She and Dennis, side by side on Southport seafront, matching sun hats tilted jauntily at an angle, ice creams in hand. They had such dreams back then. They weren't just friends and they weren't just cousins, never had been just cousins. They were brother and sister, in all but name; a happy conspiracy of two lonely, only children, there for each other in the absence of siblings.

And now Dennis was gone.

'So what happens now, oh Wise One?' She tilted her head and whispered the words in the direction of the photograph. 'Jason knows, now, about the Lancefields. He knows where you were going, Dennis. And he knows that you kept it from him.' She let out a sigh. 'You know that I'll be there for him, don't you? That I'll stand in for you, as best I can.' She raised her eyes to the ceiling. 'I was a surrogate sister to you long enough to know that I can be a surrogate mother to him. But I'm not sure for how much longer I can go on lying to him.'

She lowered her eyes to the envelope on her lap and scowled at it. Then she slipped a plump finger under the unsealed flap and pulled out the contents, a hastily-scribbled note written in Dennis's untidy scrawl. Two names were listed at the top of the paper, with two mobile phone numbers to match. Beneath, Dennis had added a third – The Regency Hotel in Bristol – with what she assumed was the number of the hotel's reception desk.

What good was it now, to know where Dennis was planning to meet with David Lancefield?

She sucked in a breath but the action failed to stifle a sob. If he'd turned down the meeting, he might still be alive. And God knows she would rather have Dennis alive than a whole army of Lancefields marching into her life. But he wouldn't be stopped. However many times they had discussed it, however many arguments she had put forward to dissuade him from responding to that damned invitation, he wouldn't give it up.

Her eyes were moist now and she turned them back

towards the picture. 'I didn't try hard enough, did I? I didn't try hard enough to stop you.' She pursed her lips inward and shook her head. 'And I'm so very sorry, Dennis, that I didn't.' She sniffed back another swell of tears. 'I can cope with the funeral.' She nodded to herself. 'I can help Jason to organise that. And I can deal with the police, and the investigation into your accident. I can protect him from that. I've even offered to identify your body tomorrow, to save him from the heartache. But this' – she tapped on the note – 'this lie, this deception… keeping it from him, going behind his back… I'm not so sure I can deal with this. God save us, Dennis, I've even lied to the police about it.'

She closed her eyes in momentary contemplation. 'The police officer who came to speak to us – Kate Jenkins – she's such a nice young woman. Keen, you know. And helpful.' Qualities that Barbara would only ever admire. 'I keep thinking about how I lied to her, how I told her that I didn't know that you were going to Bristol, and how she didn't deserve such dishonesty. And what on earth am I going to say now, if the truth comes out?' More tears were stinging wildly at the back of Barbara's eyes. 'She's given Jason the letters that were in your pocket. There was nothing I could do to stop her. Just like there is nothing I can do now to stop Jason, if he decides to get in touch with the Lancefields himself.'

Barbara pulled a crisp cotton handkerchief from the cuff of her cardigan and dabbed at her eyes with it. It wasn't completely true, of course, to say that there was nothing she could do.

The problem, really, was knowing whether or not she could find the courage to go ahead and do it.

*

Ennor put out a hand and lifted the bottle of Chablis from the ice bucket. 'So, does that change how you feel about the Lancefields, Kathryn? Now that you know they were trading in slaves as well as using them on the plantation?'

There was an uncharacteristic hesitation before she answered the question, and when she finally spoke it was slowly and with deliberation. 'I want to say "no" because I still don't believe that you can blame the present generation of Lancefields for the crimes that their ancestors committed.' She looked down at the tablecloth. 'But it was barbaric, and I know that what I have uncovered is going to deeply upset David. God knows how hard I've had to work on Richard's behalf to persuade David to agree to take on the responsibility for the estates. You know how much the source of the family's wealth already concerns him.'

'I know that it doesn't upset him enough to surrender it. He could easily give it away to charity if it bothered him that much.'

'That's not very fair, Ennor. You don't know enough about the family, or the estates, or even their history to make that kind of judgement.' Kathryn lifted her wine glass and drained off the lukewarm remnants in the bottom. 'Richard sees himself as a patriarch, the father figure of his estates. And he sees himself as responsible for the well-being of everyone who lives or works on them. Why else do you think that he's trying so hard to give Becca Smith a second chance?'

'Because he feels guilty that his granddaughter's fiancé murdered Becca's partner?'

Kathryn winced. 'I'm going to let that one go because it's been a long and unhappy day, and I'm not going to spoil a lovely supper by telling you what I think about that comment.' She put down her glass and picked up her fork, using it to skewer the last piece of crab meat on her plate. 'David is trying to see things from his father's point of view. He isn't a natural leader but he knows how important it is to Richard that someone takes responsibility for the estates and their workers. I think that when

Richard is gone, David will find his own way of dealing with his inheritance. But to do that, he has to face up to it. He has to own it before he can change it.' She looked away across the restaurant, saddened now. 'I'd really hoped that meeting Dennis Speed would help David. It wouldn't have mattered if Dennis had been uncomfortable with the Lancefield heritage. In fact, it might have given David an ally when it came to making changes.'

If only Dennis hadn't found his way under a bus. Ennor shivered at the thought. 'How has David taken today's events?'

'He's disappointed, of course. But mindful of the loss to Jason and to Barbara. I think he might reach out to them at some point and offer to attend the funeral.' Kathryn's brow relaxed and she almost smiled. 'You know, I'm quite warming to David now. He's changing, Ennor. He's always had such a bad relationship with his father, but he's really trying to make a connection with him now. And he's interested, genuinely interested in his family's history.'

'Not that you're biased, of course. You'd warm to anyone interested in all those crusty documents.' It was an affectionate jibe and Ennor knew she would take it in good part. 'These Liverpool cousins; I've never asked you what sort of people they are. Andy Drummond reckoned that Dennis was a painter and decorator. That's a bit far removed from all the Lancefield wealth, isn't it?'

Kathryn put down her fork. 'I believe that Dennis and Jason worked together as a family firm. And Barbara was the headmistress at a small primary school on the Wirral, until she took early retirement last year.'

'So what happened to their share of the Lancefield family fortune?'

'I'm still piecing that part of the family history together. Their ancestor Richard was the second son, so his brother Benedict inherited the main wealth. All the estates – the Woodlands Plantation and the estates and lands at Salvation Hall – would go to him. But Richard was well-provided for. I've established that he had a town-house in Liverpool and a country house on the Wirral. And he received a generous income from the family business throughout his lifetime. The majority of their business activities brought in huge amounts of wealth, and they were shrewd investors. They ploughed much of their Caribbean profit into English land and property.'

'Including a slave ship.'

'Don't make me regret sharing that with you.' Kathryn licked her lips. 'As far as I can make out from the documents I've been given, Benedict's brother Richard volunteered to oversee that venture. At that time, Liverpool was the centre of the slave trade in Britain, so he moved from Cornwall to Liverpool to be close to the action, and he took his family with him.' She frowned. 'I haven't put the whole picture together yet, but it looks as though *The Redemption*'s first voyage as a slave ship under the Lancefields was a financial success but a personal disaster. And it eventually led to a rift within the family.'

'Between the two brothers?'

'No. Between Richard and his son, Thomas Moses Lancefield. Thomas married against his father's wishes and was disowned by the family. Richard had another younger son, Richard Dyer Lancefield, an officer in the merchant navy. Richard's wealth passed to him and his descendants, bypassing Dennis Speed's ancestor completely.'

'I'm confused now. Why the hell do they all have to be called "Richard"? Couldn't they think of any other names?' Ennor rubbed at his forehead with his fingers. 'Do you think that Dennis knew about this, that his part of the family had been edged to one side?'

'Good heavens, no. I've pieced it all together from the original documents that Richard – the present Richard Lancefield – has given me.' She laughed under her breath. 'At this point, even Richard and David don't know the full story. I've told them that there was a rift in the family and I've told David about Thomas Moses and his unsuitable marriage. And I've shared some information with him about Lysbeth Silver Lancefield – she was Richard Dyer Lancefield's daughter, and she inherited the money that should have passed to Dennis's family. But I haven't told him why this all came about. I don't want to share the details with them until I'm certain of all the facts.' Kathryn's face began to cloud. 'Some of the evidence I've discovered is pretty distressing.'

'Then don't think about it now.' Ennor looked at her through solicitous eyes. So tired and brittle at the beginning of the evening, she was finally beginning to relax. If pushed, he might say that she looked almost happy. Talking about the past, about all that dusty, inconsequential history – it made her happy. And seeing her happy made him happy.

And suddenly it dawned on Ennor Price just how closely Kathryn Clifton's happiness was tied to his own

7

The kitchen at Salvation Hall was usually a tranquil haven, but the atmosphere that morning was brittle, and the pale winter sunlight that filtered through the large bay window was too cool and ineffective to warm the mood.

Seated in the alcove by the window, a cooling cup of coffee by her right hand, Kathryn's attention was on the small, white card resting loosely between the fingers of her left. 'I'm so sorry, David.' She lifted compassionate eyes from the card to look up across the table, to where David was calmly buttering a second slice of toast. 'I can't understand how anyone could do something so despicable.'

David spoke without taking his eyes off the toast. 'I suppose there is no accounting for the depths to which some people will sink.' He placed his knife on the table beside his breakfast plate and took up a spoonful of marmalade from a small cut-glass dish. 'To be quite honest, Kathryn, I am beginning to grow immune to the whole damned mess.' He dropped the marmalade onto his toast and flattened it angrily with the back of the spoon. 'Lucy was headstrong and foolish, and selfish beyond belief. She carried on her affair with Philip without any regard for either her fiancé or for Philip's partner, let alone his child. I might even go so far as to agree that she was, indeed, a whore.' He winced at the word. 'But she did not deserve to die, and it is not her fault that Philip is dead. My daughter was a human being, and she deserves to be treated with respect in death, whatever her faults.' He shivered, a bristle of displeasure, and then lifted a diffident eye to look up at Kathryn. 'My dear, forgive me. I have no business taking out my frustrations on you.'

Kathryn gave him an encouraging smile. 'Better me, surely, than anyone else?' It occurred to her that she had arrived at Salvation Hall that morning expecting to deal with Richard's disappointment at Dennis Speed's death. She had not been prepared for either the small white card or for the emotional outburst that it had prompted from David. 'Have you notified the police?'

'You do agree, then, that Inspector Price will have to be told?'

'Yes, of course Ennor must be told.' He must be told, although God alone knew what he would be able to do about it, given the circumstances. 'Would you like me to call him?' She watched David's gentle face run a gamut of emotions as he considered the offer and hoped that he didn't suspect her motive. 'I'm sure he would want to know.'

David's shoulders relaxed. 'I'd be very grateful, Kathryn. In truth, this is all becoming a little too much for me. First Dennis, and now the desecration of my daughter's grave.'

It was a measured understatement. Kathryn let out a sympathetic sigh and dropped the card onto the table. 'Have you mentioned this incident to Becca yet?'

David's eyes narrowed, but the hint of a guilty smile began to play around his lips. 'No, but only because my father has forbidden it. It is quite obvious to me that the Smith family are responsible, but he insists that we cannot make an accusation against them without firm proof. And I suppose that he is right.' His smile began to fade. 'Becca herself is staying out of my way. She prepared the breakfast table in silence and then absented herself upstairs. I believe she is cleaning the bedrooms.' He pursed his lips. 'I might almost think that she is too ashamed to look me in the face, but perhaps I am giving her too much credit.'

His discomfort was beginning to make way for an

uncharacteristic disdain. Kathryn thought for a moment and then decided to divert the conversation. 'Dare I ask how your father took the news of Dennis's death?'

'With surprising stoicism. He's very sorry, of course. And he agrees with me that in time we might reach out to the family to offer our condolences.' David rubbed at his temple with a finger. 'Having thought about the matter overnight, and despite feeling a degree of shame at the very idea, I can't help thinking that things have turned out for the best. Whether or not we are in any way responsible for what happened to Dennis, we are not exactly in the best of positions to welcome new cousins to the family fold. That despicable card…' He shivered and gave a sorrowful shake of the head. 'How on earth could we have explained that sort of behaviour to Dennis, or to his family?'

Kathryn shrugged. 'It might not have been necessary.'

'You think?' David sounded unconvinced. 'We are still awaiting a trial date for Marcus and, when it comes, we will have a distressing court case to deal with, as well as all the attendant publicity. Even now we are being harried by an unseen force, which may or may not be some disaffected member of our housekeeper's family who thinks we deserve to suffer. I wonder, Kathryn… I have suggested to my father that we should postpone any further attempts to connect with our wider family for the time being. Do you think you might be prevailed upon to support me?'

'Because you believe it would be the right thing to do?'

'As opposed to…?' David looked momentarily puzzled, and then he smiled. 'You suspect me of sabotaging my father's plans.' He nodded to himself. 'I know that my father has my best interests at heart. And I will concede now – given certain considerations – that having a few distant cousins in my life might be a useful thing. But if they are to come into my life, I would prefer them to be happy with the experience. As things stand, we have no choice but to sit here in silence and permit some unknown assailant to defile our graves, churn up our gardens, scratch the paintwork on our cars, and conduct whatever other petty, mindless crimes they feel like. But is that really the sort of situation into which we should invite innocent and unsuspecting members of our family?'

*

Detective Sergeant Tom Parkinson sank onto the visitor's chair beside Ennor Price's desk and let out a low whistle. 'Dead? Before they even met with him?' He scratched at his ear. 'Well, I don't think any of us could have seen that one coming.'

'Ah well, that's what happens when you have a day out of the office. You miss all the excitement.' Price lifted his arms and clasped his hands behind his head. 'How was the training course, by the way?'

Parkinson gave a noncommittal shrug. 'It was meant to improve our interviewing techniques. I can't say I was impressed. I don't think the tutor himself has ever interviewed a witness or a suspect. He probably spends most of his time writing text books.' The sergeant's eyes turned towards the in-tray on Price's desk. 'Dare I ask if I missed anything else yesterday?'

'You mean the death of a distant Lancefield wasn't enough for you?' Price chuckled. 'If you're asking whether the Lancefields were on the receiving end of any more harassment, then as far as I'm aware the answer is "no". It was pretty quiet in that respect.' He lowered a hand to retrieve a sheet of notes from the in-tray. 'How many have we had now?' He dotted down the page with his finger. 'Two instances of damage to the gardens, damage to David Lancefield's Mercedes, four pieces of hate mail in the post, and a banner of graffiti strung across the gates to the estate. I make that eight so far, not including the two episodes of verbal threats made to the family in The Lancefield Arms.' He looked up at Parkinson. 'Odd, don't you think, that there wasn't anything yesterday when David and Kathryn went to Bristol?'

'You think they might be aiming all the activity at David, so it would miss the mark if they did anything while he was in Bristol?'

'No, I'm wondering whether they turned the heat up just a little too far and made his trip to Bristol a wasted one.'

'I don't follow you.' Parkinson gave the conundrum a little more thought, and then uttered an incredulous laugh. 'Dennis Speed? You surely don't think that's connected in some way to the harassment?' He dismissed the notion with a shake of the head. 'You said that Speed had met with an accident.'

'I know I did. Funny, though, how it happened on the very day that he was going to meet with David and Kathryn.' Price tilted his head. 'What did you say to me last week, when I told you that a date had been set for that meeting to take place? If I remember rightly you said, "Bloody hell, Ennor, that's just going to wind Becca Smith up further". Am I right?'

'Well, it stands to reason, doesn't it? She doesn't want the Lancefields to find more family. She doesn't want them to have anything that will improve their lot in life. But I don't see how you could nail Dennis Speed's death on Becca or her family. Harassment is one thing, I don't deny that they're probably behind that. But murder? You think they would go that far to punish the Lancefields?'

'It's too much of a coincidence.'

'How could they pull that off in Liverpool?'

'Any number of ways.' It had been too much for Price to hope that Parkinson would buy into his theory. 'Look, just humour me on this one, will you? I want you to do a bit of digging. Go over to The Lancefield Arms and make yourself visible. See if you can find out what Becca's brothers have been up to lately. Anything that might place them with a connection to Liverpool.'

Parkinson groaned. 'Ennor, it's just a coincidence. You said yourself that it was an accident. The DCI in Liverpool thinks it was an accident. Why do you have to go looking for something more?'

Price snorted. 'Andy Drummond is assuming that it was an accident. You know that's not my way. And especially not when something like this happens on the periphery of a murder case. Our murder case.' He tapped a finger sharply on the desk. 'Assume nothing. Check everything.'

'But aren't you assuming that the Smith family will be prepared to account for their movements over the last few days?'

The inspector scowled. 'They'll account for their movements if they know what's good for them. I've given them the benefit of the doubt for long enough. If they don't play ball you can let them know that the next time I hear about Zak Smith shooting his mouth off in The Lancefield Arms, holding forth about what he'd like to do to Richard Lancefield, he'll be looking at charges of harassment and criminal damage.'

*

Emma Needham glanced around her. A motorway service area in early November was never an appealing proposition and even less so, she thought, when the journey you were making was a slow and unwilling descent into madness.

She swallowed down the thought and turned worried eyes back to Jason. He was seated at the other side of the small table, one hand wrapped around an extra-large mug of hot chocolate, the other carefully cradling his mobile phone. She watched as he swiped deftly at the phone's screen with his thumb and couldn't decide if he was oblivious to her discomfort, or just determined to ignore it.

'I wish you would let me call Barbara.' Emma kept her voice as steady as she could. 'I really don't think we should be doing this.'

Jason glanced up from the phone with a frown. 'What did I tell you this morning? If you wanted to come with me, it was on condition that you didn't call Auntie Barb until we got back home this evening.' He narrowed his eyes. 'Remember?'

Remember? Of course she remembered. Just like she remembered the other half of the ultimatum.

If you decide to stay at home and tell Barb about this, we're finished.

So much for loyalty. And so much for love.

She stretched out a hand and tried to take hold of his fingers. 'Jase, I'm really worried about you. You've just lost your dad. You're not thinking straight. We need to go back and help Barb to do the identification, and then I think you need to rest. You've got to come to terms with what's happened.'

He dismissed the suggestion with a crooked, almost self-satisfied smile. 'Auntie Barb has offered to do the identification. And there is nothing for me to come to terms with. Dad died. He died on his way to Bristol.' A blotch of heightened colour suddenly flecked its way across Jason's throat. 'What we need to do now is move on.' He held the mobile phone out towards her. 'Look, this is Salvation Hall, where the Lancefields live.' He turned the screen so that she could see it. 'Go on, take it. Look at it.'

She lifted her hand and reluctantly took hold of the phone. 'Salvation Hall.' She repeated the name as she stared down at the image that filled the screen. The house was breathtaking; a graceful mansion of rose-gold stone, a faultless blend of gables and chimneys and imposing mullioned windows. 'Is it open to the public?'

Jason sneered. 'Of course not. It's a private residence. It's not some naff place with a sticky tea room and a putting green for the kids. These people are proper toffs.'

He grumbled under his breath. 'Don't you think it's elegant?'

Elegant? Since when did the word "elegant" make its way into Jason's vocabulary? 'It looks very impressive.'

'Doesn't it?' He sounded like a child, eager and expectant. 'Our family own that. Can you imagine?'

'Your family?' Could he really call the Lancefields his family? And even if he could, what did it matter when his connection to them was so tenuous? What could such a connection do for Jason, except possibly make him dissatisfied with his own life? With the life he shared with her. Perhaps even dissatisfied with Emma herself. She handed the phone back to him with a forced smile. 'What happens when we get there, Jase?'

The simple question seemed to puzzle him. 'What happens? Well, we tell them who we are. Who *I* am. And we tell them about my dad, and what happened to him. And we say that we don't want that to stop us from getting to know them.' Jason puffed out his cheeks. 'And then I suppose we go home and we stay in touch with them. We invite them to Dad's funeral. And we move on, but with the Lancefields on our side.'

On our side? She kept the thought to herself. 'What if the Lancefields know that Dennis didn't tell you about his trip to Bristol? Or anything else about them? What if they know *why* Dennis didn't tell you about it?'

Jason's face clouded. 'Well, that will be a bonus, won't it? I mean, it's not like it's going to be anything bad, is it? It's like Auntie Barb said, he probably just wanted to check them out first. To make sure that they were on the level.' He looked down again at his phone. 'Now that Dad's gone, it's down to me. These people are going to be good for us, Emma.'

'But we won't have anything in common with them.'

'You don't know that until we meet them. They're probably really nice people.'

'But what do we do if we don't like them? Or they

don't like us?'

'Why do you always have to be so negative about everything? They *will* like us.' He sighed out his discontent. 'Look, if they don't like us – which isn't going to happen, right? – but if it does, we'll just get back in the car, go home, and forget about them.' He put out a hand and rubbed at her arm. 'Why do you always have to worry when there's no need?'

Emma forced another smile. 'I don't know, Jase. Maybe I'm just a worrier.' She folded her arms on the table and tried to look relaxed. 'I don't mean to spoil things. I just care about you.' She looked into his eyes. 'Look, we've still got over a hundred miles to go. Why don't I drive the next stretch? You could pick up a newspaper before we go back to the car.' She tried to look coy. 'And you could buy me a bag of chocolate eclairs while you're there.'

He was easily persuaded. She watched as he made his way out of the coffee area, hands in his pockets, his head held high, his pace brisk and confident, almost swaggering. In barely seconds he had vanished into a throng of customers outside the newsagent's shop, and the very moment that the back of his head disappeared she quickly thrust her hand into her bag and pulled out her mobile phone. She jabbed anxiously at the keypad and pressed the phone to her ear.

Please pick up. Please pick up. Please pick up.

The call connected and Emma drew in a sharp breath of relief, only to exhale it again despondently as the call diverted to voicemail. 'Barb, it's me. It's Emma.' She whispered loudly into the phone. 'I can't explain properly, there isn't time. We're on our way to Cornwall, to Penwithen. Jase doesn't want you to know.' She glanced up in the direction of the shop but there was no sign of Jason. 'Barb, I'm scared. He's going to see the Lancefields. He hasn't even told them that he's coming. I had to come with him. I'm scared about what might happen. I don't think he's well. But I had to agree not to tell you what he was planning.'

She felt a sudden knot of tension in her gut. It all sounded far too ridiculous. But it wasn't. God knows there was nothing remotely funny about it. 'Barb, he'll be back in a minute. I'm going to have to ring off. Please send me a text to let me know that you've got this message. But whatever you do, please don't call me back. I won't be able to take the call, and if he finds out that I've told you where we are, I just don't know what he'll do.'

8

The fire in the library at Salvation Hall had been lit in the hour before Kathryn's arrival and now, seated at the grand mahogany desk, she was beginning to feel the heat. She put a hand up to her neck and pulled on the cashmere cardigan loosely draped around her shoulders until it slipped silently down onto the carved wooden backrest of the captain's chair, and then reached down into the bag at her feet with almost-reluctant fingers. She pulled out a large, fading silk scarf and a pair of soft, white cotton gloves, and then rolled the chair forward until she was a little closer to the desk.

She shook out the scarf and then smoothed it across the top of the desk, teasing out the fabric's wrinkles with her fingers, and then deftly pulled on the gloves and reached down again into the bag to retrieve a small black velvet pouch. She could feel the contours of its contents as she lifted it onto the desk, the soft leather curves of an ageing notebook, its well-worn covers yielding and bending within her grasp as she placed it gently down on the scarf in front of her.

She rested her elbows on the edge of the desk and stared at the pouch, her chin resting on her hands, her eyes contemplating the contents with a growing sense of unease. And for a fleeting moment, she wondered whether it would be best to return this particular treasure to the bottom of a crate in the storeroom.

God knows there were horrors enough in that room – the brick-built outhouse next to the late Philip McKeith's potting shed – and for the most part, Kathryn had become almost immune to them. Her initial shock at seeing the manacles, chains, whips and stocks – the inanimate reminders of the Lancefield's distasteful heritage – had soon made way for the historian's objective curiosity, and she had examined, photographed, catalogued and packaged them all with a cold, almost clinical detachment. It was easy, she thought, to detach from such things, to see them as little more than a collection of objects, iron and timber and leather. All one had to do was deny the human context. Perform a simple trick of the brain.

But there were some things amongst them that just couldn't be denied.

She had found the notebook at the bottom of a dusty packing crate. Abandoned and forgotten, the once-supple pigskin binding had begun to flake at the corners but the pages within had defied their neglect, their story too precious to surrender to the damp and decay of Richard Lancefield's storeroom. She had opened the cover with an eager delight, keen to uncover whatever new piece of Lancefield history lay within it. But soon she had closed it again with a heavy heart. Not every story is a cause for celebration. And perhaps not every story needed to see the light of day.

She put up a hand to the reading lamp to her right and took hold of the shade, pulling the metal collar around until the beam of light settled on the top of the velvet pouch. And then slowly, carefully, she pulled the fragile book once more from its hiding place and settled it gently onto the soft silk scarf.

Did this particular story need to see the light of day?

She leaned back in the captain's chair with a sigh and folded her arms across her chest. The answer to the question, of course, was "yes". Who was she, to suppress the truth of The Redemption's first voyage on behalf of the Lancefield family? And why would she even consider such a possibility? Richard had commissioned her to document his family's history, and David was keen to own that history before deciding for himself just what to do with it. It wasn't in her gift to suppress the truth, to hide the story from Richard or David, let alone to keep it hidden from the world at large.

She looked down at the book with uneasy eyes, dismayed by a passing thought. The story of The Redemption's voyage didn't belong only to the Lancefields. Sharing the facts with Richard and David was only part of the picture. This story, the story within these yellowing, crumbling pages, belonged to another family too. Within the pages of this book lay the beginnings of a family feud, the baring of a conscience, and the anguish of a man drowning in the unfathomable depths of greed and profiteering and the unspeakable, undeniable horror of man's inhumanity to man.

This story, this book, belonged to the family of the man whose writing filled its pages. It belonged to the late Dennis Speed, to his son Jason, and to their cousin Barbara. Cousins who, without it, might never know why their lives were so different from those of Richard and David Lancefield. Who might never know why they were cut adrift from the Lancefield family, why their legacy was denied to them, and their fortunes settled on the redoubtable Lysbeth Silver Lancefield. Because this story, this book, was so much more than just the recording of a voyage, the passage of The Redemption on its way from Liverpool to Angola, and from there to St Felix by the infamous Middle Passage.

This was the personal journal of one Captain Digory Banks.

*

'I'm so sorry, Kate. I promised myself that I wouldn't get upset.' Barbara pulled a crisp cotton handkerchief from the pocket of her coat and dabbed at her eyes. 'He looked so peaceful. I just wish that Jason could have been here with me. I can't help thinking that it would have helped him to come to terms with Dennis's death.'

Instead of sulking over his breakfast and leaving someone else to do the difficult work? Kate Jenkins swallowed down the thought and turned in her seat to regard Barbara with a sympathetic gaze. 'There's no need to apologise. Identifying a body can be incredibly distressing, especially when it's someone you were close to.' They were sitting in Kate's Vauxhall outside the hospital mortuary. 'Jason will still be able to see him, once the body's been transferred to the funeral director.' She couldn't shake the feeling that there was something Barbara wanted to talk about, something more than the identification of a body. 'Were you and Dennis always close?'

'Oh, yes. We were more like brother and sister, really. Neither of us had siblings and our parents were all close. We used to holiday together as kids.' Barbara tilted her head towards the police officer. 'Of course, our relationship waned a little after Dennis married Jean. I didn't want to be a third wheel in someone else's marriage. But then after Jean left, Dennis and I became quite close again. He needed someone to help him with Jason.' She hesitated. 'To raise him, I mean. It was difficult for Dennis, trying to bring a small child up on his own.'

'I'm sorry, I didn't realise. I thought Jason's mother had passed away.' Kate tried to sound casually interested. 'And she left Jason behind?'

Barbara's nose wrinkled. 'She wasn't the maternal sort. Poor Dennis was heartbroken. But at least he had Jason.'

'And how did Jason take it?'

'Oh, he was very young at the time, only three or four years of age. Of course, it was hard for him, but we managed somehow. I just wish… well, I wish that Jason was coping better with Dennis's death. The shock seems to have hit him very hard. I tried to talk to him yesterday about the funeral and the identification, and he just wasn't interested.' She glanced at Kate. 'Don't get me wrong, I don't mind doing all these things for Dennis. It's what your next of kin is for, isn't it?'

'But Jason is Dennis's next of kin, surely?'

Barbara checked herself and then nodded with a smile. 'Of course he is. I was talking about Jason. I'm Jason's next of kin now, aren't I, now that Dennis is gone.'

'Apart from his mother?'

A sudden blush blew into Barbara's cheeks and she turned her eyes down to study her hands. 'Jean hasn't wanted anything to do with Jason since the day she left. I wouldn't even know where to find her.' Barbara looked up again. 'I don't mean to sound brusque when you've been so kind, but this is how it's always been for us. Dennis brought Jason up by himself and I did my best to fill the "surrogate mother" role whenever it was needed. Legally speaking, you're quite right. Jean is Jason's next of kin. But the likelihood of her ever making a reappearance in his life… well frankly, it's just not ever going to happen.'

Kate thought for a moment, and then she asked, 'Did Dennis and Jean divorce?'

'Yes, they did. Dennis filed a petition for desertion very shortly after she left. He knew where she was in those days. Who she had left him for and where she was living. She didn't contest it.' Barbara sighed. 'Until Emma came along, there was pretty much just the three of us. A tiny nuclear family.'

A thoughtful silence settled into the Vauxhall's interior and then Kate said, 'I'm sorry I ask so many questions, Barbara. It comes with the job, you know?' She tried to sound contrite and wasn't quite sure that she'd pulled it off. She turned her head to glance out of the car's window at nothing in particular. 'It's funny, isn't it? In terms of family, there's just you and Jason now. Like the Lancefields.' She turned back to look at Barbara, but Barbara had turned her head away. 'How do you feel about that, Barbara? Would you like to have met the Lancefields? It would have been more family for you, wouldn't it? I can't help wondering why Dennis kept that from you, as well as from Jason?'

Barbara considered the question. 'I don't know how I feel about it at the moment, to be honest. All I can think about is Dennis, and the fact that I've lost him.' It was a deflection, not an answer. 'And Jason, and what I can do to help him.' She turned back to Kate. 'At least he has Emma. And hopefully, one day, Jason and Emma will have a family of their own. And then he won't be alone, and I won't have to worry about him anymore.' She tilted her head. 'I turned my mobile phone off when we arrived at the mortuary. It seemed the right thing to do. Would you mind if I turned it back on again now? I'd like to know if Jason has tried to get in touch with me.'

'Sure.' Of course Kate minded. But she couldn't afford to push Barbara too far. 'We'd better get going anyway. I'll drive you back.' She started the car's ignition and pulled the Vauxhall away from the kerb.

In the passenger seat beside her, Barbara drew a mobile phone from the handbag on her lap, turning it on with a flick of the thumb. 'Oh, that sounds hopeful.' A familiar beep heralded the arrival of a new voicemail message, and she pressed the phone to her ear. Her smile faded in an instant. 'Oh God, no.' She turned dismayed eyes towards the policewoman. 'It's a message from Emma. There's no wonder I couldn't get hold of them this morning. They're on their way to Cornwall.'

'To Cornwall? You mean they're going to Penwithen?'

Barbara nodded, her eyes wide with concern. 'They're going to Salvation Hall so that Jason can speak to the Lancefields.' The colour drained from her cheeks. 'Oh, Kate, they mustn't. Whatever can we do to stop them?'

*

Kathryn pulled a chair away from the kitchen table and sat down on it, a reluctant actor for the task at hand. More than once she had rejected an appeal from Richard Lancefield, to take a watching brief over Becca Smith's behaviours. It was a task for which she believed herself ill-equipped, and one which fell more naturally to Richard's capable secretary Nancy, not least since Becca herself had little time for Kathryn. But Nancy was still in St Felix, and someone needed to apprise the belligerent housekeeper of the latest turn of events. Now, alone with the girl in the kitchen, Kathryn regretted accepting the challenge. 'I wanted to speak to you about Dennis Speed.'

At the other side of the room, Becca bristled with discontent. She prodded the dishwasher's on-switch with a determined finger and turned a truculent eye towards Kathryn. 'I hope you're not going to tell me that he's coming down here. I have enough work to do just looking after the house, without pandering to David Lancefield's playmates.'

'Dennis won't be coming here, Becca.' Kathryn chose her words carefully. 'The meeting didn't take place yesterday.' She braced herself for the reaction and she wasn't disappointed.

An almost-triumphant glow flashed across the girl's usually-sullen face. 'Didn't he turn up then? Didn't this Dennis Speed want to know?' She coughed out a laugh. 'Perhaps he's heard what the Lancefields are like.'

'Dennis had an accident. He was hit by a bus on his way to the train station.'

The stark declaration knocked the wind from the housekeeper's sails and she growled under her breath. 'I'm sorry.' It was a grudging apology. 'But I'm only sorry for him. I hope you're not expecting me to show any sympathy for the Lancefields. There's no need for the old man to be reaching out to strangers, looking for a new set of snooty relatives to add to his Christmas card list. He's got me and Frankie. Frankie is Philip's child. She could be a part of the family.'

Kathryn inhaled, and counted silently to ten. She had

heard this narrative so many times before. Keeping her tied cottage for a peppercorn rent, an increase in her housekeeper's salary, a "death in service" benefit after Philip's body was found, even the promise of a private education for Frankie – none of these dented Becca Smith's hostility.

Not that money could ever compensate for the loss of a lover, a partner, a friend. Frankie was too young to understand what had happened to her father, and Richard would make sure that the child was never disadvantaged in a material sense. But for Becca, no amount of money could ever take away the pain of the loss she had suffered.

And why the hell should it? Kathryn exhaled her frustration and did her best to sound kind. 'Richard cares about you, Becca. And he cares about Frankie. He thinks the world of her. And you know that he's doing his best to support you both. But at the end of the day, Philip was a friend. He wasn't a blood relation. Richard has every right to reach out to family if he wants to. Please don't hold that against him, on top of everything else.' She paused, and then dared to ask, 'How did things go here yesterday? I hope it didn't add too much to your workload, my being out all day?'

Becca rolled her eyes. 'It was alright, I suppose. Richard was holed up in the library with the dog for most of the day. But he went out for a walk in the afternoon.' There was the slightest thaw in her tone. 'I took him his morning coffee, like you asked. And his lunch, and his afternoon tea.' She turned an enquiring eye in Kathryn's direction. 'I don't know why you do that for him. I thought you were here to look into the family's history?'

'I am.' Kathryn spoke softly. 'But it's Nancy's job to assist Richard, and since Nancy is in St Felix someone has to step in and look after him. I've just tried to pick up most of Nancy's duties so that you don't have to.' She watched as Becca acknowledged the point with a grudging nod of the head. 'I do appreciate what you did yesterday.'

'I don't need thanking just for doing my job. I didn't do it as a favour. I get paid to do it.' The girl sniffed her disapproval. 'I don't do favours for murderers.'

Kathryn's shoulders stiffened. 'If that's really how you feel, Becca, then why don't you go?' The time for soft words was running out. 'You know, I understand why you feel so angry. I can't imagine what you've been through. Losing Philip must have been bad enough, but losing him the way that you did – it was brutal. What I can't understand is why the hell you stay here. If that's how you feel about Richard and the family, if you still hold them responsible for what happened to Philip, then why are you still working here? Why come here every day to be reminded, to torture yourself like this?'

Becca lifted a hand and slammed it down on the kitchen counter. 'Why the hell shouldn't I stay here? That cottage on the estate is my home, mine and Frankie's. And it has been since long before you turned up. And if Richard wants us to stay, then why shouldn't we stay? No one said anything about having to be nice while I work here. I'm just doing my job, keeping my nose clean, and picking up my wages.' She turned her head and cast a scornful eye across her shoulder. 'Maybe you should think about doing the same. I didn't ask for your opinion, but since you feel inclined to give it, maybe you'd like to hear mine? I don't understand why *you* stay here. There's been nothing but trouble since you turned up, spouting your fancy notions about families and history, and long-lost relatives. And I for one wish that you'd just go away, and leave those of us who belong here to get on with it.'

9

Price waited until David Lancefield disconnected the call and then placed the phone's receiver back down on its cradle, cursing quietly under his breath. He swivelled on his chair to face the set of metal shelves behind him and put out a hand to pull a grey lever-arch folder from the middle shelf, his growing file of harassment against the Lancefield family. The file was expanding far too quickly for his liking. Whatever he thought of the Lancefields – and make no mistake, despite Kathryn's appeals to the contrary he still considered them a spoiled bunch of aristos – they didn't deserve a hate campaign.

He swivelled back on his chair and threw the file onto his desk. He was growing tired now of the Smith family's persistent and petty campaign of intimidation. It wasted time and it wasted energy. The main antagonist, Price knew, was Becca's eldest brother Zak. And if Zak Smith had any sense he would know by now that neither Richard nor David were in any way daunted by his jibes or his threats or his mindless acts of vandalism. He might even realise how tired Price was of trying to explain that such actions might jeopardise the case against Marcus Drake. But then sense had never really been one of Zak's strong points.

The policeman wondered for a moment just exactly what Becca's brother was trying to achieve. As far as he could recall, there had been no particular friendship between Zak and Philip McKeith, no burning reason for him to care whether the Lancefields had or hadn't been instrumental in Philip's death. His current plea was that he wanted justice for his sister and her daughter, but harassing the Lancefields wasn't going to bring him that. Was this, as Ennor suspected, just a handy opportunity for a local lout to kick back at the landed gentry? He'd been caught often enough poaching on the Lancefields' land, so was this just an excuse to pay them back? Did he really believe that McKeith was innocent of Lucy's murder? Or was that just an excuse for a vindictive campaign of his own?

Price let out a sigh. Right now, did any of that really matter? Did it matter why Zak was intent on making the Lancefield family's life a misery if he had the opportunity and the motivation to do it? Apart from anything else, if Zak was busy in Penwithen yesterday, taking his prejudices out on Lucy Lancefield's grave, he couldn't have been anywhere near Liverpool, pushing Dennis Speed under a bus.

Price laughed softly under his breath. His imagination was beginning to get the better of him these days. As if Speed's death could have possibly been some part of a ridiculous Smith-family conspiracy to wreak their revenge on the Lancefields. Dennis Speed died as the result of a road traffic accident. His conversation with Kathryn the evening before had raised nothing to suggest otherwise. And long may it continue to be that way. No one knew what caused Speed to fall in front of that bus and, truth be told, Ennor didn't want to know. He didn't need to know. All he knew was that he didn't need yet another Lancefield case to juggle. A double murder and a campaign of harassment were quite enough for now. As far as he was concerned, the death of Dennis Speed could stay firmly on DCI Andy Drummond's books.

There was a page of handwritten notes on the desk and Price picked it up and slipped it into the file. At some point that morning, someone would probably confirm to Tom Parkinson that Zak Smith had been spotted in the village the day before. That would put Smith neatly in the frame for the card on Lucy's grave. Ennor closed the folder with a nod and was about to turn in his chair to return it to the bookshelf when the phone on his desk began to ring. His mood improved, he lifted the receiver with a smile and barked his name into the mouthpiece. 'Ennor Price.'

At the other end of the line, Drummond's laconic Liverpudlian drawl rang out. 'Ennor? It's Andy.'

'Mate, I'm sorry. I owe you a call. It's been one of those mornings. You know how it is.' Price tucked the phone into the crook of his neck and swivelled gently in his chair. 'I met with Kathryn last night and there's nothing to worry about. She can't think of anything that might connect the family to Dennis Speed's accident. The family are saddened by the death, but nothing more. And I'm happy to say that I can't think of anything either.' He smiled to himself. 'To be honest, I only had one possibility and something happened down here in Cornwall yesterday that I think puts paid to that. I'm expecting my sergeant to confirm that later today.' Price could barely resist sounding smug. 'So, I'm afraid it's over to you again, pal. Dennis Speed's death is a Liverpool affair.'

There was a momentary pause and then Andy Drummond clicked his teeth. 'Nice try, Ennor, but I'm afraid you're not going to be able to pass this one back to me quite that easily.'

*

The drawing room at Salvation Hall was an impressive sight. Long and narrow, it could easily be three rooms in one. Sunlight flooded in through a vast bay window to warm the cosier end of the room, a comfortable space accommodating an impressive Chesterfield sofa and a collection of mismatched but equally impressive damask-covered armchairs. Beyond, an expanse of space ran past the room's only door to a recess containing a Steinway piano. The highly polished floor was littered with Chinese rugs, silk-shaded gilt table lamps illuminated exquisite pieces of antique furniture, and a stunning collection of Impressionist art-work punctuated the simply-painted walls.

Its unquestionable elegance was something that the Lancefield family had learned to take in their stride. It was, after all, their family home. But for those unaccustomed to the finer things in life…

David watched with a sympathetic eye as Emma Needham hovered by the sofa's edge. 'Emma, my dear, please make yourself at home. I'm sure you would feel more comfortable without your coat.' He couldn't miss the anxious glance she threw at Jason, standing awkwardly beside an armchair. 'You've both driven such a long way this morning.' Probably about four hundred miles, if his reckoning was correct. 'Kathryn will be here shortly with some refreshments.'

Emma forced a smile in David's direction. 'Thank you.' She unzipped her pale blue padded coat and wriggled out of it. 'It has been quite a long journey.' Hesitant, she placed the coat down on the sofa's arm and then sat down beside it and rested her hands primly in her lap. For a moment she gazed at David with unseeing eyes, and then she flicked the eyes up to Jason and gave an almost imperceptible jerk of the head.

Jason started and slipped off his own jacket. 'I'm sorry to just turn up unannounced on your doorstep like this.' He dropped the coat on top of Emma's and then sat down beside her on the sofa. He rested his hands on his knees and looked up at David with narrowed, inquisitive eyes. 'I take it you know who I am?'

David nodded. 'Kathryn told me who you were when she came to advise me of your arrival. You're Jason, Dennis Speed's son.' He lowered himself into an armchair. 'And this is your friend, Emma.' He nodded again in the girl's direction. To call her a friend was the safest guess, though she could be a partner, a lover, perhaps even fiancée? 'Might I ask what brings you all the way to

Penwithen today?' The question sounded absurd, almost as absurd as the situation itself, but he was too well-mannered to risk embarrassing his uninvited guests.

Jason flicked his eyes towards Emma, perhaps looking for an encouragement which she didn't appear inclined to provide. He cleared his throat and turned back to David. 'I understand that my dad was meant to be meeting with you yesterday.'

'And I was very much looking forward to meeting with him. I've heard, of course, of the tragic accident at the station, and I'm very sorry indeed for your loss.'

'He was hit by a bus outside the station. On his way to meet with you.' Jason leaned forward. 'The thing is, David, I didn't know anything about it. About the fact that he was planning to meet with you. I only learned about it when the police gave me the letters he was carrying. The letters from your solicitor, and from your father.'

'I see.' David's brow puckered. In truth, he wasn't sure at all that he *did* see. 'And that's why you've come to Penwithen? To ask me about the letters that were sent to your father?' It would be too obvious to ask why Jason didn't simply pick up the phone that morning and make a phone call, especially in the wake of such a brutal and unexpected bereavement. David would have to choose his words carefully. 'This was something which you wished to discuss with me in person?'

Jason's broad forehead rippled with a frown. 'It wasn't like my dad to keep something like that from me. We discussed everything. We shared everything. We worked together day in, day out.' It didn't answer David's question. 'I thought that you might know why he kept it to himself.'

David thought for a moment and then said, 'I'm afraid not, Jason. You see, we didn't know that to be the case. If you've seen the letters then you will know that my father invited Dennis, yourself and your cousin Barbara to visit us here at Salvation Hall. And we would have been most pleased to meet with Emma too.' He offered her an encouraging smile. 'It was Dennis's idea that we should meet for lunch in Bristol, instead.'

'And he didn't tell you why?'

'I'm afraid not. We are as much in the dark about that as you.' And probably just as intrigued. 'We had assumed that Dennis was coming to meet with us alone, so that he could reassure himself that our two families were actually connected, that there was a legitimate link. And perhaps to make sure that we could be trusted. After all, my father's original letter to him will have arrived like a bolt from the blue. It isn't every day, I'm sure, that one receives a letter from a stranger claiming to be a long-lost relative.' David paused to let the notion settle, and then said, 'May I ask about cousin Barbara? Was she not disposed to make the journey with you today?' Out of the corner of his eye, he saw Emma throw Jason a cautionary glance.

But Jason just shrugged. 'We were planning to make an early start, and we didn't want to put her out.' He placed a hand on Emma's knee and patted it gently. 'And Auntie Barbara is never too keen on long car journeys. Six and a half hours on the road would be a stretch for her, wouldn't it, Em?'

The girl gave an unconvincing nod. 'We broke the journey up at Exeter services. But it's still a long time to spend in the car.'

David smiled again at Emma. He could see that she was trying to rally, but there were dark circles under her eyes that spoke of something more than a short night's sleep. The girl looked exhausted, yes, but she was anxious. There was, he was certain, something preying on her mind.

He took a moment to consider the situation – the unexpectedness of their arrival, the flimsiest of pretexts for their making the journey, and their decision not to include Barbara – and found himself unable to fathom the absurdity of it. He placed his hands on his knees and pushed himself to his feet. 'I had no idea that your journey had been so long. It's not refreshments that we need, it's lunch.' He bowed his head. 'If you'll excuse me for a moment, I'll just pop along to the kitchen and have a word with Kathryn.'

Outside in the hallway, David Lancefield drew in a breath. There was one more thing that he found himself unable to fathom, and that was Emma's obvious discomfort. His reference to Barbara had clearly touched a nerve, and that only left him wondering just exactly what he was missing.

*

Kathryn closed the door of the orchid house behind her and leaned against the doorframe. 'I've prepared some coffee and biscuits for David to take into the drawing room. He's going to try to keep Jason and Emma entertained until some lunch can be prepared.' It was humid in the glass house and she fanned her face with a hand, trying to create a cooling breeze. 'Richard, it's very warm in here. Are you sure it shouldn't be better ventilated?'

Richard, clearly amused, lifted his head from the potting bench and raised an eyebrow in her direction. 'Kathryn, my dear, you would never thrive in St Felix.' He turned his attention back to the bench and picked up an unpotted orchid. 'This is the normal temperature for early November.' He gave the orchid a shake, loosening the bark from its roots, and then set about clipping them with a pair of sharp snips. 'Dare I ask what you have done with Becca?'

'I've sent her into Penwithen on an errand. If I'm to rustle up lunch we'll need more bread and some homemade cakes from the bakery. It will keep her out of the way until we've agreed on a plan of action.' Always supposing that a plan of action could be agreed upon. 'Fortunately, there is cold ham in the fridge, and we have plenty of cheese and fruit.' Kathryn sighed. 'What is this all about, Richard? Why have they come all the way to Penwithen, unannounced?'

'I would think they have come looking for answers.' The old man gave the orchid's roots another shake. 'Yesterday should have been a momentous occasion for the family, Kathryn. The healing of a rift that has endured for over two hundred years. By rights, it should have happened here at Salvation Hall.' He shook his head sadly. 'This is not at all how I imagined things would unfold.' He reached up to a shelf to retrieve a clean plant pot. 'It's possible that the boy wants to know why his father kept my letters to himself. The question could have waited, but Jason only lost his father yesterday, and grief can often be called upon to account for the inexplicable.'

'You think he's behaving irrationally because of Dennis's death?'

'Perhaps because of the nature of Dennis's death.' Richard dangled the orchid's roots into the pot and began to add handfuls of bark. 'The death itself was both unexpected and shocking. And then to learn that his father had been secretive about his trip to Bristol, about the very fact that we had been in contact – well, it must pose many questions for the boy.' Richard tapped the pot on the bench to settle the roots and then turned again to look at Kathryn. 'You of all people know how keen I am to find an extended family. But this is not the time or place to talk to the boy about building a family connection. The shock of his father's death may lead him to say or do things which he may find he later regrets. And neither is it the time to judge his motives in coming here. Perhaps the best we can do today is offer him some kindness, answer whatever questions we can, and then send him back up to Liverpool to deal with his grief. There will be time enough to talk of family connections when his father is buried and he is able to look to the future.'

Kathryn sank onto the shabby Lloyd Loom chair beside the door. 'Do you think we should attempt to contact Barbara Gee? Do you think that Barbara even knows that Jason and Emma have come down to Penwithen today? David asked them why Barbara wasn't with them, and it seemed to touch a nerve.'

'My dear Kathryn.' Richard closed his eyes and shook his head with a smile. 'Jason isn't a child. And he isn't our responsibility. Perhaps we should just take this whole situation at face value. He wants to know why his father didn't share those letters with him. Perhaps the conundrum has given him something to latch on to, a balm to ease the pain of unexpected loss. All we can do is welcome him, and let nature take its course.'

'Is that really what you think?'

The old man's eyes creased and his cheeks began to dimple. 'Truthfully? I still cannot help wondering myself why Dennis chose not to inform his son that I had reached out to them, any more than I can help wondering whether David is right and that the reluctance is in some way connected to our family's unconventional history. There is also the question of Lucy's murder – the events in our more recent past have been the subject of much insalubrious speculation. Perhaps Dennis heard the rumours and wanted to protect his family from the notoriety.' Richard's face brightened. 'Still, they are here now, and it will be good for us to have the presence of young people in the house, at least for today.' He turned to study Kathryn's face, looking for understanding. 'Do you think I have got this wrong?'

'Wrong? It's not for me to make that call. I know how important it is for you to find a family for David. We always knew that there would be risks, and the possibility of disappointment if things didn't work out the way you'd hoped. But I understand that you have to try.'

'Then we are in accord.' Richard turned back to the potting bench and picked up a small watering can. 'David and I will have lunch with this young couple. And before we send them on their way back up to Liverpool we will give them a tour of the house, share with them a little of our history, and give them every indication that in time we will be there for them if needed. And I hope, my dear girl' – he tried, and failed, to suppress a grin – 'that we will do so with your blessing.'

10

Becca Smith dropped the empty tartan shopping bag onto the floor and slipped into a seat at the table beside the window. She took a cautious glance through the glass, craning her neck to check up and down the road outside The Lancefield Arms, and then turned towards the bar and beckoned to her brother with an enthusiastic wave of the hand.

Zak registered her attempts to attract his attention, and then lifted his glass to his lips and drained off the dregs. 'I'll have another, Harry, when you're ready.' He threw the words across his shoulder to the landlord, busy bottling up behind the bar. 'I'll be at the table in the window.' He rolled off the bar stool he'd been occupying for the last three-quarters of an hour and ambled across the almost-empty room towards his sister. 'What's up, Becs?'

She beamed at him as he dropped onto a chair at the other side of the table, her excitement barely contained. 'It's all kicking off up at the hall.'

'Is that all?' His thick lips settled into a smirk. 'The way you're carrying on, I thought you'd won the lottery.' He folded tattooed arms across his chest and lowered his head, looking up at her through thick, dark lashes. 'You want a drink?'

Impatient, she shook her head. 'I don't have time. I've just come to tell you what's happened.' She lowered her voice to an eager whisper. 'Old man Lancefield's plans have come off the rails, big time. You know that bloke, Dennis, that David and Kathryn were going to meet? They trailed all the way to Bristol yesterday, and you'll never guess what happened.'

'He didn't turn up?'

'Better than that.' Becca's eyes widened. 'He didn't even leave Liverpool. He fell in front of a bus on his way to the station.'

If she'd expected her brother to share in her joy, she could only have been disappointed. Zak growled under his breath. 'Well, that explains a lot. Your mate Tom Parkinson was in here not half an hour since, sniffing around, asking questions about the family. He wanted to know where me and Robin were all day yesterday.'

'You mean he thought you had something to do with what happened to that Dennis?'

'I dunno.' Zak scowled. 'But they're not pinning that on us. That was nothing to do with us.' He paused, and then his unshaven cheeks puffed up with a devious grin. 'You wouldn't have been disappointed though, would you? If it had been down to me and Robin? You want those privileged bastards to suffer, don't you?'

It was a possibility that she hadn't considered. While Dennis Speed's untimely death might be a cause for celebration, her brothers in the frame for his murder was not. She put out a hand and grasped at Zak's arm. 'Zak, you didn't…'

'Didn't what?' He growled the words menacingly under his breath, and then leaned back in his seat and let out a raucous laugh. 'Of course I didn't, you dopey bitch. How the hell could I? We live in bloody Cornwall. I wouldn't even know where to find the bloke.' He rolled his eyes and then leaned back down on the table and whispered to her. 'But I would have done if you'd wanted me to. You know you only have to ask, little sister.'

Becca felt an exquisite rush of adrenalin. For a moment she froze, and then she gently drew back from Zak a little and forced her lips into a smile. 'Just as well I didn't ask you then. I don't want my brother to go to prison, do I?' She tried to sound nonchalant. 'Not for me, anyway.' She pouted. 'I know you're looking out for me, Zak. But if the police are watching you, you need to cool it a bit.'

'Let them watch. What those bastards did to you was unspeakable.' His mood was swinging back to belligerence. 'That bastard Drake murdered your Philip, left you without a man and your baby without a dad. They deserve everything that's coming to them.' He growled again under his breath. 'And that bloke in Liverpool, he's better off out of it. Better off dead, than one of them. At least it will put an end to all that rubbish about finding more relatives to carry on their poncy name.'

Becca turned her head away from him to look out of the window. 'No, it won't. That's the other thing I've come to tell you. Dennis's son has turned up at Salvation Hall. He just arrived on the doorstep out of the blue, with his girlfriend in tow. And Zak, you'll never guess… they're as common as muck.'

An angry flush of colour began to show beneath the stubble on Zak Smith's cheeks. 'Common or not, they're family for the Lancefields. What's gonna happen to you, Becs, if they get their feet under the table?' He nodded, as if to emphasise the point. 'Maybe they'll throw you and Frankie out of the cottage and give it to this pair. Maybe they'll take him on as a gardener, to replace your Philip. And she can do your job.'

'Don't be so vile.' Suddenly Becca forgot her fear and she let out a punch, a jab of her fist that hit her brother square in the shoulder. 'I thought you were on my side.'

He grasped at the shoulder with his other hand. 'Bloody hell, Becs. What was that for? Can't you take a joke?'

'It isn't a joke if it isn't funny.' Her anger was beginning to build. 'Sometimes I don't think you really understand just what it's like for me. Sometimes I think it's all just one big joke to you. You don't care about what happened to Philip. You just want an excuse to cause trouble.'

'So what if I do? Does it matter to you why I do it, as long as it serves a purpose? As long as I make your precious Lancefields suffer?' He stopped rubbing at his shoulder and folded his arms across his chest. 'What do you want me to do about it? Put the frighteners on them? Drive them away?' He snuffled a scornful laugh under his breath. 'Shit, Becs, I can't do much about it when they're on the inside of Salvation Hall, can I?'

'I don't want you to do anything. I only came to tell you what had happened.' And now she wished that she hadn't bothered. She puffed out a petulant lip and grasped at the shopping bag under the table. 'I'd better get down to the bakery. If I'm not back soon they'll wonder where I am.' She pushed herself up to her feet and then took one more look at her brother. 'If Tom Parkinson didn't come to ask you about what happened in Liverpool, what did he come to ask you about?'

Zak grinned, a familiar, supercilious sneer. 'It seems like the late and unlamented Lucy Lancefield has a secret admirer. Somebody left some flowers on her grave.' He feigned a look of indignation. 'As if I'd waste good drinking money on flowers for a slut like that.'

*

'I had a call from Andy Drummond. He told me that Jason and his girlfriend were on their way down here.' Ennor Price helped himself to a piece of Cornish Yarg from the plate on the kitchen table. 'I just thought I should pop in and make sure everything was okay.'

'And why wouldn't it be okay?' Kathryn sounded annoyed. 'Do you think we can't cope with a young couple coming to visit Salvation Hall?'

'They turned up unexpectedly, didn't they?'

She gave a wry smile. 'And so did you.'

'Yes, but I only came from Penzance. They've come all the way from Liverpool.' She was sitting beside him at the table, close enough for him to be able to feel the brittle heat of her displeasure. 'You know that Jason was supposed to be identifying his father's body today?'

'How could I be expected to know that?' Kathryn threw up her hands. 'Ennor, what are you really doing here? Has something else happened? Or have you just come to be nosy?'

'Nothing else has happened. And I really did want to know that everything was okay.' He stifled a grin. 'As well as being nosy.' He nudged her arm with his elbow. 'Why are you cross with me?' He hoped it was the usual reason. Usually, when she was cross with him, it was because she was going on the defensive.

She considered the question and then her shoulders relaxed. She tilted her head and looked at him with appraising eyes. 'Are you on duty?'

'Just a teeny bit.' He held up a hand, his thumb and forefinger almost touching. 'I just wondered what they were doing here, turning up out of the blue like that.' He tried to sound casual. 'You know you can speak freely to me. I never reveal my sources.' He lowered his voice to a whisper. 'Well, maybe now and again, when the price is right.' He watched as a smile began to tug at the corner of her mouth. Any minute now…

She sighed her surrender. 'Okay, you win.' She looked down at her hands and spoke to her fingers, as if not meeting his gaze would make it better. 'Jason told David that he didn't know anything about the Lancefields, or Salvation Hall, or the meeting arranged for Bristol. He was upset that Dennis had kept it all a secret from him and he wanted to ask if David or Richard knew why.'

'And for that, he drove all the way from Liverpool to Penwithen? He couldn't just pick up the phone?'

'Yes, that's what David thought.' She puffed out her cheeks. 'I agree that it's all a bit odd, but Richard is taking a different view. He thinks that Jason is grieving, or perhaps still in shock.'

Trust the old man to be pragmatic. 'So what's the plan?'

'To be kind to them today. They're both exhausted and they're newly bereaved. Richard has the kid gloves out. I managed to rustle up the beginnings of lunch and they're taking it in the conservatory. After coffee, he's going to show them around the house and the garden, and then send them off to get some rest. He asked me to book them a room at The Lancefield Arms, at his expense. I think the intention is for them to have some supper at the pub, stay overnight, and then invite them back here to have breakfast with David and Richard in the morning before they go back to Liverpool.'

'Richard wasn't inclined to let them stay here at Salvation Hall then?'

Kathryn gave the policeman a withering look. 'He doesn't want them to be exposed to the harassment, or to Becca's bile.'

'And he thinks they'll be able to avoid that at The Lancefield Arms?' It seemed unlikely. 'How are you keeping Becca out of the way now?'

'I sent her down to the bakery in the village until we'd decided what to do. When she comes back I'll send her home for the rest of the day.' Kathryn rubbed at her temple with her fingers. 'How did Andy Drummond know that Jason and Emma were on their way down here?'

'Barbara Gee had a message from Emma, and she was worried about them making such a long journey when Jason was still in shock.' Price didn't want to say too much. 'I said that I'd drop by and make sure that they'd arrived safely so that Andy could pass the message back to Barbara and put her mind at rest.'

'I see.' Kathryn sounded unconvinced. There was something on her mind. 'They seem like a nice couple.'

'Do I detect a hint of reservation?'

'Well, Jason is a little wired but I suppose that's only to be expected.' She thought for a moment. 'It's Emma. I get the impression that she didn't want to come and I can't help thinking that she's only here to keep an eye on Jason.'

Kathryn put a hand on Ennor's arm. 'I know you'll think I'm crazy, but something doesn't feel right.' She looked up into his face with thoughtful eyes. 'Something doesn't feel right at all, but I don't know what it is.'

*

David offered the delicate cup and saucer to Emma with a smile. 'Please help yourself to sugar.' He sank into a large armchair next to the sofa. 'I very rarely have coffee after lunch myself. This is the stuff for me.' He pointed at another cup resting on the coffee table, a steaming concoction of fresh peppermint leaves and water. 'Each to his own.' He sounded cheerful; comfortable with meaningless small talk.

Richard settled deeper into his favourite shabby armchair and turned his eyes from his son to his guests. Emma and Jason were sitting primly on the edge of the drawing room sofa, Emma balancing the delicate china carefully between faintly trembling hands, Jason eyeing David intently with an attentive, brooding eye. Just what they were doing at Salvation Hall was still a mystery to the old man. He had heard Jason's explanation, discussed it with Kathryn and David, and convinced himself that – taken in the context of Dennis's unexpected death – he was almost prepared to believe it.

Almost.

He cleared his throat. 'Emma, my dear, you mentioned over lunch that Barbara has been conducting her own research into her family's history. Has she happened to mention whether that research has taken her as far back as the Lancefield connection?'

Emma blinked, startled by Richard's attention as much as by the question, and she turned her eyes to Jason. 'I think she mentioned that she'd come across the name. Didn't she, Jase?'

Jason shook his head. 'I don't remember. We don't

really encourage her to talk about it much. I mean, it's all just history, isn't it?'

'Yes, I suppose it is.' Richard raised an eyebrow in David's direction, but his son was busy averting his eyes in an attempt to suppress a smile. 'Of course, without that history, we might never have known that our two families were in any way connected. It was only thanks to Kathryn's sterling work on our own family tree that we were able to identify your father, Barbara and yourself as our nearest living blood relations.'

A faint flush of colour began to seep into Jason's pale cheeks, and he looked down at his hands. 'I suppose I should have paid more attention to what Barbara was telling me.' He ran a thoughtful tongue around his teeth and then asked, 'Has Kathryn identified any other relatives?'

'At the moment all her efforts are concentrated on the Speed and Gee lines of the family.' Richard was not inclined to grace the question with a direct answer. 'It remains to be seen whether I will ask her to research further. Our families' connection dates back a couple of hundred years, Jason, all the way back to the early nineteenth century. I am, of course, delighted that Kathryn was able to identify the link.'

Emma frowned. 'I'm still not sure that I understand why you decided to reach out to Dennis. Why do you need more family? Is it because you're lonely?'

'Heavens, no.' Richard felt a sudden pang of compassion for the girl. 'I realise that we must seem an odd set-up to you, Emma – David and I rattling around in this big old pile of bricks. But we are not completely without friends and family. I have a delightful secretary, Nancy, who lives here with us. She grew up on our estate in St Felix and is quite a part of the family. She is there on holiday at the moment, visiting her parents, or it would have been a great pleasure to introduce you to her.' He looked suddenly wistful. 'Sadly, we lost our estate gardener some weeks ago and we still haven't managed to find a permanent replacement for him. But his partner remains with us and works as our housekeeper. You met her briefly when she helped Kathryn to serve the second course of lunch. Becca lives in a cottage on the estate and has a charming little girl, Francesca – we call her Frankie.' He nodded to himself. 'And there is Kathryn, of course. She has a home in Cambridge but spends the weekdays here in Cornwall with us. She has chosen not to reside at Salvation Hall with us during the week, she prefers to stay in a hotel in Penzance. But she works here every day and sometimes well into the evening. We often have supper together.'

'And we have other relatives by marriage, of course.' David broke his silence. 'I have a charming wife, but she is my second wife, and we married late. Regrettably too late to have a family together.' He hesitated before adding, 'Stella and I have our own home in Edinburgh. But I am staying here at the moment in order to work with my father and learn more about running the estates. And in time, I hope that she will agree to spend more time with me here at Salvation Hall.'

Emma still looked puzzled. Richard rested his elbows on the arms of his chair and steepled his fingers. 'The Lancefield family is a very old, very prestigious and very privileged family, Emma. We are also rather set in our ways, and our ways do not always seem to sit comfortably with the rest of society.' He frowned. 'Perhaps I might put it another way. The rest of society does not always find it within itself to understand that our ways and our legacy are normal for us. As I mentioned to you over lunch, our family made its original fortune several centuries ago from its estates on St Felix. And we still have very close connections with the island through our Woodlands Plantation.' He let out a sigh. 'I used to make a lengthy annual trip to the estate myself but, unfortunately, old age is getting the better of me now, and my doctor forbade me the trip this year.'

'We've always wanted to visit the Caribbean, haven't we, Em?' Jason asked the question without looking at the girl, his attention wholly on Richard now.

Emma didn't answer him. Discomfited, she looked shyly up at Richard. 'That must be very sad for you. Do you think you'll be able to make the trip next year?'

Richard smiled at her and tilted his head. 'Thank you for asking, my dear. Yes, it is very sad. And no, I very much doubt that I shall see St Felix again.'

'So what will happen to the plantation?' Jason cast an irritated glance at his girlfriend as he asked the question. 'Will you sell it?'

'Good heavens, no.' Richard uttered a quiet laugh. 'We have owned the Woodlands Plantation for over three hundred years. We were amongst the original sugar producers on the island, and that is how we built our fortune. That wealth in turn was used to invest in businesses and property here in England. The estate still runs as a going concern. It produces sugar and rum, and provides employment for local people.' He laughed again. 'Well, I say "we own it". It often feels to me more that we are caretakers, managing the land and looking after our extended family who work with us.' His face softened, his train of thought suddenly cast adrift in the Caribbean. 'It's a very beautiful place, the Woodlands Plantation. And a very happy one. We are very lucky.'

Emma's brow creased. 'If your family own a sugar plantation, Richard, then at some point they must have owned slaves?'

'Of course, my dear. It wasn't possible to operate a sugar plantation without slaves in the early days. Sugar production was very labour intensive, and the climate can be fierce. I'm afraid it was just a fact of life in those days.'

The girl turned her head to Jason. 'Do you think that Barbara knows about that, Jason? From her work on the family history?'

'I shouldn't think so. And what does it matter anyway?'

Jason snapped at her, biting back his annoyance. 'I mean, it's not like the family keeps slaves now, is it?'

11

Kate Jenkins switched off her mobile phone and dropped it into her bag. Across the table, Barbara was stirring a frothy cappuccino with a wooden stick, her eyes fixed not on Kate, but out of the café's window across the quayside to where the River Mersey rippled and rolled on its way out into the Irish Sea.

Kate turned her head to follow the woman's gaze. On the other side of the glass a mist was coming in off the water, a thankless haze soaking everything in its path – cobbles, pedestrians, even seagulls were beginning to glisten noticeably with its dewy deposits. 'God, it's miserable in the town when the weather turns like this.' She took a sip of warming hot chocolate. 'I don't know how people could make themselves go to sea.'

'No? I've always loved the water, since long before I ever started studying our family's history. I suppose it made a lot of sense when I discovered there were mariners in our direct line.' She gave a soft, low laugh. 'The connection we have with the Lancefield family comes somehow from our links to the sea. Our common ancestor was in the Royal Navy.' Her brow furrowed into an unhappy ridge. 'I tried several times to tell Jason and Dennis about it, but they just weren't interested at all.' She sipped on the coffee. 'Dennis used to say that no good ever came of digging up the past.' Her lower lip began to tremble. 'It looks as though he was right.'

Kate shook her head. 'Don't upset yourself, Barbara. You've been through a lot in the last twenty-four hours.' She tried to strike a brighter note. 'Anyway, I've got some good news for you. We've heard back from DCI

Drummond's contact in Penzance. He's been over to Salvation Hall, and he's confirmed that there is nothing at all for you to worry about. Emma and Jason arrived safely just before lunch and the Lancefields are looking after them.'

'Oh, Kate.' Barbara stifled a sob of relief. 'Are they really alright?'

'A bit tired, but otherwise fine. We've been told that they travelled with overnight bags in case they decided to spend the night in Penzance. Richard Lancefield has kindly arranged for them to stay in the village inn overnight, and they'll be travelling back to Liverpool tomorrow. Kathryn Clifton – she's the lady who was travelling with David Lancefield to meet with Dennis – she's there too, and she'll let DCI Price know if there are any problems. And I'm to give you this.' Kate dipped a hand into her bag and pulled out a scrap of paper. 'This is the landline number for Salvation Hall and Kathryn's mobile number. If you're worried at all, you can call either number.'

Barbara's face clouded. 'But I'm not supposed to know that they're in Cornwall. Emma said that Jason didn't want me to know.'

'Kathryn knows that, and she'll be discreet.' Kate thought for a moment. 'The Lancefields were quite surprised when Jason and Emma turned up unannounced, but they're putting it down to the grief. Jason told them that Dennis kept the letters from him. He wanted to ask them if they knew why.' Kate watched the older woman's face as she spoke. 'They know that Jason's behaviour isn't really rational, but it sounds as though they understand. I think they're just trying to be kind.' She picked up her mug and swilled the contents around with a twist of her wrist. There was something else that she wanted to ask. 'Barbara, I'm sorry to ask you this again, but did you really not know that Dennis was going to Bristol?'

A sudden flush of colour seeped into Barbara's cheeks. She pursed her lips, perhaps to stem a tear, and then looked straight into the policewoman's eyes. 'I'm so sorry that I lied to you about that, Kate.'

'Well, I'm sure you had your reasons.' Kate could think of at least two obvious ones, but she wasn't so sure that Barbara would admit to them. 'So you knew about the letters?'

'Yes, Dennis showed them to me. And he told me that he'd arranged to meet with David Lancefield. But he swore me to secrecy.' Barbara was speaking very quietly now. 'Dennis thought it would unsettle Jason. He tends to be a bit… well, silly. Immature, I suppose.' She laughed under her breath. 'I think Dennis thought that Jason would see the Lancefield's money and their property, and not enter into the spirit of the thing. And he didn't want there to be any unpleasantness.' The truth was spilling out now. 'Jason hasn't always had the best of temperaments. Emma has been a calming influence on him, but he can be unpredictable. I think Dennis thought it would be in Jason's best interests to carry on just as they were.' Barbara narrowed her eyes. 'Too late for that now, of course, since Jason has taken it upon himself to visit them. I just hope that it doesn't all go to his head.'

'I don't understand.'

Barbara smiled. 'Dennis understood that the Lancefields were looking for friendship. They were looking for a connection. But Jason can read too much into things at times. He can get silly notions in his head. We thought it came from being abandoned by his mother.' She looked down at her hands. 'I suppose you might call it a sense of entitlement. It's an awful thing to say, especially about someone that you love. But we can't always turn away from the truth, can we? Dennis was worried that Jason might think there was some material advantage to a connection with the Lancefields.'

'I see.' Silly notions and a sense of entitlement? So neither of the two reasons Kate Jenkins had in mind, then. 'I would never have thought of that.'

Barbara looked down at her hands, and the blush in her cheeks deepened. 'It certainly wasn't a good enough reason for me to lie to you. And I am truly sorry about that, Kate, especially when you've been so kind.'

'It's alright, Barbara.' Kate gave a wan smile. 'Forgiven and forgotten.' At least, she thought, as far as the original lie is concerned. But as to the one you're telling me now… well, that one I'm not so sure about.

*

'This house is just amazing.' There was a curious, almost reverential tone in Jason's voice. 'I don't think I've ever seen anything like it.' He cast his eyes around the library and then brought them to rest on Kathryn's face. 'It's grand, and yet it feels like someone's home.'

'It is someone's home, Jason. It's Richard and David's home.' They were sitting at the large mahogany desk, Kathryn in the captain's chair and Jason on a sturdy occasional chair next to her. 'What does Emma make of it?'

The question seemed to puzzle him. 'Emma? I don't know.' And hardly seemed to care. 'She's gone out into the garden with David. Gardens are more her sort of thing, really.' There seemed to be something else on his mind. 'Kathryn, you know about the family's history. If I'm related to the Lancefields, how come they live in a place like this and I don't? Shouldn't some of the family's fortune have come to my part of the family?'

Well, at least he was direct. 'It can be for many reasons.' There was a large sheet of cream paper on the desk in front of her and she turned it slightly so that Jason could see what was drawn on it. 'Traditionally, in families like the Lancefield's, the majority of any wealth passed to the eldest son and his family. Younger sons, or daughters who married into a different family, would be provided for to some extent, but they wouldn't receive an equal share of the estate.'

'That doesn't seem very fair.'

Kathryn's eyes creased with a smile. 'It wasn't personal, Jason. It was an economic decision, to preserve the estate as a whole.' She ran a finger down the piece of paper on the desk. 'I sketched out this rough family tree for you. You can see here that your branch of the family goes back to a Richard Lancefield, who was the younger of two surviving sons. The bulk of the family's wealth went to Richard's older brother, Benedict. Richard did have property of his own but his son, Thomas Moses Lancefield, had a disagreement with the family and sadly was disowned.' She paused and waited for the obvious question.

'So what happened to Richard's property?'

Not the question she was expecting, then. 'It eventually passed to Richard's granddaughter, Lysbeth. She didn't marry and she used her wealth to travel and enjoy life. She didn't forget her uncle Thomas, and she left the remains of her estate split equally between his daughters. But there wasn't a great deal left, I'm afraid. Certainly not enough to live in the style of the Lancefield family.'

Jason glanced down at the document. 'And this is my family tree?'

'A part of it, yes.' She pointed to the line descending from his ancestor, Richard Lancefield. 'Thomas Moses married a girl called Alice Banks. She was the daughter of a sea captain. Your family descends from this line through a family called Watkins, and then Gee, until your grandmother Margaret Gee married Graham Speed.'

'Auntie Barb is into all this sort of thing.' He looked disinterested. 'But at the end of the day, they're all dead, aren't they?'

'Yes, I suppose they are.' But dead or not, Kathryn thought, without them you would have no claim to be related to the Lancefields at all. Aloud, she said, 'While we're here, is there anything else you would like to know about the family's history?'

'Yes. Did my part of the family ever live in the Caribbean?'

'Not that I'm aware of. Your ancestor Richard was born on St Felix, but he was brought back to England as a child and he never left the country again, as far as I can tell. He originally lived here in Penwithen but he moved to Liverpool for business reasons.'

Jason swept his eyes up from the surface of the desk to Kathryn's face. 'Do you know anything about the plantation on St Felix? It's called Woodlands Park, is that right?'

'Yes. I know a little bit about it, but only from the research I've done for Richard. The Lancefield family originated here in Cornwall, but at the end of the seventeenth century another, earlier Richard Lancefield was transported to St Felix as a bonded labourer. As a young man, he supported the Monmouth Rebellion.' She saw a frown begin to form on Jason's pale face, and his eyes begin to glaze. 'I won't bore you with all the details. Suffice it to say that Richard had supported a rebellion against the king, and he was sentenced to death for treason. His family managed to buy his life, but on the condition that he be sent to St Felix for seven years to work for a supporter of the king. It was a hard life but he worked hard, and in time he married a woman called Charlotte Proctor. She was the only child of a plantation owner, so when her father died she inherited the family's wealth. The couple had three children, but no grandchildren, so the estate passed across to the family still here in Cornwall. They consolidated their wealth, buying more land and estates both in England and St Felix. And they still own most of those estates today.'

Jason licked his lips. 'Yes, but the plantation itself – what's it like?'

'I'm afraid I don't know. I've been to the Caribbean, to Barbados and Antigua, but never to St Felix. Richard tells me that it's quite beautiful, on a par with the rest of the Leeward Islands, and that Woodlands Park is on the western, more sheltered coast.'

'And I suppose it will all pass to David when the old man dies?'

The bluntness of his question almost took Kathryn's breath away, but she managed a coy smile. 'That isn't anything to do with me, Jason. I'm only here to curate the family's history and heritage.'

'But you've been helping Richard and David to find their relatives. Isn't that how they came to find my dad?'

'I've been helping them to find relatives because they asked me to. And yes, I was instrumental in finding the link between the Lancefields and your line of the family. But that's where my involvement ends, I'm afraid.' She lifted the hand-drawn family tree from the desk and rolled it carefully into a tube before handing it to Jason. 'Please, take this with my compliments. Perhaps if it isn't of interest to you, you might pass it on to Barbara? And let her know that if she has any questions at all about the family's history, I'll be more than happy to answer them for her, if I can.'

Kathryn had seen and heard enough. It had been Richard's wish that she spend some time with Jason, and it hadn't taken long for her to understand why. It had been mostly thanks to her efforts that the genie was out of the bottle. And now she couldn't help wondering how on earth they were going to put it back.

*

'May I ask how long you and Jason have known each other?' David Lancefield, his gloved hands thrust deep into the pockets of his waxed jacket, swayed a little as he walked. He was trying to keep his pace slow, relaxed, in the hope that the gentlest of strolls in the fresh air would put the girl at ease.

'Just coming up for three years.' Emma answered the question quietly and without emotion. 'At least, that's how long we've known each other. We met at a friend's birthday party. But we've only been living together for a year and a half.'

'And you live in Newton-le-Willows?'

'Yes, on a new estate. Well, it was new when we bought it last spring.' She almost smiled. 'It suits us very well. It's half-way between Liverpool and Manchester, but it's quite an old town, so it has a lot of character.'

'It sounds charming.' David cast a sideways glance in her direction. She was a pretty girl, unsophisticated and unsuitably groomed for the country air. Her sleek bleached hair was beginning to frizz at the ends under the unforgiving Cornish damp, and he suspected that her fashionable padded coat – although long enough to cover her knees – was failing to protect her against the early November chill. 'Are you cold, Emma? Would you like to go back into the house?'

She turned her face towards him. 'No, I'm fine, thank you. It's nice to be outdoors, especially after sitting in the car for so long. I think the fresh air is doing me good.'

He thought he detected a shiver as she spoke. Unsophisticated, he mused, but too polite to cut short the walk. Or perhaps just reluctant to go back into the house? 'Forgive my directness, Emma, but would I be right in thinking that you didn't want to come here today?'

The question stopped the girl in her tracks, and tears began to well up in her eyes as she whispered her reply. 'Yes.'

He put out a hand and touched her gently on the shoulder. 'My dear girl, please don't be upset. It was an unforgivable question. But I had to ask.' He spoke as kindly as he could. 'Why don't we make our way back to the house and you can tell me all about it as we walk? No one will hear us and you can be as honest as you like with me. I promise I won't tell anyone.'

'You wouldn't understand.'

'Oh, I think you should try me.' He brushed her cheek with his fingers. 'You know, I've spent many, many years of my life at odds with my father. Yes, and with other members of my family. I know how it feels to not be able to speak up and to have my feelings and my wishes discounted when I do.' He let out a sigh. 'And I'm so very sorry if our clumsy attempts at trying to find our family have led to you having to make this journey against your will. It was never our intention to cause anyone distress.'

Emma's lower lip quivered, but her shoulders relaxed. 'David, I'm so sorry. You and Richard have been so kind to us. And you're right. I didn't want to come. But Jason wouldn't listen to me.' Tears were running freely down her cheeks now. 'He wouldn't tell Barbara about it. I think it must be the grief, or the shock. I only came with him to make sure that nothing happened to him.' She let out a tiny gasp. 'I didn't mean that you or Richard would harm him.' She raised her eyes skyward. 'Oh God, that sounds so ridiculous. No.' She shook her head. 'He was so… I don't know, so irrational, that I was worried about him driving all this way, worried that the grief might explode or something, that he might…'

David took a step forward and gently wrapped an arm around her shoulders. 'I think you've both been through a great deal in the last twenty-four hours. You've lost Dennis and Jason has obviously not come to terms with it yet.' David gave her a gentle squeeze. 'I think we should walk back to the house now, and I'll make you a mug of hot chocolate. And then we'll pack you off to The Lancefield Arms for some supper and a good night's sleep.' He pulled a crisp white handkerchief from his pocket and handed it to her. 'Now dry those tears, there's a good girl.'

She took the handkerchief from him and laughed softly into it as she dabbed at her eyes. 'You're very kind, David. I don't know what to say.'

'Hush. You don't need to say anything.' He began to

steer her slowly along the path, back in the direction of the kitchen door. 'We're not ogres at Salvation Hall, Emma. We're just ordinary people like you and Jason. It's just that we've been walking along a different path in life. If my father hadn't taken a running jump at this notion to find our family, our paths might never have crossed. But they have, and I'm very pleased to have met you.'

The sentiment was genuine. He *was* pleased to have met her. She was a charming young woman, and he felt sure that her heart was in the right place.

But they both knew that place wasn't Salvation Hall.

12

'Highly strung?' DCI Drummond shook his head with a laugh. 'Then I suppose it doesn't really matter whether Dennis Speed knew about the murder case, or whether he knew about the Lancefield family's murky history. Either way, if Jason is a sensitive soul you can see that the news might upset him.' The policeman leaned back in his seat and folded his arms across his chest. 'Did you tell Barbara about either of those nuggets? That her distant relatives are going through a murder case and oh, by the way, they made their money from the slave trade?'

Kate, seated at the other side of Drummond's desk, scowled into her plastic coffee cup. 'No, I didn't. She was already upset and I wasn't going to make it worse for her.' Kate lifted her head and turned reproachful eyes in Drummond's direction. 'Jason isn't that sort of sensitive, Andy. I've met him, remember?' She lifted the cup and flexed her wrist, sloshing the cooling dregs of coffee around. 'I think that Dennis kept those letters from his son because he wanted a quiet life. Barbara was hinting at a sense of entitlement.'

'Entitlement? I'm not following you.'

'Maybe that's because I'm not explaining it very well.' Kate laughed, an almost-cynical cough, and then drank off the cold, bitter coffee. She tossed the empty cup into the waste bin beside Drummond's desk. 'After Barbara admitted that she'd lied to me about those letters, that she'd known all along that Dennis was going to Bristol, I asked her how she felt about that. What it meant for her.' Kate's brow puckered. 'She's quite a sweetheart, Andy, and she's keen on all that family history stuff. This could have been a real opportunity for her. She only had Dennis and Jason, and now she's only got Jason.'

'And his girlfriend. What's her name? Emma?'

Kate dismissed the suggestion with a shrug and leaned a little closer to her senior officer. 'Emma isn't family, she's Jason's girlfriend. Barbara has been a sort of sister to Dennis and a surrogate mum for Jason, when it was necessary. She's an educated lady – a retired headmistress. And Dennis and Jason are, were, her only family. I think she would have enjoyed that connection with the Lancefields, and taken it in the spirit in which it was offered.'

'Instead of which she agreed to forego the opportunity and keep it a secret.' Drummond gave the suggestion some thought. 'You think that Dennis was worried about the impact it might have had on his son if he found out that he was related to this wealthy family?' The DCI shook his head. 'I can't see that any harm could have come of it. It might have wobbled the family a bit, I suppose. The lad might have got ideas above his station.' Drummond wrinkled his nose. 'Were they worried that he'd become dissatisfied with normal life, and turn his back on his family? Is that why Jason has taken himself off to Salvation Hall today? To see what's in the Lancefield connection for him?'

'I don't know. Everyone seems to be ascribing it to the grief but I'm not sure that I buy it. Do you really think that a decent sort like Barbara Gee would take the risk of lying to a police officer just because her nephew might have ideas above his station? She was distraught about that. I could tell after she coughed up the truth. She knew about the letters, and she knew that Dennis was going to Bristol to meet with David Lancefield. She lied to Jason and Emma about that, and she lied to me. No…' Kate gave a resolute shake of the head. 'Dennis and Barbara were worried about something enough to tell those lies. I think you're right that they were worried about how Jason would react, but I think the real worry was that he might cause trouble if the Lancefields met him and decided not to welcome him into the fold.'

'Cause trouble for who? For Dennis and Barbara, or for Richard and David Lancefield?'

Kate pouted. 'If there was a risk that he'd cause trouble, does it really matter who for?'

'It matters to me.' Drummond grinned. 'If he causes trouble for the Lancefields it'll be on Ennor Price's patch, and nothing for us to worry about.'

*

The double room that overlooked the village green was the largest and most comfortable of four that The Lancefield Arms had to offer.

Emma dropped her small, floral holdall onto the bed and spoke without looking at Jason. 'Didn't that make you feel uncomfortable? The way that girl behind the bar smirked when we checked in?' She tugged at the bag's zip. 'Did you have to make such a big deal about being related to the Lancefields?'

Busy emptying his own overnight bag on the other side of the bed, Jason gave a self-satisfied grin. 'Of course I did. The bloody pub is named after them, Em. It's called The Lancefield Arms.' He was lit up by the notion. 'What's the point in being related to the local nobs if you can't let people know about it?' He huffed out a breath. 'I can't see the problem. The landlord was friendly enough. If a few people stared, so what?' Jason dug a hand into his bag and pulled out a clean shirt. 'They're just jealous.'

'Jealous?' His girlfriend gave a quiet gasp of astonishment. 'Did you understand what Richard was saying to you when he took us around the house? They made their money out of *slavery*.' She whispered the word with a hiss. 'I mean, they were very nice people. And very kind, considering we'd just turned up on their doorstep without a word of warning. But doesn't it bother you?'

Evidently not. Jason pulled the last items of clothing from the bottom of his bag and threw them onto the bed. 'If it bothers you, don't think about it.' His brow creased into a scowl. 'You're not the one who's related to them, are you? Nobody asked you to come. You invited yourself.'

Emma flinched, stung by the jibe. She lifted her bag off the bed and dropped it to the floor. 'You didn't mind using my car to get here, though, did you? You didn't want to arrive in your van, looking like a tradesman.' The words were out before she could stop them. She stiffened, and then dared to look at him. His face was a mask, his lips set tightly together, his eyes beginning to narrow into slits. She'd seen that look before but for once she didn't feel unsettled by it. 'I think that in the morning, we should call in and say goodbye to Richard and David and thank them for their hospitality. And then we need to go home and think about your dad's funeral, and putting his affairs in order.'

Jason tilted his head, birdlike. 'So you think I should turn my back on my family?'

'Jase, they're *not* your family. Dennis was your family. Auntie Barb is your family.' A sob caught at the back of her throat. 'I'm your family.' She reached out to the bedside table, pulled her mobile phone from her handbag and held it out towards him. 'Call Barb. Please.' She leaned a little closer to him. 'Please, Jason. Let her know that you're alright. Let her know that you've met Richard and David, and how nice they've been to us. Let her know that there's nothing for her to worry about and that we'll be back tomorrow to help her sort out the funeral arrangements.'

For a moment, Jason stared at the phone in her outstretched hand. And then he shook his head with a growl. 'I'm not listening to this. I'm going for a walk to think.' His jacket was lying across a nearby chair and he snatched at it. 'Make yourself a cup of coffee or something. You need to calm down. When I come back, we'll go down to the bar for a meal.'

She watched in dismay as he stormed from the room, and listened as his feet clattered noisily down the bare wooden staircase outside. Somewhere downstairs she heard a door slam and she crossed the room quickly and pulled a curtain back from the window. She could see Jason down in the street, striding angrily out along the pavement, hands thrust deep into his pockets, head and neck tucked down inside the collar of his jacket.

Slowly, unconsciously, she stepped backwards to the edge of the bed and sank onto it, tears stinging at her eyes. She wasn't sure what was happening now, what had prompted this breach of their simple, peaceful existence. But she knew that things would never be the same again.

She settled her hands into her lap, clasping the fingers tightly together, and began to rock quietly to and fro. It had to be a breakdown of some sort. It couldn't be anything else but the shock of Dennis's death tipping Jason over the edge. He could be difficult, petulant, childish even. But he'd never been quite this selfish, never been so unkind. It wasn't just that he was angry with Emma, nor that he seemed to have almost forgotten that his father had lost his life. He wasn't giving a moment's thought to Barbara, that she must be lonely too. It had been so unfair to leave her to identify Dennis's body. To not even let her know that they were going to Salvation Hall, and to ask if she could cope with the ordeal alone.

So unfair. So unkind. So *selfish*.

It had to be a breakdown or else there was only one other possibility. Emma sniffed back her tears and lifted a hand to rub at her eyes with the sleeve of her jumper. There was the possibility that this was the real Jason. That Jason, unfettered by his father's mild and kindly influence, and unrestrained by Barbara's general common sense and quiet air of authority, might be a Jason that Emma wouldn't like.

Not just selfish, but arrogant. Not just unfair, but deceitful. Not just unkind, but *cruel*.

It was an unwelcome train of thought. Emma's shoulders stiffened and her mouth became suddenly dry. Was she witnessing a side of Jason that had hitherto been kept carefully hidden? Or was this a side of Jason that she'd always known was there and had chosen to ignore? Was Jason's volatility something that she had accepted with a loving heart?

Or had she been turning a blind eye to his faults because she didn't want to admit them?

13

It was quiet at The Zoological Hotel, so quiet that Kathryn and Ennor had the whole lounge bar to themselves.

'I suppose Richard is bearing up, all things considered.' Kathryn ran a contemplative finger around the rim of her wine glass. 'But I think he's had a wake-up call. I don't think Jason is exactly what he envisaged when he thought about finding a family to support David.'

'Not quite part of the old boy network?'

'No, it's not that. To be honest, Jason came over as quite abrasive.' Kathryn sounded unsure. 'No, not abrasive.' She looked into Ennor's face. 'Smug. Overconfident, somehow.' She nodded to herself. 'And far too interested in the material value of the estate.'

'You mean he's more interested in what the family owns than he is in the family itself?'

'Pretty much. Richard asked me to spend some time with him this afternoon, to talk about the family's heritage, and all he wanted to know about was the Woodlands estate, and who would inherit when Richard dies.'

'Do you think he sees himself as some sort of heir apparent?'

'I'm beginning to wonder.'

'And what does David make of it?'

'He's being very pragmatic. He took Emma for a walk in the gardens while I was with Jason, and he thinks she's charming. But...' Kathryn looked suddenly troubled. 'He also thinks she's anxious about the whole thing. She told David that she was very happy with their life up in Liverpool, and setting aside the fact that Jason might be behaving irrationally because of his father's sudden death, she doesn't like the idea of him getting his feet under the table at Salvation Hall.'

Ennor whistled through his teeth. 'She actually said that?'

'Not in so many words, but I think that was the gist of it.'

'So what happens now? Did they accept Richard's invitation to spend the night at The Lancefield Arms?'

'Yes. I think they were grateful for the offer.'

'Well, let's hope they still feel grateful in the morning then.' Ennor snuffled a laugh. 'Does Zak Smith know they're going to be staying there?'

'Why would he?'

'You think that his sister would keep a piece of information like that to herself?' Ennor shook his head with a smile. 'Kathryn, you can be such an innocent.' He let out a sigh. 'I'll put a call in before closing time and see if I can get a patrol car round there, just to make sure that everything is okay.' He settled back into his seat. 'What happens in the morning? Do you think Emma and Jason are going to go quietly back to Liverpool and get on with their lives?'

'I wish I could say "yes".' Kathryn looked troubled. 'But truthfully, I don't know. I know that Richard is going to sleep on it, but I think he realises now that it isn't going to be so simple to find family to support David. That finding them isn't enough, and that he needs to know that anyone brought into the family fold will understand what is expected of them, and want to support David in the right way. He needs to find someone who will embrace the family's history for what it is. Someone who won't be ashamed of it or embarrassed by it.' A faint blush crossed her cheeks. 'Someone who won't just see it as financial gain. And it needs to be someone that David is comfortable with. Someone who can understand why he tried to distance himself from the family's history, but still be prepared to support him as he tries to run the estates.'

She stared down into her glass. 'David still isn't completely comfortable with his inheritance, you know. But he's trying to think about it in a different light, to think about it as an opportunity for change. And he's doing that for his father.' She lifted the glass and swilled the wine around, irritated suddenly by the line of discussion. 'It isn't easy for him, but he's trying to overcome his objections.' She looked away. 'Which sort of brings me back to the reason I asked you to meet with me.'

Ennor grinned. 'I knew there would be a catch in it somewhere.'

She turned back and gave his arm a playful nudge. 'You're my guinea pig. I've been putting the story of the Lancefield rift together this afternoon, and I wanted to run it by you and to see how it sounds.' She offered him a teasing smile. 'You make such a good pupil.'

'So you haven't shared this with Richard and David yet?'

'They've had more than enough to contend with this afternoon. I didn't have the heart.' She leaned down to retrieve a notebook from the bag at her feet and propped it gently on the edge of the table, opening the cover and licking at a finger to ease the turning of the pages. 'I think David is going to take this quite badly. It doesn't paint the Lancefields in a very good light at all.'

'More skeletons in the closet?' Ennor was intrigued. 'Does it make a difference to the way you feel about them?'

'You asked me that yesterday, and I still don't know. It's something that happened so long ago. I think perhaps what might make a difference for me is how Richard and David react when I recount the story to them.' Kathryn forced a smile. 'Perhaps that's why I need to practise on you. I have a pretty good idea of how you're going to react, and I want to see if I'm right.'

'Then I'm flattered that you're using me as a sounding board.' Ennor put out a hand to the wine cooler on the table and lifted the bottle of Chablis to fill both of their glasses. 'Go on then. Shock me.'

Kathryn glanced at her notebook. 'Do you remember how I told you yesterday that the Lancefields had owned their own ship, and that they traded in slaves?'

'The Redemption.' Ennor pursed his lips. 'It's not something I'm going to forget in a hurry.'

'Well, they bought the ship at the beginning of the nineteenth century, when the slave trade was at its height. At the time, Liverpool was the centre of the slave trade in Britain and Richard decided to move his family up to Liverpool so that they could be right at the heart of the action. The Redemption was a sizeable vessel, two hundred and fifty tons, and could carry a decent cargo. It had already made a number of voyages and its original owner had decided to get out of the business and retire on the proceeds.'

'When you say "the business"?'

Kathryn frowned. 'When you were at school, did you learn about "the Triangular Trade"?'

'If I did, I've forgotten it.'

She cast her eyes away from the notebook and lifted her wine glass. 'I don't think you would have forgotten.' She sipped on the wine. 'The Triangular Trade is a broad term used to describe how the slave trade operated. At its most basic level, a ship sailed from a British port to Africa, carrying goods manufactured in this country. That was the first side of the triangle. Those goods would be sold or bartered for slaves, which were then transported in the same ship across the Atlantic on the second leg of the journey. Then on arrival in the West Indies, or some other point in the Americas, that cargo –'

Ennor put up a hand. 'Cargo? We're talking about human beings here?'

'I'm afraid so.' Kathryn sipped again on the wine.' I'm using the terms of the time, Ennor. Human or not, at that time they were considered cargo.' She let out a sigh. 'They were sold to plantations and other enterprises that needed the labour. The ship was then loaded up with goods produced on the plantations – sugar, rum, cotton, spices, and so on – to be shipped back to Britain for sale.' She put down her glass. 'It was a very lucrative business, because profit was made on every leg of the journey.'

'So the Lancefields bought their own ship to cash in on the boom?'

'Pretty much.' She looked down at the notebook and leafed through it again to find a particular page. 'As far as I can tell from the documents I've examined, up to this point the Lancefields exported goods from Britain to St Felix for their own use and sent their sugar and rum back to be sold on the English markets. But they bought their slaves from traders on St Felix.' She ran a finger down the page. 'They were diligent about record keeping, of course, so I've been able to compile details of exactly what happened on The Redemption's first voyage under their ownership.' She drew in a breath. 'In 1805 the ship sailed from Liverpool for Angola, carrying cloth made in Yorkshire and Lancashire, items of Sheffield steel, and iron goods made in the Midlands. The first leg of the journey ran smoothly, and those items were exchanged one way or another in Angola for three hundred and sixty-six slaves.' She dared to lift her eyes to Ennor's face and was unsurprised to see his expression. She looked back down at the notebook. 'The ship was under the command of a seasoned captain, a man called Digory Banks. Banks had captained The Redemption before, for its previous owner, and was experienced in the trade. There was no reason to expect that the second leg of the journey wouldn't run at least as well as could be expected, given how deplorable the business was. Everything points to Banks being a decent man –'

'A decent man?' Ennor shook his head. 'He was captain of a slave ship and you call him a decent man? Kathryn, how can you be so cool and logical about this?'

'Because it's what I do. I take facts and I examine them without applying any emotion.' She cleared her throat. 'I'll stop if this is upsetting you. Maybe it was selfish of me to use you as a sounding board.'

He put out a hand and placed it on her arm. 'It isn't that it's upsetting me. I just don't really need to hear the detail to know what happened next, do I?'

Kathryn studied his face for a moment and then gently closed the notebook and dropped it back into her bag. 'The second leg of the Triangle was known as "the Middle Passage". Even the best of voyages was horrific.' She blinked back the thought. 'The Redemption suffered an outbreak of dysentery just a matter of days before it was due to reach St Felix. Digory Banks was able to attract the attention of a packet boat – a ship carrying mail from England to the Caribbean – and send a letter to Benedict Lancefield, describing conditions on the ship and pleading for help. A letter was sent back immediately, making it clear what was expected of the captain, but Banks refused to carry out his instructions. He sailed on to St Felix, stood his ground against the Lancefields and refused to sail the ship back to England for them. He never worked for them again.'

Ennor's eyes narrowed. 'What was the instruction?'

Kathryn sucked in her cheeks. 'He was instructed to cast overboard any slave who was sick.'

'You mean they wanted him to throw the dead bodies over the side?'

'No.' She spoke quietly now. 'They wanted him to throw the dying over the side.'

For a few moments, Ennor was silent. And then he said, 'I can see why this is going to upset David Lancefield. And I can see why you're worried about what Richard will say. You think the old rogue will shrug his shoulders and say, "That's how it was". But how did this lead to a rift in the family?'

Kathryn offered him a faint smile. 'You know that old

saying "what goes around, comes around"? Well, the Lancefields pretty much ruined Digory Banks' reputation but while he was away on that dreadful voyage, his wife Sarah gave birth to a daughter, Alice. Fast forward twenty-five years and Alice Banks fell in love with a young man she met at a charity ball in Liverpool. The young man proposed and Alice accepted, but his family objected to the marriage and cut him off without a penny.'

Ennor shook his head. 'I still don't get it.'

Kathryn leaned a little closer to him. 'Does it help if I tell you that the young man's name was Thomas Moses Lancefield?'

*

Barbara lifted her feet onto the footstool and dropped the mobile phone into her lap. She closed her eyes and rubbed at her temples with tired fingers, hoping to ease the day's tension. And there was a lot of tension to ease.

It had been a shocking day, almost worse than the day before, if that were possible. A day which had begun with identifying her beloved cousin's body, had dragged out in hours of worry about Emma and Jason and their ill-advised trip to Salvation Hall and had culminated in admitting that she had lied to a police officer. Would it really be improved by making a clandestine call to the Lancefields?

Of course, it wasn't the Lancefields themselves that she feared. It was the turmoil the call might unleash. There could only be one reason that Jason would have travelled to Salvation Hall behind her back. He'd known that Barbara would do everything possible to dissuade him from making the journey.

'So much for your bright idea of keeping the Lancefields a secret.' She opened her eyes and cast the words across her lounge, in the direction of Dennis's photograph. 'He's gone to Penwithen anyway.' She shifted in her seat and tilted her head towards the mantelpiece. 'What would you like me to do now?'

Too late for Dennis to answer. Too late for him to know or to recognise the irony of the situation. That despite all of his efforts, Jason had not only met with Richard and David Lancefield but had visited them at Salvation Hall. 'What the hell was the point? If you'd just taken him to Cornwall, then the accident would never have happened and you'd still be here. And I wouldn't have to deal with this alone.' Barbara closed her eyes for a moment and almost surrendered to the grief. 'But at least the Lancefields are kind.'

She opened her eyes again and stared at Dennis's photograph. 'From what I've heard, they've made Jason and Emma very welcome. And they've arranged for them to stay overnight in the village.' She dropped her gaze to the mobile phone still resting in her lap. 'I've been given the Lancefields' phone number and invited to call them if I'm worried. But I've heard from Emma too, and I can't help thinking that a call from me would only make things worse.'

As if things *could* be any worse. 'Emma tells me that they've argued. That Jason has stormed off somewhere in a temper, so she took the opportunity to call me. She said that Jason is being unkind. And Emma doesn't think it's just the grief. She thinks that meeting the Lancefields and seeing Salvation Hall has gone to his head.' She sighed softly under her breath. 'You were right about that, of course. The Lancefields are wealthy. Emma says that the house is beautiful and that Jason is blown away by it all. That he wants to be a part of the Lancefields' family.' Barbara lifted her eyes to the ceiling. 'You were right all along, Dennis. But going behind his back, keeping the letters a secret, none of it stopped him, did it?'

None of it, not even Dennis's death.

She felt a sudden rush of anger. Dennis was *dead*. And Emma was right – this wasn't just about the grief. Jason was taking for himself the thing that Dennis had tried to deny him. He wasn't grieving for the father who loved him, he was washing his hands of the man who had tried to stand in his way. He didn't care who identified the body, any more than he was interested in arranging the funeral or settling his father's affairs, now that the path to the Lancefields was clear.

'I know what to do now.' She whispered the words quietly under her breath and turned her eyes back to the picture. 'I know what to do, and I promise you that I'll do it tomorrow. Jason has left you to me, and I'll take care of you. I'll arrange for the funeral director to collect you from the mortuary, and I'll talk to the solicitor about your will. Then I'll go over to the house and I'll begin to pack everything up.' Barbara's voice crackled with emotion. 'But there's one thing I can't do for you, and that's to go on lying. First thing in the morning, I'm going to call the Lancefields. And I'm going to tell them the truth.'

14

Ennor turned up his collar and thrust his hands deep into his pockets. The night air was cold, too cold in his book for a late-evening walk around the block. 'I hope we're not going far.'

'We're not. I just want some fresh air to clear my head before you head off for home.' Kathryn huddled into her warm, cashmere coat and linked her arm into his. 'I hope I didn't spoil the evening.'

'No. But I don't think I can take any more history. I don't know how you can be so calm about it all.'

'I don't know how you can be so calm about murder. Or grievous bodily harm. Blackmail, fraud, harassment… it's all man's inhumanity to man, isn't it?'

'I have to be calm about it. It's my job.'

'Just as history is my job.' She pulled a little on his arm as they walked. 'History has to be looked at without emotion, without passion, otherwise we would never get at the facts. You have to be logical about it.'

'There's nothing logical about what the Lancefield family did, or how they made their money. I don't know how you can work with it.'

Kathryn rested her head casually against his shoulder. 'Okay, as it seems to offend your sensitivities, how would it be if I told Richard tomorrow that I'd had enough? That he's on his own. I want nothing more to do with his family's history.'

'Why would you do that?'

'To please you. So that we didn't have to talk about it anymore.'

He let out a laugh. 'You would do that for me?'

'Yep.'

'Wow.' The suggestion completely threw him. 'And what would you do then?'

'Well, I'd pack my bags and I'd go back to Cambridge. For good.' She kept her eyes turned down from his face. 'It will be a shame not to have a reason to come to Cornwall, but I won't leave without saying goodbye.'

Leave? Ennor turned the word over in his mind and slowed his step. 'What sort of a game is this?'

'It's not a game, Ennor. I just wanted you to see how this thing you don't want to talk about creeps into every corner of life. If I hadn't come to Penzance to curate the Lancefield family's heritage – that heritage that you despise so much – you and I would never have met. And if I agree not to work on that heritage anymore, there won't be any need for me to be here in Cornwall, will there?'

'Won't there?' He could think of a reason. His cheeks warmed at the thought, but then caution took over and he found himself tongue-tied.

Kathryn smiled to herself, amused by his discomfort. 'I suppose I could still support the Lancefields without looking into their history. Richard still needs an assistant while Nancy is in St Felix.' She was toying with him now. 'And then there's Becca to be considered. David told me that he'd spoken to you about the card that was left on Lucy's grave. Do you think that was something to do with Becca's family?'

Ennor puffed out a breath. 'We don't know. I've asked Tom Parkinson to look into it. He spoke to Zak this morning but Smith's a slippery beggar. Tom's going to have a word with Becca tomorrow. We thought there was already too much going on at Salvation Hall today to want to stir up a hornet's nest with her. We can wait until Emma and Jason are on their way back to Liverpool.' Ennor narrowed his eyes. 'How is Becca behaving these days?'

'Still biting the hand that feeds her.' Kathryn pouted

her disapproval. 'I never thought it was a good idea for her to continue working at Salvation Hall. I'm supposed to be keeping an eye on her in Nancy's absence, but I'm not very good at it. Nancy knows how to handle her, but I don't have the patience.'

'Well, that's refreshingly honest.' Ennor chuckled under his breath. 'You know, we are pretty convinced that the Smith family are behind all the harassment that's been meted out to the Lancefields, but we have to be careful. We can't afford to let anything rock the boat until after Marcus Drake has been to trial.' He lowered his voice. 'You're not really going to go back to Cambridge, are you?'

'I might if I didn't think there was a good enough reason for me to stay on here.' Kathryn pulled playfully down on his arm. 'Of course, you could always offer me a bribe. Like all good copper's narks, I'm embarrassingly open to persuasion.'

*

David tugged gently on the dog's lead and tried to coax him away. 'Not tonight, old chap.' For a moment, Samson resisted the effort, and then he turned his snuffling attention away from the doorway of The Lancefield Arms and trotted obediently across the road, following in David's wake.

Safely on the pavement at the other side, the pair turned westward, Samson sniffing at the air as he went, David taking the opportunity of their regular evening walk to consider fate and her fickle ways.

Yesterday she'd denied him the opportunity to meet with his distant cousin, Dennis Speed. Today she had unexpectedly thrown him Dennis's son Jason, and his charming partner Emma. What had blown the impulsive Jason to the door of Salvation Hall was still to some extent a mystery. But everything in life happened for a reason, and David couldn't help thinking that the reason on this occasion was to persuade his father to stop any notion of finding an extended family.

Perhaps he was being too hard on the young man, but David couldn't warm to Jason, however hard he tried. There had to be another way of securing the family's future, a way that didn't involve strangers. He didn't wish Jason any ill will and the connection, now forged, could hardly be revoked without causing offence. And in any case, it wouldn't be fair to put a train of events like this in place, to set an expectation, without delivering something. An annual visit to Salvation Hall, perhaps, which included cousin Barbara? Would that be enough to satisfy Jason that his connection to the Lancefield family had been acknowledged?

David let out a sigh. Somehow he didn't think so. He couldn't shake off the feeling that Jason had arrived at Salvation Hall with a far more elaborate expectation. An expectation which, if pushed, David would feel disinclined to meet. That young man had no interest in preserving the Lancefields' heritage. If today's events were the yardstick, Jason was far more interested in what the Lancefield heritage could do for him.

David muttered under his breath. He would need Kathryn's assistance. Today he'd asked her to persuade his father against any notion of looking for more extended family. Tomorrow he would ask her to go a step further – to help him to come up with an alternative.

It occurred to him now that the answer could be closer than he'd realised. There was already someone who could take responsibility for the estates after he, himself, had passed on. It wouldn't be long now before Marcus came to trial. And when Marcus was found not guilty of Philip McKeith's murder – and, God willing, that would be the verdict – then perhaps he could be persuaded to come back to Salvation Hall and work with David and Kathryn on running the estate.

It was a simple idea, with only one possible drawback.

The thought troubled him, and he brushed it from his mind. One could only face so many challenges in one day.

He shivered against the thought and lifted his head. They were beside St Felicity's now, and had walked far enough for their purpose. David slowed his pace and again tugged gently on the dog's leather lead. 'Come on, boy. Time to go home.' But the dog was having none of it. He strained towards the lychgate and let out a defiant squeal.

'Whatever is the matter?' Impatient, David craned his head over the church wall but all he could see were ancient gravestones rising gloomily in the moonlight. 'There's no one there.' But the dog was excited now, his neck braced firmly against the pull of his collar, his breath coming in short, rasping gasps. Bewildered, and yet intrigued, David slowly let out the length of the lead, following the dog closely as he strained to reach the lychgate.

The gate wasn't locked and David pushed on it with his arm and dropped the lead to the floor. Samson was gone in a moment, bounding down the path in the darkness towards Lucy's grave. Could he sense her so strongly then? David watched as the animal turned at the end of the path, his small form illuminated by the light in the porch, and then froze as the dog let out a short, sharp bark.

Samson turned his head back towards his master and barked again, three, four, five times, his front paws stamping on the ground, each bark more urgent than the last.

David felt a sharp stab of panic in his gut and he stepped forward slowly into the dim glow from the porch light, turning his head down to see what had so excited the dog. It took a moment for the horror to register. His knees began to fail him first and he put out a hand to grasp at a nearby headstone to steady himself, turning his head away to stifle a sob.

It must be a mistake, there was no other explanation. A trick of the light or a quirk of the shadows. Slowly he drew in a breath and then slowly again, very slowly, he turned his eyes back to look at the scene.

There was no mistake, and neither the light nor the shadows deceived him. Emma Needham's lifeless body, shrouded in the now-familiar pale blue padded coat, lay gracelessly spread-eagled across the precious marble slab that marked his own late daughter's grave.

15

'Is it true?' Drummond's voice sounded solemn at the end of the line. 'The girl's dead?'

It was going to be a long conversation. Price regarded what remained of his bacon-sandwich breakfast with a pang of regret and reluctantly pushed the plate to the edge of his desk. 'I saw for myself.' He tucked the phone's receiver into the crook of his neck and stretched out a hand for his coffee. 'I'd been out for a drink with Kathryn and I was just about to head for home when the call came through. We grabbed a cab out from Penzance to Penwithen. Kathryn came with me.' He hadn't been sure how the evening would end. But he knew that standing in the churchyard of St Felicity's, gazing down at Emma Needham's lifeless body, hadn't been one of his preferred outcomes. 'David Lancefield found her. He was out walking the dog and it dragged him into the churchyard. He was pretty shaken up, but he didn't waste any time in calling us out.'

'Was it an accident?'

Price snuffled a cynical laugh into the receiver. 'What do you think?' He sipped on his coffee. 'She'd been strangled with her scarf and her body had been arranged over the top of Lucy Lancefield's grave.'

'Fully clothed?'

'It wasn't that sort of crime.' Price wasn't sure yet just what sort of crime it was. 'But I'd be interested to know what you make of it. Maybe I'm too close to the Lancefields to see clearly.' He swivelled his chair gently to and fro. 'Lucy was strangled with her scarf. It's the same method.'

'It could be a coincidence.'

'Or you could wait until I've got the end of the story.' Price struggled to keep the irritation out of his voice. 'Yesterday, anonymous flowers were found on Lucy's grave. There was a card attached to them with one word on it: "whore". We put it down to the ongoing hate campaign against the family.' He paused to give Drummond time to catch up. 'When Emma's body was found, there were fresh flowers on the grave beside her but this time the card…' He hesitated, still disturbed by the memory. 'There was a card with the word "slut" written on it. But it wasn't attached to the flowers this time. It had been inserted into Emma's mouth.'

'Ennor… mate…' Andy Drummond sounded suddenly remorseful. 'I didn't take this Lancefield business seriously enough, did I?' He fell silent for a moment and then asked, 'What can I do to help?'

'We haven't informed the family yet. We could do with a liaison point at your end.'

'Consider it done. I'll speak to Kate Jenkins. We'd better inform Barbara Gee as well, she'll need to know.' Drummond was silent for a moment, and then he asked 'What about Jason Speed? Is he okay?'

'That depends on what you mean by "okay". He's safe. Kathryn came with me to The Lancefield Arms, to inform him of the death.' If he closed his eyes, Ennor could still see the numb shock taking hold as the young man took in the news; the stiffening of the shoulders, the eyes glazing over, the colour draining from already pallid skin. 'He's had to face two unexpected deaths in as many days. It's a lot for anyone to take in. We only questioned him briefly last night and he was too shaken to give us any meaningful answers.'

'So where is he now?'

Price glanced at his watch. 'Hopefully on his way to Salvation Hall. He didn't stay at The Lancefield Arms last night. We didn't want him staying alone so close to the crime scene.' Nor did Price want him surrounded by members of the Smith family. 'Kathryn took him back to the hotel that she uses in Penzance. That way she could be on hand if he needed anything. She's going to drive him over to Penwithen this morning, and we're going to take a statement from him there.'

'Ennor, there's a piece here that I don't understand. How the hell did the girl come to be on her own in that churchyard in the first place?'

'We don't know. Jason told us that after they checked into the pub, he went out for a walk by himself just to get some fresh air. Emma didn't go with him because she wanted to unpack and run a bath. When he came back to the room she wasn't there. He tried her mobile but she didn't answer, so he went down to the bar to look for her. But the story is that no one saw her. There is a rear entrance she could have used to go out. It's possible she could have come down the stairs from her room and gone out that way into the car park behind the pub. It was unlikely anyone would see her if she did that.'

'But *why* would she go?'

'How the hell should I know?' The words came out too sharply and Price bit on his lip. 'Sorry, Andy. I just feel like I've screwed up. There's no way this can be a case of "wrong place, wrong time". It can't be a coincidence. That young woman was only down here in Cornwall because of her partner's links to the Lancefield family. And she's died by the same MO as Lucy Lancefield. It just feels like murder is following the Lancefields around. I should have known when Dennis Speed died. I should have realised then that it wasn't an accident.'

Drummond sucked in a breath. 'Speed's death *was* an accident, mate. I'd stake my pension on it. He slipped on the ice and went under a bus. And in any case, there was no motive for his death.' The DCI paused and then added, 'But I can see why you'd be worried about this latest turn of events. There are plenty of people down there with a grudge against the family. I suppose the question is, does the grudge run deep enough for one of them to murder a completely innocent woman?'

*

Richard placed the mug of coffee down on the kitchen table beside Kathryn's hand, his fingers trembling dangerously in his effort to grip the delicate china handle. 'I'm afraid these old bones are not as dexterous as they used to be, my dear.'

'Then I consider it a privilege that you offered to make the drinks yourself.' Kathryn smiled as he sat down on a chair beside her. 'I would have been quite happy to do the honours.'

'Tush.' Richard clicked his teeth. 'You've been through quite enough in the last few hours.' He wrapped a hand carefully around his mug of tea. 'I'm pleased that you've brought Jason back to Salvation Hall. Is he safely deposited with David?'

'Yes, they're in the library.'

'Good, then we are free to talk privately.' Richard sipped on his drink and nodded to himself, a pensive bob of the head. 'I cannot tell you, Kathryn, how sorry I am that this dreadful thing should have happened. Emma was a charming young woman and, while she might not have been close to us, it is because of us that she was in Penwithen. I saw no reason not to accommodate those young people in The Lancefield Arms, but I fear that my decision may have been ill-judged.'

'You think that Emma's death is something to do with the family?'

The old man raised a fading eyebrow. 'What other conclusion could we draw? The manner of her death, the desecration of Lucy's grave, that appalling card that was left between her lips – everything points to us.' He turned his eyes towards Kathryn. 'David says I shouldn't blame myself, but now I am beginning to wonder. I was so intent on thinking only of myself, of my determination to ensure that David wasn't left without any family connections, it never occurred to me for one moment that I might be disrupting other people's lives. That I might even be putting those lives at risk.' He looked old beyond his years at the thought, his eyes sunken with sorrow. 'Emma was afraid of us, wasn't she?'

'Heavens, no.' Kathryn placed a reassuring hand on the old man's arm. 'I think you are right that she feared her life being disrupted. But not that she feared you, or David. You were kindness itself when they arrived unannounced on the doorstep.'

'But it was my actions that brought these young people down to Salvation Hall, and I fear that they have somehow become caught up in the Smith family's feud against us. You know, I am not a negative soul, and I tried and better tried to reassure David that we were not responsible for the accident that befell Dennis Speed. But now I am not so sure. As a result of my letter to Dennis, Jason has lost both his father and his partner.' Richard turned rheumy, troubled eyes to Kathryn. 'Is this a curse, Kathryn? Are we being cursed for the sins of our fathers? For our part in what others believe to be a dark history?'

Kathryn squeezed the frail arm beneath her hand. 'No, you are not being cursed. You invited Dennis, Barbara and Jason to connect with you for the best of reasons. It was Dennis's choice to travel to Bristol, not yours. And it was his choice to travel by train. And Jason chose to visit Salvation Hall uninvited, and to bring Emma with him. You're not responsible for that.'

'I fear that Jason may not agree with you. Does he believe that we are to blame?'

'He hasn't said so. To be honest, Richard, I think he's still in a state of shock. It's come so suddenly after Dennis's accident, I'm not sure that the news has sunk in.'

Kathryn resisted the temptation to add that Jason Speed was something of a closed book. 'I told him that he could call on me at any time during the night if he needed anything, even if he just needed to talk, but I didn't see him again until the morning. We agreed to meet in the breakfast room at eight o'clock and he was already there and ordering breakfast when I arrived.' She cast her mind back, remembering. 'He was subdued, but then he's faced two close bereavements in as many days. It's bound to take its toll.' She let out a sigh. 'He told me that he had a decent night, all things considered. He was grateful that we had moved him away from The Lancefield Arms, because he didn't want to be close to where it happened.'

'Have you spoken to Inspector Price this morning?'

'No, not yet. I know that Ennor is happy for Jason to stay here with us during the day. He'll be over here mid-morning to take a statement.'

'Then I suppose the best we can do today is to keep Jason company and keep him occupied until the inspector arrives.' Richard sipped thoughtfully on his tea. 'Did he talk very much about Emma?'

'No, I can't say that he did. I tried asking him about Emma's family, and whether he wanted to be the one to break the news to them. He looked dumbstruck and said that he didn't think he had the strength. He wanted to leave it to the police. Ennor's already offered to speak to his colleagues in Liverpool.'

'And cousin Barbara?'

'I wondered about that. It will hit Barbara as hard as it hit Jason, two close bereavements in two days. But I believe Jason has abdicated that task to the police too.'

'He doesn't plan to break the news himself?' Richard pursed his thin lips. 'Then perhaps it was wrong of me to assume that Dennis and Jason and Barbara were close as a family. I wonder… do you think it's possible that there was a disagreement between them somewhere? Is that why Dennis decided not to share the details of my letters with his son and his cousin and chose to travel to Bristol alone?'

*

Barbara Gee turned to face Kate Jenkins. 'Is it Jason?' She asked the question so quietly that Kate could barely hear the words.

'No. Jason's fine.' Kate gestured towards the sofa. 'Perhaps we could have a seat?' She watched Barbara's face as she considered the suggestion and noted the puzzled, fearful expression as the woman sank silently onto the couch.

'Emma then?' Barbara's voice was low.

Kate sat down beside her and took Barbara's hand in her own. It wasn't the sort of thing a detective constable would do, but Barbara's bewildered expression suggested that she knew bad news was coming. Kate had turned up at her front door unannounced, with DCI Drummond in tow. It wasn't going to be good news, was it? 'I'm so sorry, Barbara.' The officer squeezed the plump, warm fingers within her own. 'I'm afraid she died last night.'

The words hung in the air and Kate shot a glance at Drummond, hovering awkwardly beside an armchair.

'We understand that her body was found in the churchyard in Penwithen village.' Drummond kept his voice low and steady. 'Kate tells me that you knew they would be staying there overnight?'

Barbara didn't answer him. Instead, she turned her eyes towards Kate. 'When was she found?'

'During the evening. Around eight o'clock, I think.' She knew what Barbara was thinking. 'Jason was in a state of shock, Barbara. The Lancefields looked after him. He was taken to a hotel in Penzance, to stay with Kathryn Clifton. It was quite an ordeal for everyone concerned.'

'But he didn't call me.' The hand beneath Kate's was beginning to tremble. 'Emma died, and Jason didn't call to tell me.' She nodded to herself with a sigh. 'But of course, you're right. He wouldn't have been thinking straight, would he?' She turned her head now and forced a smile in Drummond's direction. 'Thank you for coming to tell me. Can I ask if Emma's family have been informed yet?'

'Yes, they have. I spoke to them myself, earlier this morning.' He moved a little closer to the armchair and sank uninvited to perch awkwardly on the edge of the seat. 'The investigating officer in Penzance – his name is DCI Ennor Price – tells me that Emma's mobile phone has been examined and that she made a twenty-minute call to your mobile phone yesterday evening. Is that correct?'

Barbara's cheeks flushed. 'Yes. She called to tell me that she was unhappy. She wanted to come home.'

The police officers exchanged glances and Kate picked up the baton. 'Was she worried about something in particular?'

'She was worried about Jason.' Barbara drew her hand away from Kate's. She pulled on the sleeves of her cardigan, stretching them over her hands, and then folded her arms across her chest. 'We were both worried about Jason. The Lancefields had been very kind and Emma confirmed everything that Kate had shared with me yesterday. They'd arrived safely in Cornwall, the Lancefields had been surprised to see them but had been very hospitable. And they'd arranged for Emma and Jason to stay overnight in a hotel in the village. The Lancefield Arms, would that be right?' She laughed softly under her breath. 'Jason can be very impressionable and he's still in shock after his father's death. Emma thought that the whole Lancefield thing was going to his head. He had begun to talk about extending their stay in Penwithen and Emma didn't think it was a good idea. She travelled to Cornwall with him because he wouldn't be dissuaded from making the trip, and she wanted to make sure that he arrived there okay. But she didn't think it was a good idea for them to outstay their welcome.'

'So she called you to ask for advice?'

'She wanted me to speak to him, but I didn't think it would do any good.' Barbara tilted her head towards Kate. 'We spoke about that yesterday, Kate, didn't we? That Jason wasn't returning my calls?'

'Yes, we did.' Kate shifted in her seat. 'Was it just Jason that Emma was worried about? Did she say anything to you about the Lancefields themselves?'

'She said they were charming. Very welcoming, given the circumstances. And they had invited Emma and Jason to go back this morning and have breakfast with them before making the journey back to Liverpool.'

'And what about The Lancefield Arms? Was she concerned in any way about the welcome they received there?'

'A little, yes. She said that the landlord seemed friendly enough, but some of the staff were… well, she thought that she and Jason were being laughed at. Although I don't know why she would think that.' Barbara's voice suddenly cracked with emotion and her face began to crumple. 'Poor Emma.' She tried to blink back a tear. 'She was only trying to keep Jason safe. Why on earth did she have to die? And so soon after Dennis's accident.'

Kate and Drummond exchanged another glance, and Kate nodded at him. If anyone was going to have a shot at explaining to Barbara why Emma might have died, it wasn't going to be Kate. Only the day before, Drummond had been boasting about the fact that if anything happened to Jason Speed, it wouldn't be on their patch. Well, it was damn well on their patch now. And all because Andy wouldn't listen to her intuition. She widened her eyes and, with an almost imperceptible jerk of the head, she flicked them in Barbara's direction.

Drummond hesitated, and then took the hint. 'Miss Gee… Barbara… I think you need to be prepared to offer some additional support to Jason. Emma's death wasn't accidental. I'm afraid she was murdered. The investigation into her death will be led by DCI Price. And it's particularly relevant that Price should be the senior investigating officer.' Drummond paused and licked his lips. 'Because this isn't the only murder case he's investigating which involves the Lancefield family.'

16

Richard strode purposefully across the terrace, the ever-obedient Samson following quietly in his wake. 'The view from here is magnificent, Jason.' He turned with a smile and lowered himself onto a nearby bench. 'I never tire of it.' He pointed out towards the lake with an unsteady finger. 'In the summer, the surface of the water is a sea of colour. Water lilies, you know.' His voice became wistful. 'Water lilies and orchids were the basis of my friendship with Philip McKeith.'

'Philip was the gardener here. Is that right?'

'Yes, Philip was the gardener.' And so much else. Richard cherished the memory for a moment, and then glanced up at Jason and patted the bench with his hand. 'Take a seat, boy. I don't bite.' He watched as Jason sat down awkwardly on the seat beside him. 'It's a fine morning, we might as well take advantage of the fresh air and get to know each other a little better. There's a tragedy to be faced and a police investigation to be undertaken, and neither are for the faint-hearted. I should know. This will be my second such trial in a matter of months.'

Jason shivered and huddled deeper into the inadequate warmth of his jacket. 'Kathryn told me last night about what happened to your granddaughter. And to the gardener. I'm very sorry.' The sentiment sounded like an afterthought.

'Nothing for you to be sorry about, Jason. Lucy lived her life the way she chose. I miss her with all my heart, as I also miss Philip, but it's the living we need to look to. Did Kathryn tell you about Marcus?'

'She told me that he was Lucy's fiancé and that he'd been charged with Philip's murder.'

'That's right. He's up in Edinburgh at the moment, awaiting trial. The man building the case against him – DCI Price, you met him yesterday evening – he's the same man who will be investigating what happened to Emma.' Richard paused, and thought for a moment. 'He's a sound man. The best. If anyone can find Emma's killer, it's Ennor Price.'

'You must be relieved that Marcus Drake is going to pay for what he did.'

Richard let out a short, sharp laugh. 'Must I?' He leaned a little closer to Jason and lowered his voice. 'The tragedy that befell our family was a crime of passion. Philip murdered Lucy. We'll never know why, although I'm sure we could guess, since my granddaughter was capable of driving the calmest of men to the limit.' There was no point in denying the truth. 'Marcus stumbled across the scene, saw Philip leaning over Lucy's body, and challenged him. Believing Lucy was still alive, Marcus lashed out at Philip in the hope of defending her. We have explored a number of avenues, and when the charges are read to him in court, the plea will be voluntary manslaughter, and the mitigating factor will be temporary loss of control due to extreme provocation. We hope for a suspended sentence and for Marcus to spend a year or two managing our estates in St Felix to get the taste of the justice system out of his mouth.'

'You mean you support his acquittal?'

'Technically it won't be an acquittal, of course. But if you are asking if I support Marcus's right to his freedom and a fresh start, then I can only say that I am doing everything I can to ensure it.' Richard chuckled. 'Marcus is a good man, Jason, and he's a part of the family. He is David's stepson. Philip was my friend, and a great loss to me, but I cannot blame Marcus for what he did. Marcus loved Lucy, and he believed that he was defending her. Regardless of the law, no man can be blamed for doing whatever he can to stay true to his beliefs. Especially where love is concerned.' Richard put out a shaky hand and patted Jason's arm. 'Emma was a charming young woman and she did not deserve to lose her life. Inspector Price will find the degenerate scoundrel responsible for her untimely death, I have no doubt of that. And when he does, we will do all that we can to see that justice is done. You have my word on that.'

Jason lowered his head. 'I loved her so much, Richard. I should have taken better care of her, shouldn't I?' He sniffed, and then lifted his eyes to the sky. 'We argued yesterday evening, because she wanted to go home and I wanted to stay the night. She thought the people at The Lancefield Arms were laughing at us. And it really upset her.'

'I'm sorry, my boy. Truly I am.' Richard sighed out his sorrow. 'I know there are people in the village who don't care very much for the Lancefield family. But I didn't for one minute think that they would take out their resentment on yourself or Emma.' He saw a bewildered frown make its way across Jason's brow. 'You know that our housekeeper, Becca, was Philip's partner. And Becca's family are angry that Philip has been accused of murdering Lucy. They believe that Marcus was responsible for both deaths. I have grown accustomed to their belligerence, which I attribute to their ignorance. But I will not tolerate that hostility spilling out onto the innocent. And no one could regret more than I do what happened to Emma yesterday evening.'

Jason's eyes widened and he turned to look squarely at Richard. 'Are you saying that someone in Becca's family might have been responsible for my Emma's death?'

'Let's just say that I have my suspicions.' The old man looked down at his hands. 'But whoever the killer turns out to be, we will do right by her, Jason. Inspector Price is not a man to let things rest. And neither am I.'

*

'I thought talking about the family's history might take my mind off our latest misfortune. If nothing else, I thought it would keep me distracted until DCI Price arrived.' David, seated beside the mahogany desk in the library, leaned back wearily and rubbed at his brow with a finger. 'If I had known that it would present me with not just another tragedy, but a further damning indictment of our family's despicable past, I may well have thought better of the idea.'

'You did insist that I tell you about the rift.' Kathryn looked down at the yellowing documents in front of her with a wry and knowing smile. 'And I did try to warn you that it wasn't a heart-warming story.'

'Heart-warming?' David repeated the phrase in astonished tones. 'If I've understood the tale correctly, Digory Banks captained The Redemption on its first voyage for the Lancefields and found himself adrift in the Atlantic aboard a floating cesspit.' He nodded towards the papers on the desk. 'Do they tell the whole story?'

'Digory's journal provides a detailed account of the facts as he saw them. The letters explain the Lancefield point of view.' Kathryn gently lifted the uppermost page from the desk and examined it with a practised eye. 'It's quite remarkable that these documents have survived when you consider that they were written at the beginning of the nineteenth century.'

'They explain that my ancestors deceived and manipulated Banks for no other reason than to line their own pockets. They sent him to Angola not just to trade goods, but to buy slaves. Three hundred slaves, in fact. But on arrival in Angola, he found a letter from the Lancefields waiting for him, with instructions to buy not three hundred, but three hundred and sixty, far more than the ship could reasonably carry. Surely they must have been aware of the risks?'

'Of course. But they would also be aware that other traders were running those risks and making a far greater profit.'

'Why on earth didn't he refuse?'

'Because he couldn't afford to. Don't forget that Digory Banks wasn't a wealthy man. He couldn't pick and choose his opportunities. The Lancefields had offered to pay him well, considerably more than he had earned on his previous voyage.'

'But they tricked him. They offered him those generous terms and then tried to change the basis of the agreement after the journey had begun.' David scowled. 'They backed him into a corner and threatened him with ruin if he didn't follow their instructions. It appears to me that he had no choice but to act against his better judgement.' David threw up his hands. 'The story would be bad enough for me, if it ended there. But the tale you have recounted to me… are you sure there could be no mistake?'

If only she could be.

Kathryn sifted through the documents and pulled out a faded, hand-written letter. 'I've matched the various pieces of correspondence against the evidence recorded in the journal. During the voyage across the Atlantic, the ship was beset by sickness. The conditions on board were horrific and sailors, as well as slaves, died on board from the disease. They arrived off the coast of St Felix three days behind schedule, and with a much-reduced cargo.'

David winced. 'They were human beings, Kathryn, not "cargo".'

'To you and me, yes. But not to Benedict and Richard Lancefield. To them it was business. The men and women aboard that ship represented a significant capital investment. How else could you explain such inhumane behaviour?'

'I hope that is a rhetorical question.' The last of the Lancefield line sucked in his cheeks and drew in a breath. 'You say that Banks asked for help and my ancestors refused.'

'His first entreaty was sent during the voyage, by packet

boat, and it was met with a firm refusal. On arrival at St Felix he anchored the ship offshore and sent two crew members to land in a small rowing boat. They carried a second letter to Benedict Lancefield, pleading for medical supplies and help to care for the sick on board. Benedict sent back instructions to jettison any sick individuals overboard and then bring the ship into harbour. It was made clear that if this instruction wasn't followed, Banks would be charged with dereliction of duty and held responsible for all financial losses incurred on the voyage.'

'So he followed the instruction?'

'He did.' Kathryn sighed. 'But the experience broke him. He argued with Benedict Lancefield and refused to carry out any further duties. There is a letter from Benedict back to his brother Richard in England, which confirms that Banks chose to work his passage back to England on another ship, leaving the Lancefields without a captain for the return voyage.'

David sucked in his cheeks. 'He jettisoned living human beings, the sick and the dying, overboard into the sea, to drown?'

'Yes.' Kathryn could hardly believe it herself. 'They later persuaded a doctor on St Felix to bolster their argument, by claiming that it would have been dangerous to bring the disease on land.' It was a half-hearted attempt to sugar-coat the most bitter of pills. But it didn't work.

'Did they jettison any of the sick sailors overboard?'

'I don't believe so.' She had hoped that the point might have escaped him. 'Their argument was –'

He held up a hand. 'Thank you, Kathryn. I don't think I wish to hear anymore.'

A small mercy for which to be thankful. If he didn't wish to hear any more then she was spared from sharing the rest – that the Lancefields had mercilessly claimed the financial losses from their insurer. 'I'm so sorry that this has upset you, David, but you did ask me to tell you the story.'

'I know.' He leaned forward in his seat and regarded her with concern, his anger abating. 'Does this make you feel differently about our family, Kathryn?'

Kathryn flinched. It wasn't the first time she'd been asked that question in the last twenty-four hours, and she still wasn't sure of the answer. 'It doesn't make me feel any differently about you, David, or about Richard. I don't believe that you're responsible for the crimes of your ancestors. What matters to me is what you do now.'

'How many people died? Do we know?'

'Forty-three of the slaves being transported, and eight of the crew.' She stopped short of telling him that twenty-seven of those souls had gone over the side while still alive.

'And Richard Lancefield's son went on to marry Digory Banks' daughter, Alice? Little wonder that there was no love lost between the two lines of the family.' He thought for a moment. 'Do you think that Jason or Barbara has any idea of all of this?'

'I very much doubt it. Everything that I have told you is based on documents in the possession of the Lancefield family.' She turned her eyes down again to the papers on the desk, and gently pushed them to one side to reveal a notebook of her own underneath. She opened it and flicked through the pages. 'The rift wasn't all one way. As far as I can deduce, Thomas Moses Lancefield made no attempt to reconcile with his family. They did make overtures to him on several occasions after his marriage to Alice, but he rebuffed all attempts.' Kathryn found the page of notes that she was looking for. 'That's why Richard's legacy eventually passed to Lysbeth Silver Lancefield.' She looked back at David with a smile. 'Thomas was determined to do everything he could to disown his family's shameful behaviour. He signed up for the Royal Navy.' Kathryn tapped a finger on the notebook. 'I've found details of his naval record and I think that you would approve.' She leaned a little closer to David.

'Because Thomas didn't just join the Royal Navy, he volunteered to serve in the West Africa Squadron.'

*

DCI Price gently closed the outer door of the kitchen behind him and paused to reassure himself that he was quite alone. Investigating Lucy's and Philip's deaths back in September had given him a good working knowledge of the layout of Salvation Hall, and he'd long since learned that if he wanted to sense the atmosphere, and the mood of those within it, then the best thing to do was park to the side of the house and let himself in surreptitiously.

In the early days of his visits to the hall, Richard's secretary, Nancy Woodlands, had shown no hesitation in challenging his method of entry. And he had never baulked at brazening it out, happy to commit the offence first and make a feeble apology for it later. It was essential, he reasoned, in his line of duty to cross the line now and again.

He moved away from the door and began to make his way across the room, heading for the hallway and signs of life. He was barely halfway there when Becca Smith blew angrily into view, flouncing into the room through the inner doorway, her arms full of towels that were destined for the washing machine.

She halted in the doorway and eyed him with a scornful smile. 'Breaking and entering again, Inspector Price?'

'I was looking for Kathryn.'

'What, again?' Becca drew her eyes away from him and headed towards the utility room to her right. 'Seems to me that you never do nothing else, except come looking for that Kathryn.' She threw the words over her shoulder as she walked. 'I would have thought your time would be better spent looking for the man who killed that girl last night.' She kicked open the utility room door with a swift jab of her foot and pushed on it with her shoulder to open it fully. 'Still, I suppose it keeps you in work, associating yourself with the Lancefields. There's always going to be someone getting themselves murdered.'

Price felt his jaw clench at the jibe. 'The last thing I wanted was to be here again investigating another death.' Especially as he hadn't yet managed to achieve justice for Lucy and Philip. He drew in a steadying breath. 'Emma Needham didn't deserve what happened to her. I want to see whoever committed that atrocity brought to justice.'

Becca shoved the towels into the washing machine and slammed the door shut. 'What, like you're bringing Marcus Drake to justice for what he did to my Philip?'

'I'm doing everything I can to achieve justice for Philip. The process takes time, there's nothing I can do about that. We're expecting a trial date to be announced this week. As soon as we have one, I'll let you know.' Price leaned against the kitchen counter. 'In the meantime, we'll be questioning everyone in the household here about what happened yesterday. I've come to talk to Richard and David, to Kathryn, and most importantly to Jason.'

'And no doubt, after that, you'll be piling the pressure on me.' She backed out of the utility room and turned to look at him.

Price permitted himself a smile. 'Ah, no. I've decided to leave that pleasure for Detective Sergeant Parkinson. Tom will come and see you this afternoon. He's a tad busy at the moment talking to the staff of The Lancefield Arms. He's trying to establish where your brothers were yesterday evening.'

The inference touched a nerve. Colour flushed into Becca's cheeks and she stepped forward, her hand held up, her finger pointing warily in the direction of Ennor Price. 'You leave my brothers out of this.'

'I'm afraid we can't do that, Becca, any more than we can leave you out of it. We already know that you were drinking in The Lancefield Arms with Zak around the time that Emma went missing. Tom Parkinson will be questioning you both about that, and I know that we can rely on you to cooperate as fully as you can.'

'Cooperate? To help the Lancefields?' She dismissed the idea with a snort. 'Those bastards deserve everything they get.'

'Still biting the hand that feeds you?' Price shook his head and laughed gently under his breath. 'Emma Needham wasn't a member of the Lancefield family, was she? So if someone murdered her to get at the Lancefields, the gesture fell well and truly short of the mark. All they managed to do was deprive Jason of his partner, her parents of their daughter and her siblings of their sister.' He narrowed his eyes. 'I met Jason last night and I didn't see any Lancefield airs and graces. All I saw was a hard-working young man who'd unexpectedly lost his father, and then had his partner cruelly snatched away from him by some lowlife who not only took her life, but also robbed her of dignity in death.' Ennor pushed himself away from the kitchen counter and began to move towards the door that led into the hallway. 'In case you didn't hear, Becca, they spread-eagled Emma's body across Lucy Lancefield's grave.'

The colour in Becca's cheeks deepened. 'I didn't know.' She turned her head away and cast her eyes glumly towards the floor.

'Of course you didn't know.' Price had reached the doorway and he turned to look at her over his shoulder. 'Two wrongs never make a right, Becca. I hope you'll remember that when Tom Parkinson comes to see you.'

17

'I do appreciate you taking my call, Kathryn. To be honest, I've been worried sick.' Barbara sounded anxious at the other end of the phone line. 'And I wish that I'd contacted you before now.' She paused to draw in a breath. 'I've had a visit from the police this morning, to tell me what happened to Emma.'

Kathryn closed her eyes. 'I'm very sorry for your loss, Barbara. For both your losses.' And sorry that it should have taken two deaths for Barbara Gee to finally make contact with the Lancefields. 'We were all saddened to hear of Dennis's death, and I know that Richard and David planned to reach out to the family in time to offer their condolences.' She spoke slowly, choosing her words carefully, unsure how much Barbara already knew. 'Events rather overtook them when Jason and Emma arrived here unexpectedly. I know that nothing I can say will stop you from worrying, but we are doing our best to look after Jason.' Too late now to look after Emma. 'On the surface, he's coping very well, but it's obviously been a terrible shock for him, coming so soon after losing his father.'

'Did Jason tell you why he'd decided to make the journey to Penwithen in the first place?'

It was a curious question, and Kathryn relaxed back into the captain's chair to consider it. 'Jason told us that he wanted to know why his father kept Richard's letters a secret from him. He thought, perhaps, that Richard and David may have discussed it with Dennis.'

'And had they?'

'No. Until yesterday, we weren't even aware that Dennis hadn't shared the letters with you and Jason.'

Barbara was silent for a moment. And then she said quietly, 'The police officers who visited me told me about the murders of Lucy Lancefield and her lover. I have no way of knowing whether Dennis was aware of them. I suppose it's possible that he was, and that in some way he was trying to protect us.' She paused, and then added, 'They also made me aware that the family is being harassed. That some sort of hate campaign is underway. Is that true?'

'It is.' There would be no point in denying it. 'But it is a very personal vendetta. Nothing to do with Dennis or Jason, or yourself.'

'Or Emma.' The words hung in the air, and then Barbara said, 'Emma called me yesterday evening, Kathryn. She called me from The Lancefield Arms, to tell me that they would be staying in Penwithen overnight.'

'Richard felt that it was the least he could do for them. They had driven such a long way to get here, and they both looked so tired. I don't think any of us thought it would be a good idea for them to make the journey back to Liverpool until they had rested.'

'So you put them up in a public house?' There was a hint of acidity in the question.

Kathryn smiled to herself. 'Richard wanted to keep Jason and Emma close by, and The Lancefield Arms is just a short walk from Salvation Hall. It might be a pub, but as the name suggests the business belongs to the family.'

'Emma told me that she was afraid. She told me that you had all been very kind, but she didn't feel safe there. She said there was some unpleasantness – an "atmosphere", she called it – when they checked in.'

'I'm sorry to hear that. I wish we'd known.' And if they had known, what would they have done? 'Was Jason troubled by the atmosphere too?'

Barbara gave a sharp intake of breath. 'I don't think so. Emma hinted that he thought she was overreacting.'

He still hadn't spoken directly to Barbara then. But

Kathryn couldn't help thinking that he needed to. 'Jason didn't stay at The Lancefield Arms last night. We all thought it would be best to put some distance between him and the place where Emma died, so we moved him to The Zoological Hotel, in Penzance. It's a very good hotel and it belongs to a friend of the family. I stay there myself when I'm in Cornwall. In fact, we wondered if you would consider coming down to Penzance and staying there yourself, as Richard's guest? We're doing all we can to support Jason but he barely knows us, and I can't help thinking that he could do with the support of his family.' Kathryn reconsidered her words. 'The support of his *close* family.' She gave Barbara a moment to consider the suggestion. 'I'd be happy to book you a train ticket, on the family's behalf.'

'Oh, Kathryn, I don't know…'

'Barbara, Jason needs you.' Kathryn spoke gently now. 'I know that he hasn't been in touch with you. but that doesn't mean that he doesn't need your support.'

'I don't want to make things worse.'

Make them worse? Jason's father was dead, his partner murdered and he was alone, hundreds of miles away from home, about to face questioning by the police about what might have happened to Emma. However hard she might try, Kathryn just couldn't see how it could possibly get any worse for Jason Speed than it already was.

*

Price took a good long look at Jason Speed and tried to muster some sympathy. The young man looked weary this morning, huddled miserably into an armchair at the side of the drawing room fireplace. Dark circles had embedded themselves beneath his eyes, and his skin, though clean shaven, bore that dry, grey pallor that spoke of a restless, endless night. And yet still the sympathy that Ennor sought wasn't forthcoming.

'I'd like to go over a couple of things in the statement that you gave us yesterday evening, but I'll try to keep it as brief as possible.' Seated on the sofa directly opposite the young man, the policeman offered what he hoped was a reassuring smile. 'I just want to make sure that we haven't missed anything.' His notebook was resting on his knee and he flipped it open and consulted it. 'Yesterday evening, you told me that you argued with Emma after checking into The Lancefield Arms, because she wanted to go home to Liverpool rather than spend the night in Penwithen. Is that correct?'

'Yes. She thought that people in the bar were staring at us when we checked in. She could be a bit sensitive about things like that.'

'So why did she think they were staring at you? Was it because you were related to the Lancefields?'

'Yes.'

'And it made her feel uncomfortable.'

'Yes.'

'But you decided to stay there anyway?'

Jason's frown deepened, and he shrank a little further back into the chair. 'I didn't want to drive home. I was too tired to drive and so was she. We wouldn't have got back to Liverpool until well after midnight, and we'd been up since five o'clock.'

So he had wanted his own way. Price nodded with a smile and referred back to his notes. 'Can you remember who was in the bar when you checked in?'

Jason thought for a moment. 'There was a big, bearded bloke behind the bar, I thought he must be the landlord. And there was the girl who took our details for the register. Blonde. Long fingernails and dangly earrings.'

'What about customers? Was the bar busy, or was it empty?'

'It was pretty quiet. I think there was a couple in the window seat, having a meal. And a bloke on a bar stool, drinking a pint.' Jason's frown deepened. 'He looked as though he'd had a few already. He was watching us.'

'Can you remember anything about his appearance?'

'He had dark hair, quite short. I think he was wearing jeans. He looked about my age.'

'Anything else?'

'What's this got to do with Emma's death?'

Price smiled again. 'It might not have anything directly to do with her death, Jason. But we have to investigate every aspect of what happened yesterday evening. It helps us to build up a picture.' He paused, then asked, 'So, anything else about this bloke that was sitting at the bar? Anything that might help us to identify him?'

'He had a tattoo, an anchor. It ran all the way down his forearm, the arm that was holding his pint.'

Zak Smith. Ennor pulled a pen from his pocket and scribbled in the notebook. 'Did *you* think that people were staring at you, Jason?'

'Of course. But they're southerners, aren't they? They only have to hear a Scouse accent and they look at us like we're from another planet.'

Ennor let the jibe go. 'You say you checked in at around six o'clock and went up to your room to unpack. And at about six thirty you went out alone for a walk around the village to clear your head.' He looked up at Jason. 'Can you remember which route you walked?'

'Route? Does it matter?' Jason's pale brows beetled forward. 'I turned right out of the pub and walked along the main street, past the chemist and the newsagents. And then I think I turned down a side street and just followed my nose around the block.' He looked up at the ceiling. 'I just wanted to clear my head. I didn't like that we'd argued. I know I can be a bit short-tempered sometimes, especially when I'm tired. I wanted to calm down so that we could have a proper conversation.'

'And you were out for about thirty minutes.'

'Yes. When I got back to the pub I went in through the back door from the car park, and straight up to the room.

Emma wasn't there so I waited for a few minutes to see if she would come back. After about ten minutes I started to worry and I called her mobile, but she didn't answer. So I walked back down to the bar, in case she'd just gone for a drink.'

'Did you go into the bar?'

'No, I stood in the doorway and looked through. I didn't want to go in if she wasn't there.'

'And then what?'

'I tried the car park, in case she'd gone to sit in the car, but she wasn't there either. So I came back in and opened the door to the bar again, and looked through. I know I'd already looked there, but I couldn't think where else she might be.'

'And again, you didn't go into the bar?'

'Not at that point.' Jason's face looked suddenly drawn. 'That was when I really started to worry. I went back to the room to get my coat, and then I went back out into the village to look for her. I couldn't think what else to do.' He frowned, remembering. 'I walked around for about a quarter of an hour but I couldn't see her, so I tried her mobile again. Twice, I think. And then I sent her a text.' The thought seemed to trouble him. 'I said I was sorry for arguing with her, and I asked her to come back to the room so that we could talk.'

'And you went back to the room again.'

'Yes. I checked the car again on my way back, and then the room. And then I went down to the bar to speak to the barmaid. I told her that Emma wasn't in our room and I asked if anyone had seen her.' Jason looked down at his hands. 'The bloke on the bar stool was listening and he laughed. He said something about the Lancefields not being able to hang on to their women. I didn't know what he was talking about.' Jason looked back at Price. 'Was that some sort of reference to what happened to Lucy Lancefield?'

Price had wondered when Lucy's name would come

into it. 'Is that what you think?'

'Kathryn told me about it last night. About the murders. And Richard mentioned it this morning. He told me that the family were being victimised because of it, by people in the village.' Jason sounded suddenly aggrieved. 'Is that why Emma was murdered, Inspector Price? Because we belong to the Lancefield family?'

How easy it would be for Ennor Price just to say "yes". And how many reasons for him not to fall into the trap. He slipped his pen back into his pocket and folded his notebook closed. 'It's far too early to speculate.' If only he had a pound for every time he'd fallen back on that platitude. 'Did the landlord and the barmaid know that you belonged to the family, Jason?'

The question elicited an unexpected response. A violent flash of colour burst onto Jason Speed's neck and spread slowly up his throat towards his chin. 'Well, Kathryn booked us in, didn't she?' Suddenly he sounded defensive. 'She must have told them when she made the booking. How else would they have known?'

18

'Well, I suppose if he says they checked in here at six o'clock, then they must have checked in here at six o'clock.' Amber Kimbrall pulled a pint glass from the rack behind the bar and turned towards the pump without looking at DS Parkinson. 'I can't say I was bothered enough to notice what the time was.' She jammed the glass under the tap and pulled down on the pump lever with a slow and deliberate hand. 'And even if I had been, it wouldn't get you any closer to knowing who killed that girl, now, would it?'

The policeman leaned his elbow on the bar and watched as the ale flowed smoothly into the glass. 'It might. We won't know that until we get the full picture of what happened.' It wasn't the first time that he'd dropped into The Lancefield Arms to question the barmaid, and he pretty much doubted that it would be the last. She'd been Zak Smith's girlfriend for nigh on two years now, and they both knew that being questioned by the police sort of went with the territory. 'Did you see her again after they checked in?'

'No. I already told you that last night.' She carefully removed the glass from the tap and slid the pint across the bar towards him with a tilt of the head. 'I thought you weren't supposed to drink when you're on duty.'

'I'm only on duty while I'm questioning you. The sooner you answer my questions, the quicker I can knock off and enjoy my pint.' He dug into the pocket of his trousers, fishing for enough coins to pay for the drink. 'I know Zak was here in the bar when they checked in.' He dropped the coins onto the bar. 'Was he still here when

Jason Speed came in to look for Emma?'

'I can't remember.' Amber scooped the coins up, curling her fingers skilfully around them. 'I suppose he might have been.' She thought for a moment. 'Yes, he was here at the bar all the time. Right up until your mates in uniform turned up to question us.'

Parkinson suppressed a smile. She'd become so accustomed to giving Zak an alibi that she'd begun to produce them without being asked. 'Did he speak to them? To Emma and Jason?'

'How should I know?' A puckish smile tugged at her lips, dimpling her cheeks as it went. 'I'm his girlfriend, not his keeper.' She folded her arms on the other side of the bar, leaning forward and enveloping the policeman in a cloud of musky perfume. 'She seemed a nice girl, Sergeant Parkinson. Not what we expected.' Amber's voice softened a little. 'When we heard they were coming to stay here, we just assumed they'd be like the rest of the Lancefields. Stuck up, and full of themselves. But they looked so ordinary.'

'Down to earth?'

'I suppose so.'

'Both of them?'

She considered the question. 'Yes.' There was a hint of hesitation in her voice. 'They didn't look happy. I got the feeling that the girl didn't want to be here. She looked nervous.'

'Nervous? Could she just have been tired, maybe?'

'No. She was twitchy.'

'Maybe she could sense that she wasn't welcome.'

The barmaid bridled. 'We were polite enough. What more did they want?' She sucked in a guilty breath. 'I'll admit that we didn't exactly roll out the welcome mat. But there was nothing said. I just took their details for the register and gave them the room key.' She turned warm, brown eyes up towards his face. 'I'm sorry about the girl. She didn't deserve what happened to her.'

'No, she didn't.' Parkinson focused on the pint glass in front of him. 'The way I heard it, she didn't even want to come to Penwithen.' He put out a hand and wrapped it around the glass. 'You know she wasn't related to the Lancefields? She was just Jason Speed's girlfriend. She only came down to Cornwall to keep him company.' He lifted the glass to his lips and sipped on it. 'That's the thing about some relationships, isn't it? It's so easy for the innocent to get caught up in the crossfire.'

Amber Kimbrall wasn't to be so easily snared. 'You mean like poor Philip got caught up in the crossfire between Lucy and that Marcus Drake?'

'I wouldn't call Philip McKeith an innocent.'

'Becca was innocent. And so was little Frankie, poor little mite. Left without her dad. What had she ever done to deserve that?'

'What had Emma Needham done to deserve being strangled and spread-eagled across Lucy Lancefield's grave?' Tom Parkinson slammed his glass back down on the bar. 'She'd barely been in Cornwall five minutes. She didn't know a soul here. And yet, within an hour of checking into this pub, she was dead.' He growled under his breath. 'She didn't know a soul, but you knew who she was. And so did Zak. Or at least, you both thought you did.'

Amber shrank back from the bar, suddenly wary. 'So what if we thought she was a Lancefield? That don't mean that one of us killed her.'

Maybe not, he thought. But it gives you a reason. And that will do fine to be going on with.

*

'It always boils down to motive, means and opportunity.' Still at Salvation Hall, Price rested his elbows on the kitchen table. 'At some point yesterday evening, Emma wandered into the churchyard at St Felicity's and found herself face to face with a killer. What we don't know is whether she encountered that killer by accident, or whether she was lured into the churchyard.'

'So, she was murdered either by someone she knew, or someone she disturbed?' Kathryn was sitting across the table from him, her fingers wrapped loosely around a mug of coffee. 'If it was someone she knew, that would narrow the field significantly, wouldn't it?'

'Not necessarily, if we use the word "know" in its loosest sense. She met plenty of people yesterday – yourself, David, Richard, Becca, the landlord and barmaid at The Lancefield Arms, and any customers sitting in the bar when she checked in.'

'So I'm a suspect? You seem to forget that I have the perfect alibi. I was with a Detective Chief Inspector when the killer struck.'

Price groaned. 'I was making a point. We know that David found the body, and I wouldn't for one moment suggest that he could be responsible. And Richard wouldn't have been capable, he's just too frail.'

'Someone from The Lancefield Arms then? The barmaid and the landlord were presumably behind the bar all evening, so that lets them out. That narrows it down to Becca or her brother.'

'Or Jason.'

'Jason?' Kathryn drew in a breath. 'Is that meant to be a serious suggestion?'

'He had the opportunity. We already know that he had gone out for a walk around the village. And he didn't try to hide the fact that they had argued. But I got the feeling that he was playing it down. He claims that he went for a walk to clear his head because he knows he has a short fuse and he wanted to defuse the argument. Does that sound likely to you?'

'You ask that as if you expect me to know the answer.' Kathryn eyed the policeman with a wry smile. 'Which is a tall order, given that I only met him for the first time yesterday.' She thought for a moment. 'I could certainly imagine him having a short fuse. I'm not sure about diffusing the argument. He doesn't strike me as the caring sort.' She narrowed her eyes. 'Are we having an official conversation, Ennor?'

'Not yet. Let's call it a chat during my lunch break.' He studied her face. 'How did he behave after you took him back to The Zoological last night?'

'He was withdrawn, but what else would you expect? He's had two unexpected bereavements in the space of forty-eight hours. He barely said a word on the way back to Penzance. I stayed with him in the bar for half an hour after he'd checked in, to have a nightcap. I thought it might help him to sleep. He did tell me that Emma had been uncomfortable at The Lancefield Arms, and he asked me if there was any reason why the staff might not have been friendly. That's why I told him about Lucy and Philip. I thought he deserved an explanation.'

'How did he take the news?'

'Quietly. He said he was sorry to hear what had happened, but he couldn't see how it would reflect on himself and Emma. Of course, I didn't tell him about the harassment.' She leaned a little closer to Ennor. 'Did I do wrong? Should I have kept that information from him?'

'No, I don't think so. He would have found out, sooner or later.' Price leaned back in his seat. 'Did he say anything to you about Emma?'

'No. And I didn't ask him anything. I thought it best not to. I wasn't sure if the death hadn't hit him yet, or whether he was trying to keep his emotions in check.' Kathryn sipped on her coffee. 'After he went up to his room, I didn't see him again until breakfast. He was still subdued, but he told me that he'd slept. And that he was grateful to us for moving him to another hotel.'

'Did he say anything about talking to Emma's family? Or to Barbara?'

'No.' Kathryn was troubled now. 'Is this a serious line

of enquiry, Ennor?'

He swerved the question. 'They're not a close family, are they? Dennis kept secrets, Jason made the trip down here behind Barbara's back, and Andy Drummond tells me that Emma didn't even tell her own family that they were making the trip to Cornwall.'

'Well, if Jason made the decision to come here on the spur of the moment, and Emma decided just as impulsively to come with him, maybe she didn't have the time. And they did set off very early in the morning. Perhaps she didn't want to disturb the family.'

'But why tell Emma not to get in touch with Barbara?'

Kathryn raised an eyebrow. 'Did Jason do that?'

'We believe so. Andy's colleague, Kate Jenkins, was with Barbara when she picked up the message from Emma. She said that Emma sounded anxious, and she worried that Jason would find out that she'd made the call.'

'Are you trying to suggest that Emma was frightened of him?'

'Let's just say that I'd be happy to know that she wasn't.'

Kathryn lifted her coffee mug to her lips. 'So, your hypothesis is that Jason either walked with Emma into the churchyard, or lured her in there, and then strangled her with the scarf she was wearing.' She sipped on the coffee, her eyes still focused downwards. 'Where does the card come into it? The card that had been slipped into Emma's mouth.'

'I don't know.' Ennor shook his head. 'You do realise that most of my job consists of gathering facts and constructing theories, and then trying to rip them apart?' He laughed softly, a self-deprecating chuckle. 'We don't have much yet in the way of suspects, and even less to go on when it comes to motives. I have no choice at this stage but to come up with assumptions, and see whether they make any kind of sense.'

'I can see that Jason could have had the opportunity to

murder Emma. But I can't see that he had a motive. At any rate' – Kathryn sipped again on her coffee – 'not as much of a motive as the Smith family. Zak makes no secret of his animosity towards the Lancefields, and we all know that he's behind the harassment campaign.' Kathryn put down the mug. 'Have you established yet whether or not he left those flowers on Lucy's grave yesterday?'

'Not yet. He's been questioned about it but, of course, he denies it.'

'And you don't think the most obvious hypothesis about this case is that the person who left those flowers has taken their hatred of the Lancefields just that bit too far? Isn't that obvious from the card that was left between Emma's lips?' Kathryn let out an exasperated breath. 'Emma was even murdered in the same way that Lucy was murdered, she was strangled with her own scarf.'

'You're suggesting that this was a copycat killing. That the killer was trying to make a point by replicating Lucy's murder?' Ennor shook his head. 'The Smith family aren't sophisticated enough to come up with that idea.'

'Then what other possibility could there be? That the modus operandi being the same was just a coincidence? Because let's face it, Ennor, you're not going to want to consider the third possibility are you?'

'Which is?'

'That neither Philip McKeith nor Marcus Drake was responsible for Lucy Lancefield's death. Because the killer is still out there.'

*

Richard settled deeper into the old Lloyd Loom chair in the corner of the orchid house and rested a gnarled hand gently across the shoulder of the dozing terrier curled up in his lap. 'That's right, Samson old chap. You have a snooze.' He muttered the words quietly to himself. 'I'm just going to sit here for a while and think about our little problem.'

He cast his eyes across the glasshouse to the potting bench and the small mahogany clock that perched so incongruously on the shelf amongst a jumble of clay pots and rusting seed tins. It was almost a quarter to two. He had fifteen uneasy minutes to consider the situation and gather his thoughts ahead of his interview with Detective Chief Inspector Price.

He drew in a breath and closed his eyes, the better to remember the morning. He'd walked around the grounds with Jason Speed, and spent time with the boy in an attempt to get the measure of him. He'd listened to Jason's grief and offered his support. And he'd made him a promise, the promise that whoever was guilty of Emma's murder, the killer would be brought to justice.

It hadn't been an empty promise. Richard had meant every word. And he knew that DCI Price would be of the same opinion. Adversaries they may be in the case against Marcus, but Price was a worthy opponent, a man up to the fight, and an advocate of justice. A man to help Richard keep his promise.

If only he could have made the same promise for Lucy.

Richard scratched thoughtfully at his chin with a bony finger. He liked DCI Price. He admired the man's integrity and courage, and his drive to achieve the truth. But it was easy to admire such qualities when the truth might never be known. Almost as easy as it was to delude oneself into lying for the greater good.

In his heart of hearts, Richard knew that Philip could never have murdered Lucy. But the tale was told, the trail was set and the story must be defended at all costs if Marcus was to go free. There was no evidence to be presented to the contrary, no material proof to be submitted to support the view that someone other than Philip had been responsible for Lucy's death.

And they both must hold fast to the story. Should that

story ever be called into question — should he ever give in to the notion that Marcus, or perhaps even an unknown assailant — was responsible for his granddaughter's death, then his own integrity would be challenged, and the defence for Marcus would collapse.

An unknown assailant?

Richard opened his eyes. Emma had been murdered by an unknown assailant. That the girl might have been murdered simply because she had links to the Lancefield family, that in itself was a troubling enough thought. That she had been murdered by the same opportunistic method of killing…

Could he really bring himself to believe that Emma's death was a clumsy attempt by the Smith family to mirror Lucy's murder? Did she have to die simply so that Becca's family could extract some sort of vile revenge on the Lancefield family? Had they misunderstood her relationship to the family, believed her to be a blood relative or perhaps an in-law by marriage? Or was the method of her death intended to convey a subtle, far more sinister suggestion?

Whatever the case, which of Becca Smith's unscrupulous relatives would have been likely to carry out the deed? God knows there were enough of them to choose from, all with their various axes to grind. But which of them would have had the strength to twist the life out of that lovely, innocent young woman? Who had the muscle to tighten the scarf around her throat, the determination to wrestle her writhing body to the ground, the sheer desire to persist in squeezing the breath from her lungs until she lay limp and lifeless at their feet?

And above all, who had the all-consuming motive?

19

Tom Parkinson pulled the Audi onto the garage forecourt and tucked it neatly between a rusting, once-white transit van and dark grey Ford Mondeo with a missing headlamp and a dent in the offside wing. He turned off the engine and pulled the key from the ignition and then tilted his head to look out of the window. He had seen Zak Smith in his field of peripheral vision, leaning under the open bonnet of a Vauxhall Cavalier just inside the garage workshop, and he knew that Smith had seen him. Just as he knew that Smith was too cocky to make himself scarce.

He opened the car's door and stepped out onto the forecourt. 'Just the man I was looking for.' He flicked the key fob towards the Audi to activate the locks. 'Amber said that I'd find you at work.'

'Did she?' Smith kept his eyes on the Vauxhall's engine. 'She's a good girl, my Amber. I hope you haven't been upsetting her, Sergeant Parkinson.' He dipped a hand into the engine bay and tugged unconvincingly on a tangle of wires. 'Know anything about the electrics on a Cavalier SR4i? I can't get this bugger's lights to work.'

The policeman smiled to himself, a wry curve of the lips. 'Nothing at all, Zak. But then you wouldn't expect me to, would you?' He'd reached the open door of the workshop now and he leaned against the door frame. 'I'd like to have a word with you, about what happened to Emma Needham yesterday evening.'

'Is that her name? Emma Needham?' Smith leaned a little further across the engine. 'I thought she was a Lancefield.' He sniffed. 'Nice girl, by all accounts. Shame about what happened to her.' He lifted his eyes from the wiring to Tom Parkinson's face. 'Not sure why you think I can tell you anything about it. I was just having a quiet drink in The Lancefield Arms. My Amber will have told you that already.'

'What time did you arrive?'

'Arrive?' Smith sucked in his cheeks.' Let me see, now. I reckon it was about five o'clock. And I was there until long after eight.' He straightened his back. 'Time enough for three or four pints. I saw that Emma and her bloke check in, and I saw him go out for a walk. But I didn't see her again after that. I didn't see her go out, and I didn't see what happened to her.' He smiled, a condescending grin of sharp, white teeth. 'Lucky I was in the pub really, cos I had planned to go out and do a spot of poaching, and it's not so easy these days to get an alibi from a dead rabbit.'

Parkinson narrowed his eyes. 'Where was Robin?'

'Robin?' Smith gave a noncommittal shrug of the shoulders. 'I'm not my brother's keeper, Sergeant Parkinson. You'd have to ask him yourself.'

'Oh, don't worry, I will.' Parkinson folded his arms and rebalanced his weight against the door frame. 'And what about your sister, Zak? Where was Becca last night?'

'Becca? She had a drink with me at one point, and the rest of the evening she was at home with little Frankie, I should think. Or round at our mother's.' His grin widened. 'Are you really that short of clues, Sergeant? You must be clutching at straws if you think my little sister had anything to do with it.'

'Must I?' The policeman pushed out his lips. 'I don't think so. There's nothing desperate about following up the obvious leads, is there? Emma Needham's murder was the same MO as Lucy Lancefield's. My boss reckons our starting point is to look at the suspects we discounted for Lucy's murder before we came to the conclusion that Philip or Marcus was in the frame.' He paused to give Smith time to register the implications. 'Obviously, Philip couldn't have been responsible this time, since he's already dead and buried. And Marcus is up in Edinburgh with a bail condition that requires him to check in daily with the local constabulary. So that leaves Becca and Robin.'

Zak Smith growled. 'You leave my little sister out of this. She's been through enough thanks to those bastards.'

'You mean those bastards that put a roof over her head and pay her wages?' Parkinson stepped forward into the workshop and put his hands on the wing of the Vauxhall. He leaned across the engine bay and stared into Smith's face. 'As I said, that leaves Becca and Robin. Or yourself.'

'I've got an alibi.'

'You've got a tame girlfriend. We'll be checking on your alibi with everyone else that was in The Lancefield Arms yesterday evening.' He pushed himself away from the car. 'In the meantime, if you want to help your sister, I suggest that you stop being an idiot and keep your nose clean. We know that you're behind the harassment that's been meted out to the Lancefields, and we suspect that you're behind those vindictive cards that have been left on Lucy Lancefield's grave.' The policeman narrowed his eyes again. 'The question is, are you responsible for putting one of those cards in Emma Needham's mouth after she was murdered?'

Smith stiffened. 'What the hell are you talking about?' The words came out in a defensive snarl. 'What bloody card in her mouth?'

'Whoever murdered that girl left a card in her mouth, just like the card that was left on Lucy's grave. The card said "slut". That was it. Just one word. Just like the other card said "whore".' Parkinson lifted his hands from the Vauxhall and straightened his back. 'Those cards are going to lead us to Emma Needham's killer. If you left those cards, Zak, you'd better spit it out now. And if you didn't, but you know who did, then you'd better think twice before covering up for a killer.'

*

'Jason needs the support of someone close. We've invited cousin Barbara to travel down to Penwithen at our expense, but I fear that she will not accept.' A frown of disappointment etched itself across David's brow. 'We're doing our very best for him, Chief Inspector, but we cannot seem to forge a connection.' He uttered a low, self-deprecating laugh. 'It's ironic, really, when you consider that we only reached out to Dennis, Jason and Barbara in the hope of forming a bond.'

Price cast a thoughtful glance around the kitchen, and then offered a smile of encouragement. 'The best laid plans of mice and men?'

'Indeed.' David put out a hand to the freshly poured mug of coffee in front of him and slipped his fingers through the handle. 'There is no doubt in our case that those plans have gone awry.' He lifted the mug to his lips and sipped pensively on the brew. 'I suppose you would like to question me again about what I found in the churchyard?'

'No. I'd like to know more about Emma. Kathryn tells me that you spent some time with Emma yesterday, and I'd be interested to know what you made of her.'

David's frown deepened. 'She was charming, Inspector Price. A little gauche, perhaps.' He considered the word and then shook his head. 'Unsophisticated, I should say, rather than graceless. But a young woman of good manners and kind intention.' He balanced the coffee mug on the edge of the kitchen table. 'It was blindingly obvious to all of us that the last place she wanted to be was Salvation Hall, but she had supported Jason in his wish to come and visit us, and she seemed determined not to spoil the occasion by asserting her own needs.' He tilted his head towards the policeman. 'My father asked Kathryn to spend some time with Jason after lunch, so I invited Emma to take a turn around the lake with me.'

'Did she tell you that she didn't want to stay in Penwithen overnight?'

'Yes, she did. But our offer was made from genuine concern. All three of us – my father, Kathryn and myself – believed it would be unwise for them to attempt the long drive back to Liverpool without a decent meal and a good night's rest. They admitted to bringing overnight bags with them, in case they chose to spend the night in Penzance. There was no ulterior motive on our part, Chief Inspector. And we certainly didn't bring any pressure to bear.'

Price sucked in his cheeks. The Lancefields may have not applied any pressure, but the same couldn't be said of Jason Speed. 'You didn't consider inviting them to stay at Salvation Hall?'

David blushed, a faint tinge of pink across the cheek. 'Consider it? Yes, it was considered. But they had arrived unexpectedly and frankly, Chief Inspector, there was an awkwardness about the occasion that… well…' He let go of the coffee mug and gave it an almost petulant shove across the kitchen table. 'You cannot know how many times today I have berated myself for not inviting them to stay here with us.' His eyes looked suddenly moist. 'That lovely young woman might still be alive if we had extended our hospitality and encouraged them to stay in our home.'

Price shook his head. 'It was kind of you to accommodate them at all. You were under no obligation.' He paused, choosing his words carefully. 'But I can't help thinking that The Lancefield Arms might not have been the best place to put them.'

'Inspector Price, you cannot condemn us more for that misjudgement than we have each condemned ourselves. We are well aware that owning The Lancefield Arms does not render us immune to the jibes of its staff and its customers. But we had not imagined for one moment that their contempt for us would spill over onto our guests.' His face clouded at the thought. 'Jason, I think, would have weathered the storm. But poor Emma…' He shook his head. 'I will forever hold myself responsible.'

Price muttered under his breath. 'It's not your burden

to bear, Mr Lancefield. If anyone should feel responsible, it's Jason Speed. He's the reason Emma made the journey to Penwithen, and he's the reason that Emma was alone when the killer struck.' The policeman had another question to ask. 'Have you given any thought to what might have happened to her? To why she was alone in the churchyard?'

'To why she was alone?' David appeared to find the question puzzling. And then he said, 'I assumed that she had gone for a walk.'

'That she had followed Jason?'

'That she had followed him? Ah, I see. In the hope of patching up their argument?' He considered the possibility for a moment. 'And you think that perhaps in walking around the village in search of him, she was unfortunate enough to encounter her killer?'

That was one way of putting it. 'Did you see anything yesterday that might suggest a crack in Emma and Jason's relationship?'

The question hung in the air for a moment and then David said, 'I have already told you that Emma only came to Penwithen because she couldn't dissuade Jason from making the journey, and she didn't want him to travel alone. She was concerned for his welfare, not least because he had just lost his father. I wouldn't call that behaviour suggestive of a crack in their relationship.'

Price placed his elbows on the edge of the kitchen table. He folded his hands together and leaned his chin on his fingers. It was time for a curved ball. 'Why do you think that Barbara refused to come to Penwithen to support Jason?' He watched as David winced and looked away. 'According to Kathryn, Barbara doesn't want to "make it worse". What do you think that means? If Barbara is close to Jason, and the obvious person to support him, how could her presence here at Salvation Hall possibly "make it worse"?'

*

Barbara settled back into the train's uncomfortable seat and stared blankly at the mobile phone resting loosely in her hand. The phone was vibrating with a persistent pulse and on any other day she would have been glad to take the call.

But this wasn't any other day. And this wasn't a call that she welcomed.

With tired eyes, she watched the screen for a moment as the phone rang four, five, six times and then blinked as the call – like the one before it – transferred to voicemail.

He was going to leave another message then.

The thought unnerved her and she shivered into her thick, woollen cardigan. Another voicemail message would mean three messages in all. She nodded to herself. Five calls and three messages; all of them too little, and all of them too late.

There was a soft, capacious leather bag on the empty seat beside her and she slipped the mobile phone into it and folded her arms across her chest with a sigh. The first call had come through barely an hour before and been so utterly unexpected that a momentary panic had rendered her incapable of answering. But her anxiety had abated when the call disconnected after scarcely two or three rings. Her natural instinct had been to return the call, but when her phone began to ring again almost immediately, she found herself strangely reluctant.

It had been almost forty-eight hours since her last conversation with Jason and in that brief span of time he had all but erased her from his life. And not just her, but his father too; Dennis, that calm and undemanding soul who had always been there for his son through thick and thin.

She pursed her lips and turned her head to the left, to gaze out through the train's window. She wasn't prepared to listen to any more of Jason's messages. After the third call, she had persuaded herself to listen to his rambling, almost incoherent mutterings of apology. He was sorry, he said, that he hadn't called her before now. Sorry that he hadn't called her himself to break the news of Emma's death. But not sorry enough, Barbara thought with uncharacteristic bitterness, to apologise for leaving her to deal with the identification of his father's body. Or to apologise for unexpectedly disappearing to Cornwall without uttering a word of explanation.

He was sorry for himself, there was no doubt of that. There had been an unmistakable tone of self-pity in the voice that had mumbled the words and, for the first time in her life, Barbara had found herself unmoved by her only nephew's plight. She was keeping her sympathy for those who deserved it – for Dennis, who had lost his life so cruelly in Tuesday morning's accident, and for poor Emma, who had strayed into the wrong place at the wrong time the evening before and found herself face to face with a killer.

Angry tears began to sting at the back of Barbara's eye. Jason's second message had almost beggared belief. He wanted to let his aunt know that she wasn't to worry about him. To let her know that Emma's death had broken his heart, but that the Lancefields were going to look after him, and he was going to stay with them in Penwithen for a while. That he knew he could trust her to take care of Dennis's affairs, while he stayed at Salvation Hall with his family.

With his *family?*

A knot of tension began to build in Barbara's gut, just as the mobile phone in her handbag began to vibrate with yet another unwanted incoming call. She dug her hand angrily into the bag to retrieve the phone and muttered under her breath, peering down at the screen with petulant eyes, ready to swipe away the call. But her anger was misplaced and her pulse quickened at the sight of the number calling.

Because this particular incoming call wasn't from Jason.

20

'And where is Jason now?' Richard tilted his head towards Kathryn as he spoke.

'He's in the drawing room. He asked if there was somewhere quiet he could sit to make a phone call. David is in the kitchen with Ennor and I knew that you were here in the library, so I didn't really know where else to put him.' Kathryn sat down on the captain's chair. 'I'm beginning to run out of ideas to keep him occupied.'

'And still no news from cousin Barbara?'

'I'm afraid not. I've tried calling her a second time but she didn't answer, and I don't want to make a nuisance of myself. If she doesn't want to come to Penwithen to support Jason, then I'm afraid we'll have to respect that.'

The old man let out a heartfelt sigh. 'So it falls to us to keep things on an even keel until this distressing turn of events plays out?' He dropped a hand to the side of his chair, where Samson was peacefully dozing, and ruffled the dog's ear with his fingers. 'Inspector Price tells me that there is no official need for Jason to stay in Penwithen. He's already made a formal witness statement and, notwithstanding their conversation today, the inspector is happy for him to return home when he is ready. Arrangements have been made for the officers investigating Emma's death to remain in contact with him when he returns to Liverpool. The key question, of course, is just when he will be ready to leave us. Perhaps when you have supper with him this evening, you might gently sound him out about his plans? While I do not wish to be unkind…'

'You think it would be better for him to return home to

Liverpool?'

Richard turned his head towards the fireplace and thought for a moment. Eventually, he said, 'I would appreciate your opinion, Kathryn. This venture, this attempt to extend our family, hasn't quite brought me the result I was hoping for.' He hesitated, and then coughed out a disparaging laugh under his breath. 'Forgive me, my dear.' He turned back to look at Kathryn. 'I did not intend to sound so inconsiderate. Emma's death is a most unhappy tragedy but, regardless of that tragedy, I am struggling to see Jason as a member of the Lancefield family. And I cannot for the life of me see how to turn things around.'

'You still haven't found common ground with Jason, but that's understandable, Richard. Circumstances have overtaken you. No one could have foreseen Emma's death. Perhaps you just need to take a little time for the dust to settle.'

Richard's mouth curved with a knowing smile. 'I fear, my dear girl, that your humanity will always far outweigh my own. There was nothing sentimental in my attempts to find an extended family. It was, and always will be, a business matter for me. To find suitable distant cousins to support David and secure the future of the estate when I am gone.'

'Then it appears that the remit of my work has changed. I understood that we were looking for distant relatives. I don't ever remember the word "suitable" coming into it.'

He closed his eyes and bowed his head. 'And there you have me, Kathryn. It was an old man's foolishness not to think about the consequences. And perhaps an old man's vanity to believe that any Lancefield, however distant the connection, would be a gentleman of good manners.' He sighed out his disappointment. 'I hope you know me well enough by now to know that there is no question of my cutting Jason adrift without the family's support. I know that Inspector Price will stop at nothing in his efforts to find out who was responsible for poor Emma's death. And I have already given my word to Jason that we will provide him with the best possible legal support when the killer is discovered. But I cannot escape the inevitable truth – Jason is not interested in the Lancefield family's heritage, any more than he will be interested in supporting David in the future.'

'Perhaps when he has spent more time with the family?'

Richard put up a hand. 'Tush, my dear. I make no judgement on his feelings regarding Dennis's and Emma's deaths, but I do not believe that he came to Penwithen looking for answers. He came to Penwithen to get the measure of us. He has shown scant interest in our history and our heritage. That in itself I may have been able to overlook. But he makes no secret of his interest in our wealth and our various properties.' The old man clicked his teeth. 'Jason Speed has come to Penwithen for one reason alone. He has come to see what the Lancefield connection can provide for *him*.'

'And doesn't that make him a Lancefield?' Kathryn watched Richard's face as the arrow met its mark. 'Didn't you reach out to Dennis and his family in order to see what they could do for *you*? And now that you've decided that Jason isn't quite enough of a gentleman to meet your needs, and you no longer have a use for him, you want him dispatched back to Liverpool so that he doesn't get in the way of your plans?' She thought for a moment and then asked, 'Did David share Digory Banks' journal with you?'

'Journal?' Richard, stung by her outburst, looked momentarily bemused. 'Yes, I've seen the journal. But I don't understand the relevance.'

'Digory Banks put himself at odds with the Lancefield family because their primary goal was profit. Self-interest.'

'But that was a completely different situation. There is no room for sentimentality in business. You cannot judge the past on today's sentiments.'

'I'm not sure that David would agree with you.' A warm flush of anger began to work its way into Kathryn's cheeks. 'I wonder what Jason would think if I shared the story of Digory Banks with him? Or the fact that the rift between his family and yours came about because Thomas Moses Lancefield dared to lower his social and economic status by marrying Digory's daughter?' She lowered her voice. 'Perhaps it might help Jason to understand why the present Lancefield family has decided not to welcome him into the fold?'

Richard raised his eyes to the ceiling. 'I very much doubt that Jason would be interested in the story, but I thank you for the challenge, Kathryn. I am always in need of a friend who speaks their mind.' He licked his lips. 'May I suggest that we sleep on the matter? I have offered Jason our support, and I will not renege on that. I take full responsibility for setting in motion a chain of events which may have led to the loss of his father and his partner. And I will seek to make amends. But not by welcoming him into the family firm. He is not made of the right stuff.'

'And who would be, Richard? What is "the right stuff"?'

Richard turned his eyes back to her face, and he pursed his lips. 'I do not see the Lancefield backbone in Jason Speed.'

'I see. And are we to repeat the exercise with more distant cousins, and work our way through the entire extended Lancefield family, looking for that elusive attribute?' Kathryn was exasperated by the thought. 'Just how many families do you intend to disrupt, Richard? How many offers will you make and withdraw? How many hopes will you build up, only for them to be destroyed? And why is this even necessary, when you have a legitimate heir who knows the family, is part of the family, and who would go to the ends of the earth to support David?' She chewed angrily on her lip. She had come this far, there was no going back now. 'Why can you not just acknowledge that Nancy isn't just your secretary, but your granddaughter?'

*

Price levered the plastic lid from the top of his takeaway coffee, and grimaced as the bitter aromas of a poor-quality Americano wafted up to meet his nostrils. 'How many sugars?'

Parkinson grinned. 'Three brown.' He fished in the pocket of his jacket and pulled out a Mars bar. 'There's something to take the taste away.' He placed the chocolate bar on the dashboard in front of his senior officer. 'I suppose we should consider ourselves lucky that a convenience store offers hot drinks at all.'

They were sitting in Parkinson's Audi, parked up in Penwithen beside the lychgate of St Felicity's. The car was facing the centre of the village and Price, settled into the passenger seat, was surveying the scene with a studious frown. 'There's nothing to this village, Tom. What the hell was Jason Speed doing for half an hour? He's supposed to have walked around for thirty minutes. He came out of the pub, passed the chemist and the bakery and then turned right down Silver Street. He said he walked around the block, which would have taken him along Back Lane and back up Quintard Street to the back of The Lancefield Arms. It's barely half a mile. Ten minutes at the most.' Price turned to look at Parkinson. 'Where else could he have gone?'

The sergeant shrugged. 'There's a lane runs off the end of Silver Street, I suppose he could have walked along there for a while.'

'What's up there?'

'Half a dozen houses. If I remember rightly there's a row of farm cottages, a farmhouse and then a large, detached place at the end of the lane.'

Price screwed up his face. 'Why would he walk up there

in the dark?' The policeman turned his eyes across the road, where The Lancefield Arms was lit ready for the evening trade, and tried for a moment to imagine Jason walking out of the door and turning towards the heart of the village. 'He comes out of the pub, walks along the pavement and then…' Price frowned. 'He could have crossed the road to the churchyard.' Price bent his neck forward and tilted his head to peer up through the windscreen at the tower of St Felicity's. 'That would have killed a bit of time.'

'So why not mention it?'

'Maybe he didn't want to be connected with it. Maybe he thought it would sound suspicious, given that Emma was murdered there.'

Parkinson stared into his coffee. 'What do you make of him?'

'I don't know, I can't get the measure of him. Last night, when we broke the news of Emma's death, I thought he was genuinely shocked. And he made all the right noises when I spoke to him this morning. But I can't warm to him. And neither can the Lancefields. Or Kathryn, for that matter.' And Kathryn's opinion was the one that mattered to him. 'They've invited Barbara Gee to come down to Penwithen to support him, but she doesn't want to come. She says it might make things worse.' Price chewed on his lip. 'Kathryn thinks that's because she wouldn't have approved of Jason making the trip to Penwithen, so it's just some sort of family squabble. He hasn't exactly done right by Barbara, has he? They're a small family unit by all accounts, and he's left her to deal with the aftermath of his father's accident. She's been left to identify the body and to field all the police enquiries.'

'Not a very loving family then.' Parkinson gave a wry smile. 'Mind you, neither are the Lancefields. It must be in the blood.' He turned to look at Price. 'Could you see him as a suspect?'

'I've tried, but he doesn't have a motive. Not grieving

his father, ignoring his aunt, arguing with his girlfriend… it's all pretty unpleasant behaviour, but it doesn't make him a killer. It just makes him insensitive.'

'So where does that leave us? He might have lied about walking for thirty minutes, but does that place him in the churchyard at the time of Emma's death?'

Price sucked in his cheeks and considered the question. 'I had a call from Kate Jenkins this afternoon, Andy Drummond's DC. She's been acting as unofficial liaison for Barbara Gee. Barbara has confirmed that Emma's call to her yesterday evening lasted for twenty minutes and ended at around five past seven. We don't know where she was when she made the call, but she can't have been in The Lancefield Arms or the car park, or Jason would have seen her. He claims that she wasn't in the room when he got back from his walk. That would be seven o'clock.' Price turned in his seat to look at Parkinson. 'David Lancefield found the body at twenty to eight. He tells me that he didn't hear anything untoward as he walked through the village towards the churchyard, so we can probably assume that the murder didn't happen during the five minutes immediately before his arrival there. That gives us a murder window of roughly half an hour.'

'Zak Smith was in the bar at The Lancefield Arms. Amber Kimbrall's confirmed that.'

'She'd confirm the sky was pink with green dots on if it kept her in Smith's good books. Did anyone else see him?'

'I suppose, if you think about it, Jason Speed saw him.'

Price let out a laugh. 'Now there's a notion. We're considering two suspects and each is the other's alibi? Even I couldn't have seen that one coming.' He shook his head. 'I think we need to call it a day.'

'If only.' Tom drained off what was left of his coffee and snapped the plastic lid back onto the paper cup. 'I've still got Becca to question.' He reached behind him for the seatbelt. 'I can't say I'm looking forward to it.'

Price smiled. 'You can handle her better than I can. But

don't be too easy on her.' He sipped on his coffee. 'I want her alibi for yesterday evening, specifically between seven and seven forty-five. And I want to know what, if any, conversation she had with Emma and Jason yesterday.' He paused and thought for a moment. 'I want her alibi for the day before yesterday too.'

'Tuesday? What for?'

'The day Dennis Speed died.'

'You're not serious?'

'The Smiths have a motive for both murders: their hatred of the Lancefields.' He tapped the paper cup on the edge of the dashboard. 'Andy has requested the CCTV footage from Lime Street station for the hour leading up to Dennis's death. I want that footage inspected frame by frame when it comes through to us.'

'And what are we supposed to be looking for?'

'Anything that remotely resembles a member of the Smith family.'

*

Richard shook out the soft, woollen rug and draped it gently over his knees. It was warm in the sitting room at the Dower House, but still his ageing bones could feel the cold.

He stretched a hand across to the small walnut table next to his chair and retrieved a glass of port, something to heat the inner parts of him that the blanket couldn't reach. The glass was cool and he wrapped his hands around it to tease the aromas from the wine, breathing in the subtle smokiness before lifting the drink to his lips.

He was pleased to be alone, save for the ever-present Samson dozing quietly in his basket next to the fireplace. He'd had his fill of human beings for the day, even those he cherished. What he wanted now was peace. Peace and solitude to consider the folly of his ways.

You can choose your friends, Richard. But you can't choose your family.

He closed his eyes and rested his head against the wing of the armchair. What a wise girl Kathryn Clifton was. He'd chosen the plain-speaking Philip McKeith to be his friend, just as he had extended the hand of friendship to Kathryn herself when Philip had been lost. And he was honoured that she had accepted the invitation.

But he would not have chosen Jason Speed to be his family.

He opened his eyes and sipped thoughtfully on the port. Yes, Kathryn was wise. Clever enough to find the family that he desperately sought for David, and strong enough to challenge him about the wisdom of the quest. They had found Dennis Speed and lost him in a heartbeat, never to know whether he would have made a friend or foe. But Jason? Jason, who had presented himself in his father's place, who had failed to mourn his father, shown himself impervious to the feelings of his partner, turned his back on his aunt…

Richard stared down into his glass. A flush of heat was creeping into his sallow cheeks, and he hoped against reason that it was the wine that had warmed him, and not a discomfiting blush of shame. Until meeting Jason, Richard had convinced himself that any direct descendant of the Lancefield family would show themselves to be a credit to the Lancefield family name. He was proud of his family. Proud of its heritage and its work ethic and its astonishing commercial achievements. And, above all, he was proud to be its patriarch.

And are you proud of all the Lancefield descendants, Richard?

Trust Kathryn to drive home the one point that might shatter his illusions. He couldn't imagine himself being proud of Jason Speed. The boy had barely tried to make a secret of his interest in the family's material fortunes. His father lying dead in a Liverpool mortuary, and his partner cruelly murdered in a deserted churchyard, miles from the safety of her home, and all the boy could think about was how many acres the family owned in Cornwall and St Felix, and who would inherit them when David was gone.

No, there was nothing to be proud of with this particular descendant of the Lancefield family. But what about the others?

A guilty tear stung at the back of Richard's eye. You could never say of Kathryn that she shied away from the truth.

Are you proud of Honeysuckle, Richard? And of Nancy?

Of course he was proud of them. His illegitimate daughter Honeysuckle had wanted for nothing, and neither had his granddaughter Nancy. They'd had every material comfort, a good home in St Felix, a private education at the island's foremost academy and well-paid jobs on the family's estates. Everything they could possibly need.

Except, perhaps, to be recognised as members of the Lancefield family.

He rubbed at his brow with a finger. It occurred to him now that there were three choices before him. One, to draw the line at Jason Speed and admit the foolishness of seeking cousins so distant that they couldn't possibly have any common ground. Two, to support Jason from a very safe distance, and continue with his quest along another line of the Lancefield family tree. Three…

Richard's lips began to turn inwards, guarding against the eruption of an almost inevitable sob of frustration. Why could he not bring himself to acknowledge Nancy as his granddaughter? He adored the girl, she lit up his world with her quick wit and her self-assured smile. And still, he couldn't tell the world what Kathryn Clifton had already guessed.

Come along now, Richard. Pull yourself together.

Curse himself for a prejudiced, bigoted old fool. It was too late now for him to face his demons, however much Kathryn had set out her stall to beleaguer him about it. And in any case, wasn't Jason Speed the exception that unhappily proved the rule?

That Lancefield blood running through the veins wasn't enough to make just anyone a Lancefield?

21

Tom Parkinson cast his eyes around the untidy living room of Becca's cottage, looking for somewhere to sit, but apart from the sofa, already occupied by Becca herself, there were only a couple of shabby wooden chairs pushed up against the wall. He reached out a hand and pulled one of the chairs towards him, twisting it around so that he could sit astride it. He rested his forearms on the back of the chair and waggled the fingers of his right hand in the direction of the toddler playing happily in the middle of the floor. 'Hey there, Frankie, remember me?'

Evidently not. The child puffed out her lips in a puzzled pout and, without wasting any further effort on the question, turned her attention back to the small plastic tea set beside her on the floor.

The sergeant turned his eyes to Becca. 'They grow up so quickly, don't they?' He was trying, without much success, to warm up the atmosphere before getting to the point of his visit. He cleared his throat and tried a different tack. 'She looks well, Becca. And so do you.' All things considered. 'I'm glad things are going okay.'

'We don't want for anything. Except for Philip.' Becca delivered the pronouncement with a sour twist of the lips. 'But I'm sure that's not what you've come to talk to me about today, is it, Sergeant Parkinson?'

'It's a fair cop.' He grinned at her, but the effort was wasted. 'I was hoping to talk to you about Emma Needham, the girl that died in the churchyard last night.' He glanced down at his fingers. 'What did you make of her, Becca?'

'Me?' Becca shrugged her disinterest. 'I didn't really

speak to her. I saw her in the conservatory when she was having lunch, and then she went for a walk around the garden with David Lancefield. And I only saw that through the kitchen window.' Becca's lips curved into a bitter smile. 'They weren't exactly toffs, were they? Her and that Jason. That must have been a poke in the eye for the Lancefields, finding out that their newfound relatives were as common as the rest of us.'

'She was still a human being, Becca. And she wasn't related to the Lancefields. It's Jason Speed who has the connection. Emma was just an innocent victim in all of this.'

'Then I hope that you and Inspector Price make a better job of finding her killer than you did of finding Lucy Lancefield's.' Becca put a thumb up to her lips and chewed on her thumbnail, suddenly subdued. 'Can I ask what happened to the girl?'

'You mean you haven't heard?' He found that hard to believe. 'She was strangled with her scarf, Becca. Just like Lucy. And her body was laid out across Lucy's grave.'

For a moment Becca's face softened and her lower lip gave an almost imperceptible tremor. And then she clenched her jaw and snarled at him. 'Well, it serves her right for cosying up to the Lancefields.'

'I don't believe you really mean that. Emma Needham never did you any harm.' Parkinson lowered his head and rested his chin on his hands. 'You know, the key to cracking any murder case is working out who stands to benefit from the death. Once we work out why Emma was murdered, it will be a lot easier to work out who did it.'

'But nobody around here knew her. So nobody here could have had a motive.'

'Are you sure? I can think of any number of people around here who had a motive. Beginning with anyone who harbours a grudge against the Lancefields.'

Becca's face folded into a scowl. 'Maybe she was just in the wrong place at the wrong time. Maybe she just got unlucky. There could have been some nutter in the churchyard, just looking for a random victim.'

Parkinson let out a laugh. 'Some random nutter? Is that the best you can come up with? In a village of no more than two hundred inhabitants, most of whom are related in some way?' And related to Becca Smith at that. 'No, it's far more likely to be someone with an axe to grind against Richard and David Lancefield.' The policeman tilted his head. 'Your elder brother, for example.'

Becca's cheeks flushed with an angry blush. 'You're not going to pin this on Zak. He was in The Lancefield Arms all of yesterday evening.'

'I know. I've already spoken to him.' Parkinson watched her face carefully as he spoke. 'But I'd be interested to know where he was the day before.'

'The day before?' She pushed out her lips. 'I don't know. I'm not his keeper, am I?'

'But you know about the flowers on Lucy's grave, don't you? And the spiteful card that went with them? We know that's down to Zak.'

'So what?' She gave an angry shake of the head. 'Your boss has already been on my case about that. So what if Zak did leave those flowers? It doesn't mean that he killed that girl.'

'She was found spread-eagled across Lucy's grave.'

'DCI Price has already told me that. It still doesn't mean anything.'

'Did he tell you that there was a card in Emma's mouth? The same kind of card that had been left with the anonymous flowers?' Parkinson lifted his head. 'The card that Richard Lancefield found yesterday on Lucy's grave bore the word "whore". The card in Emma's mouth said "slut".'

'So?'

'The handwriting on both cards was the same.' He gave her a moment to think about it. 'We know your brother is harassing the Lancefields, and we know that the

Lancefields are tolerating it for your sake. But their patience won't hold out forever, and if Zak has gone too far…'

'Zak wouldn't kill anybody.' Becca turned her head away and focused her attention on Frankie. The child was playing silently with her tea service and her dolls, blissfully oblivious to her mother's growing discomfort. 'He isn't that stupid.'

'And what about you, Becca? Where were you last night?'

'I had a quick drink in The Lancefield Arms and then I picked Frankie up from my mum's. After that I was here with Frankie all evening, minding my own business.'

'Can anybody corroborate that?'

'Corroborate?' Becca uttered an astonished laugh. 'You're not serious? Are you suggesting that I left Frankie here on her own and nipped down to the churchyard? How would I even have known that Emma Needham would be there?' She wrapped her arms defensively around her body. 'I thought you said the key to finding a killer was all about the motive? What motive could I possibly have to murder a girl I didn't know?'

'Isn't revenge a motive? We all know that you want revenge on the family for Philip's death.'

'Do you really think I could do that to someone?'

'Maybe you didn't act alone. Maybe you had help.'

'You already know that Zak was in the pub.'

'And where was Robin?'

'Robin? You know how gentle Robin is. He couldn't do a thing like that.'

'So that brings us right back round to you.' Parkinson observed the girl with a keen and appraising eye. She was still an angry little ball of venom. Nothing much there had changed. He could remember her grief at Philip's unexpected death, and how quickly that grief had been obliterated by her rage at the injustice of her unexpected loss. Her anger at the Lancefields ran deep and unabating.

But did it run deep enough for her to murder Emma Needham?

*

'I can't remember whether I mentioned that Marcus worked here at The Zoological Hotel for a time. He was at university with the owner's son.' David glanced around the bar. It had been a last-minute decision to join Kathryn and Jason for dinner, and now he was beginning to wonder why he'd suggested it. 'Marcus was the business development manager. But, of course, he won't be coming back here.'

At the other side of the small table, Jason was listening intently. 'It must be a very difficult situation for you.'

That would be putting it mildly. David lifted his whisky and soda to his lips and sipped. 'Marcus is a fine chap and more than a stepson to me. It will be a relief when his case comes to court to be settled.'

'Richard said that you were planning to send Marcus to St Felix, to manage the estate out there.'

David smiled. 'His mother isn't keen on the idea, but she will be able to go out and visit him whenever she wishes.'

Jason's tongue ran thoughtfully around his lips. 'I suppose if he goes to St Felix, that will leave you without anyone here in Cornwall to support you.'

'Perhaps.' David's cheeks began to burn. He had an inkling where this particular line of conversation was heading and, in truth, he didn't want to go there. He lifted his hand and glanced at his wristwatch. 'It's not like Kathryn to be unpunctual. I'm sure we agreed to meet at eight o'clock.' It was a clumsy attempt at deflection. 'We'll have to find something else to discuss until she joins us.' He turned back to Jason and forced a smile. 'Perhaps we might talk about your own plans? You must feel ready to return to Liverpool now?'

The question appeared to catch Jason off guard. He bridled slightly, and gave an almost imperceptible shake of the head. 'I'm not in any rush to get back to Liverpool, David, and I'd rather be here in Penzance with you and Richard while DCI Price investigates what happened to Emma.'

'I see.' David settled back in his seat. 'But surely your father's affairs will need to be attended to? I suppose cousin Barbara must be taking care of that for you at the moment, but you will want to pick up the reins yourself.'

'Barbara was very close to my dad. They were more like brother and sister.' There was a note of unexpected bitterness in the young man's voice. 'She's not doing me a favour by looking after his affairs. She wants to do it. Even if I'd still been up there in Liverpool, she would have wanted to control everything.'

'I'm sorry, Jason. I had assumed that you were all quite close as a family.'

'Well, she was close to my dad. But she's just a sort of aunt to me. We've never been all that close. I suppose I'm pretty much alone now that Dad and Emma have gone.' Jason stared down into his drink, and then flicked his eyes swiftly back up to David's face. 'Apart from yourself and Richard, of course. You have no idea just what a relief it is to know that I have some other family. Especially when I know that you and Richard were looking for me.'

The heat in David's cheeks intensified, and he bowed his head in an attempt to hide his embarrassment. 'I wonder if I might ask you, Jason, about your mother?' He lifted his eyes to look at the young man's face. 'Do you have many memories of her?'

Jason's throat flared with a sudden flash of crimson. 'No, I can't say that I do.' The question seemed to irritate him. 'She died when I was very small. I never really knew her.'

'I'm very sorry to hear that. May I ask her name?'

'Her name?' Now Jason sounded confused. 'It was

Jean. Jean Carver.' He fell silent for a moment, and then made his own attempt to change the topic of conversation. 'Can I ask how long Kathryn has worked for the family?'

David smiled. 'Kathryn doesn't work for us, Jason. She's a consultant.'

'But she prepared the lunch for us yesterday. And today.'

'I can see it must look a little odd. She came here as a consultant to work for my father on the family's history and heritage. But, happily, she has become a friend to the family in the process, and she is supporting my father with general household duties while Nancy is away in St Felix.'

'Nancy? That's Richard's secretary, isn't it?'

'Yes, but then Nancy is also really a part of our extended family.'

'But none of these people are really family to you, are they? I mean, Marcus is your wife's son, Kathryn is a friend and Nancy is a secretary.' Jason licked his lips. 'Unlike me. I mean, I'm related to you by blood. Kathryn has proven that, hasn't she?'

Regrettably the answer was "yes". David drew in a cautious breath. 'Yes, Kathryn is certain that both you and Barbara, and of course, your late father, are direct descendants of Thomas Moses Lancefield.'

'So in law, that makes me your heir?'

The audacity of the question rendered David Lancefield momentarily speechless. It took him a moment to recover his equilibrium, and then he calmly lifted his head to put his glass to his lips and drained off what was left of his whisky. 'I'm afraid that your understanding of the law is incorrect.' He placed the empty glass gently down on the table. 'As far as I am aware, the connection between us is too distant to be recognised in law, at least in regard to the laws of inheritance.'

'But even if it weren't, Jason, I think you might find that I would precede you.'

A woman's voice, completely unfamiliar to David,

broke into their conversation and the effect on Jason Speed was as dramatic as it was immediate. The crimson flashes on his neck flared north, the colour suffusing angrily across his chin, his cheeks and his forehead. He shot an anxious glance at David, and then checked himself and rose to his feet to stare open-mouthed at the newcomer to the room.

David, bemused, turned his head to see to whom the unexpected voice belonged. A plump, middle-aged woman was standing in the doorway of the bar. She was staring at him with kindly eyes and a smile that was firm, but not unfriendly. He opened his mouth to speak but she put up a beringed hand to silence him.

'I'm sorry to descend on you unannounced like this, Mr Lancefield. And I'm sorry that Jason seems to have lost his manners, and that I need to introduce myself.' She stepped forward and extended her hand towards him. 'I'm Dennis Speed's cousin, Barbara Gee. And I'm very pleased indeed to finally meet you.'

22

Ennor Price placed the empty paper coffee cup down on his desk and swivelled gently on his chair to look thoughtfully out of the window. Outside, an insidious grey November drizzle was drenching everything in its path. He craned his neck a little, to get a better view of the street below, but there wasn't much to see first thing in the morning. The street was narrow, an unassuming cut-through between the three-storey concrete block that housed the police station and a long row of low, untidy lock-up garages. The sort of untidy lock-up garages that were used for temporary storage, or inhabited as temporary workshops when the occupant couldn't afford to rent something better.

Like the untidy lock-up garages that were used by Becca Smith's brother, Zak, for running what he claimed to be a legitimate car repair business.

Price swivelled back to his desk and turned his eyes down to a page of handwritten notes. Try as he might, he still couldn't shake off the notion that there was a connection somehow between Dennis Speed's accident up in Liverpool and Emma Needham's murder on his own patch, any more than he could shake off the notion that the Smith family were somehow responsible.

This had to be about revenge against the Lancefields. It had to be. It couldn't be just sheer coincidence that Speed met his death on the day he planned to meet with David Lancefield. And there was such obvious spite against the family in the way that Emma's body had been laid out over Lucy's grave. It suggested that her connection to the Lancefields led to her death. More than that, it suggested that the Lancefields were somehow *responsible* for her death.

It suggested that being connected to the Lancefields was dangerous.

Zak Smith's name was at the top of the page of notes and Price picked up his pen and drew a ring around it. Zak had an alibi for Emma's death. He was in The Lancefield Arms, and for once there were plenty of witnesses to corroborate his statement. But at this stage, as far as Price could see, Smith didn't have an alibi for the morning of Dennis Speed's death. Unless…

He stretched out a hand to the phone on his desk and picked up the receiver, and then jabbed at the keypad to dial a familiar number. The call was answered immediately. 'Tom, it's Ennor. Are you on your way into Penzance?'

Parkinson's voice crackled cheerily down the line. 'I'll be with you in about ten minutes. What's the panic?'

'No panic. I want you to go over to Zak Smith's garage and find out where he was on Monday evening, and into Tuesday morning.'

'I thought we knew where he was on Tuesday morning. He was in the churchyard at St Felicity's, leaving those flowers on Lucy's grave. Becca virtually admitted to me that Zak was responsible for that.'

'Responsible, yes. But what if he delegated the task? What if someone else did it for him?'

'Even then, it would be too fantastic to think that he could drive all the way from Penzance to Liverpool to shove Dennis Speed under a bus. Apart from anything else, how would Zak have known about him, let alone recognised him?'

'Becca could have told him. If he had access to Dennis's address, he could have staked him out and followed him to Lime Street station.'

'And how would he have obtained access to Dennis's address?' Parkinson let out a long, low groan. 'You're obsessed with this, boss. You have to let it go.'

'No, I don't. Just because I'm obsessed with it doesn't mean I'm not on the right track. Becca and Zak could have been working together. She could have obtained Speed's address from Salvation Hall and passed it on to her brother. She was here in Penwithen on Tuesday. Who's to say that she didn't leave those flowers on the grave?' Price tapped an impatient finger on the desk. 'Look, if nothing else we need to eliminate the two of them from our enquiries. We can't eliminate Becca from Emma's murder yet, because she doesn't have a solid-enough alibi. And we can't eliminate Zak from our enquiry into Dennis's death until we know where he was first thing on Tuesday morning.'

'At the risk of stating the obvious, sir, we're not investigating Dennis's death. That's on Andy Drummond's plate.'

Price drew in a sharp breath. 'Thanks for the reminder.' He balanced the phone's receiver in the crook of his neck. 'So Becca pretty much admitted to you that Zak was responsible for the flowers?'

'She did. But that doesn't make him a murderer, does it? Actually, she looked concerned when I suggested it. I can't help wondering whether we might have some leverage there. Perhaps he might admit to the harassment if it gives him an alibi for the murder.' The sergeant paused, and then asked, 'Do you still want me to go and talk to him?'

'Yes. I want his alibi for Monday evening and Tuesday morning, and an alibi for Robin Smith too, while you're at it. And before you object, just humour me, Tom, can't you? When you've got their alibis, you can poke me in the eye with them.' Price glanced down again at his notes. 'While you're dealing with the Smiths, I'll chase Andy Drummond. He promised us a copy of the CCTV footage from Lime Street station for Tuesday morning and we still don't have it.'

'Boss, what are we going to do about Jason Speed? Are

we going to speak to him again?'

'You can leave Jason to me. That's my piece of news for this morning. I had a call from Kathryn late yesterday evening. Barbara Gee turned up unexpectedly at The Zoological Hotel and, by all accounts, young Jason wasn't particularly pleased to see her.'

'I thought she'd declined the Lancefields' invitation to come down to Cornwall?'

'Apparently, she decided to make plans of her own. I'm hoping to have a chat with her this morning, over at Salvation Hall. I think she knows more about this whole sorry affair than she's been letting on to Drummond and Jenkins. She's admitted to knowing that Dennis was travelling to Bristol to meet David, but she'd been asked not to share that news with Jason. It might be nothing more than a family squabble, but I'm not going to take the risk. If nothing else she can tell me what Emma Needham said to her on that last call before the poor kid met her death.'

*

Richard lifted the photograph to his eyes and squinted at it. 'And this was taken when?' The light in the drawing room at Salvation Hall was unusually dim, and he tilted the frame to catch a stray beam of weak winter sunlight from the window behind his armchair.

Barbara, seated nearby on the edge of the vast Chesterfield sofa, leaned forward a little to answer him. 'About ten years ago. Jason was only in his early twenties then. We took a camping holiday in North Wales.' She smiled at the memory. 'I thought you might like a picture of the three of us, and that was the happiest image I could find.' There was another snap resting in the soft, plump fingers of her right hand and she offered it to Richard. 'This is one of Jason and Emma, taken last year. I'm afraid it isn't framed.'

'Then we'll find it a frame befitting a family treasure.' Richard's voice was gentle as he took the offering from her hand. 'Emma was a charming young woman, and I think she cared a great deal for Jason.'

'She was good for him.' Barbara sighed. 'I still can't quite believe that she's gone, any more than I can believe that Dennis is gone.'

'It has been a trial for all concerned.' Richard rested the photograph on his knee, his eyes still fixed on it as he spoke. 'I have to admit to a sense of relief at your arrival, Barbara. Of course, I could have wished for a happier circumstance for our first meeting, but you are here at Salvation Hall now, and that is what matters.' His face clouded. 'We had quite given up hope that you would come to our rescue.'

'Heavens, is that what I've done?' Barbara blushed. 'I'm sorry that I turned down your initial invitation. You know, after I'd spoken to Kathryn yesterday, I stopped to think what Dennis would have wanted. He wouldn't have wanted Jason to go through this dreadful ordeal on his own.'

'I don't think that Jason is the only one dealing with an ordeal.' Richard nodded to himself. 'Barbara, my dear, I hope that we will have many opportunities ahead of us to get to know one another. But in the light of Emma's death, we must focus on the matter at hand, and I fear I must speak plainly. Before you arrived at Salvation Hall this morning, I heard from DCI Price, the officer leading the investigation into Emma's murder. He plans to visit Salvation Hall this morning in the hope of speaking with you.' Richard let go of the photograph and leaned across to take hold of Barbara's hand. 'He and I may not always see eye to eye, but I believe the inspector to be a good man. Among the best.' Richard hesitated for a moment, and then said, 'I believe the circumstances surrounding the death of my granddaughter, Lucy, have already been explained to you.'

'I heard about it first from DCI Drummond in Liverpool.' Barbara stared at the gnarled hand that was cradling her own. 'I'm very sorry for your loss, Richard, but you can't seriously think that it had anything to do with what happened to Emma?'

'Truthfully, we don't know what to think. But it is a possibility.' Richard hesitated again, unsure of his ground, and then instigated a subtle change of direction. 'David tells me that your unexpected arrival at the hotel yesterday evening didn't elicit the response from Jason which might have been expected.'

Barbara smiled and turned her head away. 'Just tell it like it was, Richard. Jason wasn't pleased to see me.' She turned back to look at him. 'He wasn't pleased to see me, because since his father died… since Dennis has been out of the picture, Jason has been quite determined to distance himself from both me and from his life in Liverpool.' She blew out a breath. 'Well, actually, that's not quite true. I don't think it's because Dennis died. I think it's because of the letters that Dennis was carrying in his pocket when he met his death.'

'The letters which Dennis received from myself and my solicitor?'

'Yes.'

'You are of the opinion that Jason's head has been turned by my attempts to build a bridge between my own family and yours. And for that, I can only apologise.' Richard let go of her hand and leaned back in his seat. 'There is no other reason why Jason might not have been pleased to see you?'

Barbara turned her eyes away again, to look across the vast expanse of the drawing room at nothing in particular. And then she turned them down to look at her hands. 'Jason is very impressionable, Richard. It's my belief that Dennis knew the effect your invitation would have on him, and that's why he kept it to himself. Jason is apt to…' She frowned. 'He's apt to romanticise. I think Dennis feared that Jason would get the wrong idea about your invitation for the families to connect.'

It wasn't a direct answer to Richard's question. But the absence of a direct answer, perhaps, was all the explanation that Richard needed. 'Dennis feared that Jason would be impressed by our home and our lifestyle, and think that he would expect to benefit from the connection in some material sense.' Richard watched Barbara's face as he spoke and could see that she understood only too well what he was suggesting. 'I believe you were present yesterday evening when Jason asked my son if his connection to the Lancefields would make him the heir to our estates.' The old man's thin lips curled into a smile. 'David also told me of your response to the suggestion. I hear that you quite took the wind out of Jason's sails.'

Barbara relaxed a little and smiled. 'I was hoping to put Jason in his place. Like Dennis, my interest in your invitation was solely to know whether we could be of support to each other.' She looked embarrassed. 'I think I understand why you are trying to find some additional connections for David. Our family in Liverpool is a small one, too. There was just Dennis, Jason and me. And of course, we hoped that Emma would become family in time. Now there is just me and Jason.'

'I'm afraid I have to disagree with you there, my dear. There is Barbara and Jason, and Richard and David.' He meant the words kindly. 'You have already met our very dear friend, Kathryn. And in time you will meet Nancy, my amanuensis, and David's wife Stella and his stepson, Marcus. Our family is growing.' Richard let out a sigh. 'It will always be a regret to me, you know, that I didn't have the opportunity to meet with Dennis.' He glanced down at the photographs resting on his lap. 'May I ask what kind of man he was?'

'He was a decent, down-to-earth man with a very strong work ethic. And a gentle soul. Rather serious, with a strong, old-fashioned sense of right and wrong. I think he would have been very pleased to meet with you, Richard, and taken your invitation in the spirit of its intention.'

If only it hadn't been for Jason? Richard parked the thought away. 'When Kathryn investigated our connections with the Liverpool branch of the family, she discovered that Dennis had a brother.'

'Yes, Gordon.' Barbara's eyes saddened. 'Gordon was the elder by three years, but he died in infancy before Dennis was born.'

'How sad. And still more sadness, I believe, for Dennis to have found himself a widower while Jason was still quite young?'

'A widower?' Barbara's eyes took on a puzzled look and she shook her head. 'I'm afraid Kathryn must have made a mistake there, Richard. Dennis's wife didn't die. I'm afraid the marriage failed.' She nodded. 'Poor Dennis took the news very badly. He and Jean had only been married for four years and Jason was barely two at the time. Of course, I did my best to step into the breach and help Dennis to bring Jason up. But it was a bitter blow to both of them, to be left behind because Jean would rather spend her life with someone else.'

*

'Why did Richard want to be on his own with Barbara?' Jason asked the question quietly as Kathryn busied herself at the library desk.

She suppressed a sigh and swung around on the captain's chair to face him. 'I wouldn't read too much into it, Jason, it's just Richard's way. He gets quite tired these days, and I think he likes to keep things calm.' It wasn't a lie, as such. 'I can't imagine they'll spend too long together anyway. We're expecting DCI Price to be here by ten o'clock.'

Jason's brow furrowed. 'He's coming to speak to Auntie Barb too, isn't he?' The idea seemed to trouble him, and then he forced a smile. 'I suppose I made a fool of myself yesterday evening, didn't I? I didn't mean anything by asking David if I was the heir to the estate. I don't really understand how these things work.' He lifted a hand to his mouth and bit nervously on the side of his thumbnail. 'Who *will* the estate pass to, when David dies, if there isn't anyone else left to inherit?'

'Richard has drawn up a very elaborate will, to put the estates into a trust. He's done that to ensure that the estates remain intact and that the family's heritage is preserved well into the future. It's Richard's wish that Woodlands Park continues to produce sugar and rum, and to provide employment and homes for all the existing workers and their families.' Kathryn swivelled the chair gently from side to side as she spoke. 'And he wants pretty much the same for Salvation Hall. The estate here is mostly made up of farmland that's rented out to tenant farmers, and residential and commercial property.'

'Like The Lancefield Arms?'

'Just like The Lancefield Arms.' Kathryn smiled and nodded. 'Richard owns most of the property in Penwithen and rents it out to tenants. And he owns some commercial property in Penzance, and some of the other surrounding towns and villages, and a stretch of commercial waterfront on the coast between Penzance and Newlyn.' She stopped short of mentioning the family's possessions further afield – the commercial properties in London's Docklands district, the additional farm lands in Dorset and Gloucestershire, their stocks and shares and sundry investments in the City. When it came to Jason Speed, there was no question in her mind that less was definitely more. 'It's Richard's wish that everything should go into a trust, to be managed by a number of trustees. They will have ultimate responsibility for the day-to-day running of the estates but, for the most part, things will just trundle on as they do at the moment.'

'And how many trustees are there?'

'At the moment, there are three.'

Jason lifted an eyebrow. 'Just three people to take control of all of that property?'

'Not to control it, Jason. To take care of it. A trustee holds something "in trust". They look after it. Take responsibility for it. Act in its best interests.' There was another obvious question to come, one that Kathryn knew she didn't want to answer. She rolled the captain's chair back towards the desk and reached out a hand to retrieve a page of handwritten notes. 'You know, if you really want to redeem yourself with David, you might show a little more interest in the Lancefield family's history. I've been doing some digging into the history of the West Africa Squadron.'

'Auntie Barb mentioned that yesterday evening, didn't she? That's the part of the Royal Navy that our ancestor Thomas Moses Lancefield went into?'

'That's right.' Kathryn offered him the page of notes. 'When Britain stopped participating in the slave trade, other countries continued to trade, and slaves were still smuggled into the British West Indies until slavery itself was abolished. So Britain used the Royal Navy to enforce its ban on slave trading by closing down the shipping routes, seizing slave ships, and liberating the poor souls on board.' She paused for a moment to let Jason think about it. 'To begin with, Royal Navy ships operated out of the Cape of Good Hope, but a dedicated West Coast of Africa Station was created in 1819, and by 1825 there were seven ships stationed there. Your ancestor, Thomas Moses Lancefield, joined the squadron in 1832, just two years after he married Alice Banks.'

'Why on earth would he do that?'

'I think he was a man of very strong principles. His family had indulged in some pretty inhumane practices when they ran their own slave ship. He knew this to be true because his father-in-law, Digory Banks, had been the captain of the Lancefields' ship. The Lancefields didn't hesitate to cut him adrift when he married Alice Banks, and I think he decided to poke them in the eye by joining the very squadron that would injure their chances of procuring slaves for their plantation by an illegal route.' Kathryn paused again, and then said, 'The conditions for seamen serving with the squadron were often as brutal as conditions on a slave ship. They spent long months cruising offshore in a difficult climate, and dealt with violence, death and disease on an almost daily basis. It certainly wasn't a job for the faint-hearted. But Thomas Moses served in the squadron for almost six years before taking up a post back at home in England.'

Jason bit again on his thumbnail and offered Kathryn a withering glance. 'You mean he chose to go through all of that just because of his principles, rather than stay in England with his family and inherit Salvation Hall?'

Kathryn forced a smile. 'His father was the second son of the family, Jason. As I've already explained to you before, whether he had any principles or not, there was never any possibility that he would inherit Salvation Hall.'

23

David Lancefield was relieved to get out of the house and volunteering to take Samson for his morning walk down to the village had not been a hardship. He could feel the storm clouds gathering again, and he wanted to clear his head before DCI Price arrived to interview Barbara and Jason.

Memories of the evening before were hanging heavily in his mind. His own initial pleasure at the unexpected arrival of Barbara had quickly been tarnished by Jason's evident displeasure at the unforeseen turn of events. There had been no question in David's mind that Barbara should join them for supper, and he and Kathryn had made every effort to keep the conversation as light as present tragic circumstances would permit. And for her part, Barbara had risen to the occasion. She had apologised for turning up at The Zoological unannounced and talked freely and with affection about Dennis and Emma, expressing her sorrow at their loss and her regret that her first meeting with a member of the Lancefield family hadn't been in happier circumstances. David couldn't have been more relieved at her arrival. But Jason?

Jason had been… perturbed?

David toyed with the word in his mind as he strode into Penwithen village, uncomfortable with his own definition. Did he mean "perturbed"? The young man had been agitated, twitchy almost, and yet Barbara was supposed to be there to support him. She had already carried a burden on his behalf; she'd identified his father's body for the police and set about making arrangements for Dennis's funeral. And now she had come all the way to

Cornwall to ease his grief, to help him cope with the brutal loss of his partner and the coming investigation into Emma's untimely death.

So why was the dynamic between Jason and Barbara so brittle, so strained, so downright awkward?

David muttered under his breath and pulled gently on Samson's lead, steering the dog away from The Lancefield Arms and across the road towards St Felicity's. At first, the animal seemed reluctant to follow him and then a figure emerged from the lychgate and Samson let out a bark.

'Good morning. It's Amber, isn't it?' David smiled at the girl. 'Amber Kimbrall?'

The barmaid's eyes darted away across the road toward The Lancefield Arms. 'Yes, I'm Amber.' Her voice was low, her words hesitant. 'Good morning, Mr Lancefield.' She stepped quickly across the pavement, away from him. 'It's a lovely morning, for the time of year.' She threw the words over her shoulder as she went, reluctant to prolong the conversation.

David watched her as she sped across the road and into the pub. 'Well, Samson, what do you make of that?' He turned his attention back to the lychgate and a discomfiting thought occurred to him. From what he remembered of her, Amber Kimbrall wasn't the sort of young woman who was likely to frequent a churchyard. At least not alone, he thought pithily, and not during daylight hours when she might be seen. He pulled gently again on Samson's lead and made his way through the lychgate, and down the churchyard path to the sheltered spot that harboured his daughter's grave.

His heart sank at the sight of a newly-placed bouquet, a luxurious arrangement of lilies and roses and frothy, delicate gypsophila. It was an expensive offering, and far removed from the cheap, sad affair of wilting chrysanthemums that had been left on Lucy's grave the night that Emma Needham met her death. But a closer inspection revealed a familiar white card placed loosely among the blooms and, with a heavy heart, he bent down to retrieve it, lifting it up to his eyes. A single word was written in the now-familiar script; the same neat, tidy handwriting that had previously so cruelly insulted his daughter. The card said simply – "*Sorry*".

*

Barbara Gee wasn't quite what DCI Price had expected. She was already in the drawing room when he arrived at Salvation Hall and had risen to her feet to greet him with a smile and warm shake of the hands. Dressed in a burnt-orange jumper dress, an oversized fluffy affair that hung loosely atop a pair of casual brown jersey leggings, she cut a curiously Bohemian figure against the formal grandeur of the Lancefields' sophisticated residence.

'Thank you for agreeing to speak to me.' Price lowered himself onto the edge of the Chesterfield sofa and waited for Barbara to settle back into her armchair. 'I know this is a difficult time.' He cast a glance around the room's luxurious expanse, then turned towards her with a smile. 'So, what do you make of Salvation Hall and the Lancefield family?'

'To be honest, Inspector Price, I haven't really had the chance to form an opinion yet.' She spoke with a quiet authority. 'What do *you* make of Salvation Hall and the Lancefield family?'

'Touché.' Price laughed softly under his breath. 'Are you asking my opinion as a policeman or as a human being?'

'Is there a difference?'

'Of course. As a policeman, Salvation Hall and the Lancefields have become the bane of my life. In the last couple of months, I've seen Lucy Lancefield's body floating amongst the water lilies in the ornamental lake, and I've watched her murdered lover, Philip, hauled out of the same lake wrapped in a set of iron manacles that I'm reliably informed date back to the eighteenth century. I've charged Lucy's fiancé with murder, and I'm still building the case against him while I wait for a trial date. In the meantime, I've got Philip's grieving partner and her family harassing the Lancefields on a daily basis and, as if that's not enough, another young woman has been murdered and her body laid out across Lucy's grave, suggesting that her death in some way relates to her connection with the Lancefields.'

Barbara nodded sagely to herself. 'And as a human being?'

'I've always thought the Lancefields to be a set of spoiled, over-privileged aristos who made their money from the misery of other human beings. But, partly thanks to the influence of Kathryn Clifton, I have warmed slightly – only very, very slightly, mind – to both Richard and David as human beings. No one deserves to experience the losses and harassment they've endured over the last couple of months, and they are bearing the pain with a remarkable display of fortitude, kindness and dignity.'

The explanation appeared to satisfy her. 'And Salvation Hall?'

'Taken with the Woodlands estate, and all the other trappings of the family's wealth, I think it's a grade-A motive for murder.'

It clearly wasn't the answer she was expecting. An unmistakable blush rose to Barbara's cheeks and her eyes widened for a moment. 'Did you have a particular murder in mind?'

'I'm afraid I was thinking of Emma. Salvation Hall and the Lancefields, and all the privilege they represent, elicit a malicious kind of jealousy in these parts. Most of the people who live in Penwithen work for them, in one capacity or another. Or rent property from them. But they do it with resentment, not gratitude.'

'Because of the way the family made their wealth?'

'I think more likely because of the sheer amount of

wealth. There's something almost obscene about wealth that seems endless, isn't there?' Price looked down at his fingers, suddenly aware that the conversation had taken a most unexpected turn. 'But that's not what I came to discuss with you.' He flicked his eyes back up to her face. 'I'm sorry that you've had to endure two bereavements so close together. I learned of Dennis's death the day it happened. I had a call from DCI Drummond. He was following up on the letters in Dennis's pocket.' Price narrowed his eyes. 'DCI Drummond is convinced that your cousin's death was an accident. I wondered if you agreed with him?'

There was a hint of hesitation before Barbara answered. 'Yes, of course. What else could it have been?'

'Dennis told you about the letters, and you knew that he was travelling to Bristol to meet David Lancefield?'

'Yes.'

'But you didn't tell Jason.'

'No.'

'Did Dennis know about Lucy's and Philip's murders before he made the journey to Bristol?'

'I don't believe so, no.'

'Did you?'

'I didn't know about them until yesterday. DCI Drummond told me himself when he broke the news of Emma's death.' Barbara tilted her head. 'Do you believe that Marcus Drake was responsible for both of those murders, Inspector Price?'

'I'm keeping an open mind. I think it's very likely, but we have no proof. I can't charge him with Lucy's murder, only Philip's. And I have to get a conviction for that. I owe it to Becca Smith.' He paused, and then asked, 'Have you met Becca yet?'

'I wouldn't say I'd met her. I saw her earlier this morning when she brought coffee into the drawing room. She looks an unhappy creature.'

Unhappy was hardly the word. 'Becca has a little girl,

Philip's daughter, innocent in all of this. It doesn't sit well with me, the thought of that child going through life thinking her father was a murderer when he may have been only a victim.'

'Forgive me, Inspector Price, but I don't see what this has to do with Dennis's accident. Or Emma's death.'

'I have to explore the possibility that all of the deaths are connected in some way. And I have to ask myself if anyone else connected with the Lancefield family might be at risk. Jason, for example. And possibly yourself.' He didn't want to distress her unnecessarily, but forewarned was forearmed. 'I'm looking very closely at the Smith family, and I would caution you to be wary of what you say to Becca Smith while you're here at Salvation Hall.'

'Are you saying that Becca's family may have been responsible for Emma's death?'

'I certainly believe that Jason's connection with the Lancefield family was the reason for it.' Price leaned back in his seat and folded his arms. 'Emma didn't want to come to Salvation Hall, did she?' He watched Barbara's face and saw a hint of suspicion creep into the soft, kind eyes.

'Jason's decision to drive down to Cornwall immediately after his father's death was irrational, to say the least. Emma was worried about his state of mind and didn't want him to travel alone.'

'The way I heard it, Jason forbade her from telling you that they were going to make the journey. I also heard that the staff at The Lancefield Arms didn't make them particularly welcome.' Price unfolded his arms and leaned forward. 'What was she afraid of, Barbara? Did something happen at The Lancefield Arms? Something that made her fear for her life?'

*

'Cousin Barbara is more than I could have hoped for.' Richard turned up the collar of his coat against the cold November air and then sank his hands into his pockets. 'She is charming, she is prudent and, above all, she is kind.' He chuckled to himself and cast a mischievous glance in Kathryn's direction. 'I think I have found Soteria to stand with Minerva.'

Kathryn let out a groan. 'I hope you're not casting me as Minerva. I could never claim to be as wise and learned, as my next question will confirm.' She was walking slowly beside him across the terrace. 'Who on earth was Soteria?'

'My dear girl, she was the goddess of safety and salvation. Of deliverance, and preservation from harm.' His pace slowed a little, and then he paused to stare out over the ornamental lake. 'If only she had arrived while Emma was still alive. She might have delivered us from this latest atrocity.' He turned tired eyes to Kathryn's face. 'She is with Inspector Price now. I can only hope that she is able to help him.'

'And help us?'

'She tells me that she plans to take Jason home to Liverpool as soon as possible. She is going to speak to him over lunch. I've arranged for Becca to serve them in the conservatory, and plan to leave them to it.' Richard resumed his walk, his pace slow and deliberate. 'I think it unlikely they will travel today, so perhaps we should arrange for another night at The Zoological, and perhaps sound Barbara out about her plans for travelling home. I understand that Jason and Emma drove down to Penwithen in Emma's car, and I assume that Barbara and Jason plan to drive home in it together. But one never knows how things will pan out.'

'Did Barbara give you any indication this morning why Dennis didn't tell Jason about your letters?'

'She is sticking to her story that Jason is impressionable, and apt to jump to the wrong conclusions. I, however, do not buy that as an explanation.' Richard drew in a breath and sucked in his cheeks. 'I realise I may offend you by asking this, Kathryn, but is there any possibility at all that your research into the family tree could have led us down the wrong path?'

The question took Kathryn by surprise. 'Are you suggesting that I made a mistake? That there was no connection to Dennis Speed?' She laughed at the notion. 'I'm not offended, Richard. But I stand by my work. If nothing else, my conversation with Barbara yesterday evening confirms it. She has conducted her own research, completely independent of mine, and has come to the same conclusion. She and Dennis and Jason are direct descendants of Thomas Moses Lancefield, and he was the nephew of your direct ancestor Benedict Lancefield.' Was Richard so determined to put the genie back in the bottle that he would abandon Barbara and Jason? 'I had hoped that you would be keen to keep Barbara in the fold. I watched the way that she and David spoke to each other over dinner yesterday evening. They took to each other almost immediately.' Kathryn cleared her throat. 'I realise that I might risk offending you now, Richard, but I would respectfully suggest that turning a blind eye to Jason's obvious shortcomings would be a small price to pay to have Barbara on David's side when you are gone. Assuming that she's happy to keep up the connection.'

Richard stopped abruptly and stared out again across the lake. 'You are quite right, of course. And I should take into account that Barbara will know best how to handle her cousin.' The old man shivered against the cold. 'I fear that I have underestimated the weather. Perhaps we might walk back towards the house?' He turned on his heel. 'I think I might call for a taxi and take a trip into Penzance. There is something I want to follow up with old Mayhew.'

'Is it something that I could help with?'

'No, I would prefer it if you would stay here. David still hasn't returned from his walk with Samson, and I would prefer not to leave Barbara and Jason alone in the house with Becca.' Richard drew in a breath. 'We know that Barbara is with Inspector Price. Do we know where Jason is at the moment?'

'I left him in the library, reading about the West Africa Squadron. I persuaded him that it might be useful to develop an interest in the family's history. I think he's hoping to impress David with his new-found knowledge after lunch.' She tilted her head. 'Don't you think it's strange, Richard, that he doesn't seem to be grieving for Emma?'

'Perhaps. Perhaps not. You thought me a cold fish the day that Lucy died because I asked you to continue your work in curating my family's history. As I recall, I insisted on working with you, because it took my mind away from the grief. We all have our own way of dealing with our pain. When Jason and Emma arrived here, I drew the conclusion that he was still too shocked by the loss of his father to begin the grieving process. Perhaps the same could be said of his current loss. Perhaps he has not yet acknowledged that Emma has gone. The boy has his faults, but we cannot judge him to be cold-hearted simply because he has not yet begun to grieve.'

They had reached the rear of the house now, and Kathryn pushed gently on the outer kitchen door. 'I sincerely hope that you're right.' She stepped over the threshold and held the door open for Richard to follow her, muttering quietly under her breath as she did so. 'And how I wish that I shared your conviction.'

24

The lounge bar of The Lancefield Arms was deserted, save for a sullen-looking barman polishing his way through a crate of pint glasses. David Lancefield, seated at a table in the window, considered offering the man a pleasantry, and then thought better of it, turning his eyes instead to his companion under the table. 'Just settle yourself down, Samson, there's a good chap. We won't be long.' He wiggled his fingers at the dog, and Samson gave them a cursory lick before following his master's instructions.

Somewhere behind the bar, a door from the kitchen swung noisily into action. David looked up to see Amber Kimbrall approaching, and he watched in silence as she set a coffee tray down on the table in front of him.

'Coffee, milk and sugar.' She enveloped him in a cloud of musky perfume as she bent forward to empty the contents of the tray onto the table. 'I brought you white and brown sugar, Mr Lancefield, as I wasn't sure which you'd want.' She lifted the cup and saucer from the tray and set them down in front of him, the thin gold bangles on her wrist jangling noisily as she did so.

'Thank you, Amber. And please don't be so formal. You know my name is David.' He offered her a reassuring smile. It would be difficult not to notice that her hands were shaking. 'I wonder, you couldn't spare me a couple of minutes, could you? There's something I need to ask you.' He pointed to the empty chair at the other side of the table and raised a hopeful eyebrow.

'I'm a bit busy this morning, I'm afraid. Getting ready for the lunchtime trade.' She turned away quickly and began to make her way back to the bar.

But he wouldn't be dissuaded. 'I know what you were doing in the churchyard. Just now, when I bumped into you at the lychgate.' His words brought the barmaid to a halt. 'The flowers were a lovely thought, as was the card.'

Amber spun on her heel and stepped back towards the table. 'I don't know what you're talking about.'

'The flowers that you left on Lucy's grave. They were beautiful, and it was a very kind thought.' He pointed again at the empty chair opposite and this time she sank reluctantly onto it. 'You must have gone to a great deal of trouble and expense.'

She shook her head. 'I didn't leave any flowers.'

'There's no need to deny it. I'm not angry with you. I know how difficult these past few weeks have been for Becca and her family, and I think it was very brave of you to make the gesture to apologise.' David lifted the milk jug and added milk to his cup. 'I recognised the handwriting on the card. It was the same as the others. The ones which… well, which weren't quite so kind in their sentiment.' He set about pouring coffee onto the milk. 'Would you like to bring another cup, and join me? There's something I'd like to ask you. About the flowers and the cards. You might as well share my coffee while we talk.'

Amber shook her head a second time. She leaned forward, her clear blue eyes troubled under a wave of bleached-blonde tresses. 'I didn't leave the other flowers, Mr Lancefield. Those were left by Zak. But I'll admit that I wrote the cards for him. He thought it would be too easy for the police to identify him as the culprit if he wrote the cards himself.' She blinked back what might have been a tear. 'That other girl, that Emma, she didn't deserve what happened to her. And it breaks my heart to think that someone took the card I'd written and put it in her mouth. That card was meant for…' She broke off, suddenly remembering who was at the other side of the table.

David nodded with a smile. 'The card was meant for Lucy. I know.' He added sugar to his coffee and then stirred it. 'I know what you all think of my late, unlamented daughter. For my part, she and I were never that close. But she didn't deserve what happened to her.' He picked up his cup and sipped on the coffee. 'And I think you know that, Amber, in your heart of hearts. The hurt was never going to land on Lucy. Lucy's dead and gone. For what it's worth, it didn't particularly hurt me either. But my father has been quite distressed by it, especially when he's tried to do so much for Becca and little Frankie.' David looked at the barmaid over the top of his cup. 'But leaving those flowers for Emma, and letting her know that you're sorry, he will appreciate that as a gesture of genuine remorse.'

'Are you going to tell the police that I wrote those cards?'

'Oh yes, I'm afraid I must. But I don't want you to worry. I very much doubt that we will take any further action on the matter. And you can pass that message on to Zak. If the harassment stops, we will let the matter drop. I will square it off with my father and with Detective Chief Inspector Price.'

Amber offered up a rueful smile. 'Mr Lancefield… David… how can you be so kind, after what we've done?'

He stretched out a hand and patted the young woman's arm. 'Because I can never see the point in being *un*kind, Amber. What possible purpose is to be served by doing something mean, just to make another human being feel wretched?'

*

Jason was still in the library at Salvation Hall when Becca wandered into the room unannounced. He was sitting at the large mahogany desk, a small set of handwritten notes spread out in front of him, and the squeak of the heavy oak door behind him alerted him to the newcomer. He turned his head to look over his shoulder and eyed her with suspicious, narrowed eyes. 'Did you want something?'

Becca shuffled her feet. 'I'm sorry, I didn't know there was anyone in here.' The lie was a feeble one. 'Do you mind if I water the plants? Only Richard gets annoyed if they're left to dry out.' She was carrying a small, brass watering can and she lifted it up to show him.

Jason scowled, first at the watering can and then at Becca herself. 'It's not very convenient at the moment, Becca. Could you come back later, when I've finished?'

Come back later? Who the hell did Jason Speed think he was? Becca's jaw clenched, but now wasn't the time to demonstrate her temper. She ignored his request and crossed to the fireplace. 'There are only two or three plants to do in here. There's this peace lily here on the mantelpiece' – she dropped a splash of water into the pot – 'and the two parlour palms over by the window. I'll just do those and then I'll be out of your way.' She turned to him and forced a smile. 'While I'm here, can I just say how sorry I was to hear about Emma?'

'About *Emma*?' Jason almost spat the name back at her.

Becca blushed. Had she got that wrong? 'I thought that was her name? Emma Needham?' She licked her lips, a nervous flick of the tongue. 'I'm talking about the girl who came with you yesterday. The girl who was murdered in the churchyard.'

'I know who you're talking about. I'm just trying to work out what you think gives you the right to talk to *me* about it.' There was a hint of malice in Jason's voice. 'The way I heard it, one of your scumbag relatives was responsible for my Emma's death.'

'No, that can't be right.' Becca stepped towards him. 'It wasn't one of my family. Nobody knows who murdered her.'

'That's not the way I heard it. The way I heard it, your family have got it in for my family. You all thought that Emma was a Lancefield, like me. But she wasn't. You've taken your anger out on the wrong person this time.' Jason put his hands on the chair's arms and pushed himself to his feet. 'And one way or another, I think you're going to be sorry.'

His words were designed to provoke, and provoke is what they did. The blush in Becca's rounded cheeks flushed crimson, and anger twisted her lips into a cruel and angry snarl. 'It's the Lancefields who are going to be sorry. You don't know what you're getting into, getting mixed up with them. It's all because of Lucy and that bastard Marcus Drake that my daughter is growing up without her daddy. They killed my Philip, the two of them.'

'That's a lie. Philip McKeith murdered Lucy Lancefield. He murdered one of my family. Everybody knows it. And then, thanks to Marcus Drake, he got what was coming to him.' Jason's face lit up with a smug, self-satisfied smile. 'Anyway, what are you going to do when Marcus comes back here? Because he will come back, once they get him off the murder charge. It's better all round that you just go now. The family aren't going to want you back here when Philip is named for Lucy's murder.'

'Of course they want me here, just like they want Frankie here. Frankie is Richard's goddaughter. He won't give up on her, just because the likes of you suggests it.' Becca shook her head. 'You don't know what you're talking about.'

'And you do?' Jason hissed through his teeth. 'One minute you're moaning about the Lancefields and what they did to your precious Philip, and the next you're rabbiting on about how much they want you here.' He took another step towards her. 'So which is it, Becca? Are you here because they want you here, or are you clinging on here because they're rich? Because they're loaded? Because they're throwing money at you and your kid, to make up for your partner being murdered?'

'You don't know what you're talking about.'

'Oh, I think I do.' Jason's nostrils flared and he tipped

his head back. 'You're still here because you're milking the Lancefields. But I don't like the idea of my family being milked.'

'I only came here to tell you how sorry I was about Emma.'

'Well, now you've said it. But it doesn't make any difference. We all know that your brother Zak killed my Emma in the churchyard. And when he goes down for it, everything is going to change for you and that kid you drag around with you.' He flicked a dismissive finger in the direction of the library door. 'You'd better get out there and enjoy your last few days working at Salvation Hall because you're not going to be here much longer, not if I have anything to do with it.'

*

Price sank into the passenger seat of Parkinson's Audi and slammed the car door behind him. 'I would have suggested lunch at The Lancefield Arms, but I can't help thinking it would give me indigestion.' The Audi was tucked down a lane at the end of Penwithen village and Price nodded towards the pub as he spoke. 'Did you get anywhere with Zak Smith?'

'If you mean "did I get a reasonable alibi" then I'm afraid the answer is "yes".' The sergeant barely turned his head as he spoke, his eyes still fixed on the view through the Audi's windscreen. 'He was playing snooker at a club in Newlyn until after midnight on Monday, and he's provided the names of the three blokes he was playing with. As for Tuesday morning, he opened up the garage early to start repair work on a Fiat Punto that needed a new exhaust. He's given me the name of the customer, and shown me a copy of the paperwork that he drew up and signed at eleven o'clock on Tuesday morning when the car was picked up.'

'And Robin?'

'Robin was in Hayle on Monday night, staying over at his girlfriend's. I've spoken to both her and her mother, and they both corroborate his story. Before you ask, I haven't spoken to Becca yet this morning, but we already know she was at Salvation Hall on Tuesday.'

'She still needs an alibi for Wednesday evening.' Price breathed out a sigh of resignation. 'I had a conversation with David Lancefield before I drove over here to meet you. Amber Kimbrall has admitted to him that she wrote the cards that were left with the flowers. She did it for Zak.'

Parkinson's eyes widened and he turned to the senior officer. 'How the hell did he get her to admit that?'

'He saw her this morning, leaving more flowers on Lucy's grave. This time the card said "sorry". She reckons she bought the flowers herself, by way of an apology for the way Emma Needham was treated.' Price shook his head. 'Some people just don't know when to stop, do they?'

'I guess not. But I don't suppose we should be surprised that Amber was involved somewhere along the line.' Parkinson shifted in his seat and folded his arms, his eyes back to staring through the car's windscreen. 'How did you get on at Salvation Hall this morning?'

'I've spoken to Barbara Gee. She's quite a character.' And that, thought Price, was another understatement. 'But she's very level-headed. I think Richard and David have landed lucky there, if she's inclined to stay in touch with them. And yet I still have the feeling that she's hiding something.'

'About the Lancefields?'

'No, about Jason. I asked her about the phone conversation she had with Emma on Wednesday evening and she grew very cagey.' Price turned to look at Parkinson. 'When you spoke to Amber Kimbrall, she admitted that they didn't exactly put out the welcome mat for Emma and Jason, didn't she?'

'Something like that.'

'Well, according to Barbara, that's not quite how it happened. In Emma's version of events, Jason swaggered into The Lancefield Arms and started boasting about being related to the Lancefield family and that caused a great deal of amusement amongst the locals. Emma said that people were staring at them and sniggering behind their pints. She felt humiliated.'

'Did it bother Jason Speed?'

'I very much doubt it.' Price turned his head and glanced out of the car's window at nothing in particular. 'Barbara said that Emma was uncomfortable with the Lancefields, too, although she was at great pains to say not with Richard and David as human beings. She said they had been very kind, and hospitable beyond what might have been expected, given the circumstances. No, she was upset by the idea of them making their money from slavery.'

Parkinson grinned. 'And I suppose that didn't bother Jason either?'

'No.'

'So just what do you think Barbara is keeping from you?'

Price spluttered a laugh. 'Well, if I knew that she wouldn't be keeping it from me, would she?' He shook his head and turned back to look at his sergeant. 'Until she decides to cough it up, there are other things for us to focus on. I've had a couple of messages from Andy Drummond this morning, one to tell me that the CCTV footage from Lime Street has been sent through for your attention, and one to warn me that Emma's family are on their way to Penzance to quiz us about the death. If you can take a look at the footage, I'll start to make preparations for receiving the Needhams. They didn't know anything at all about the trip to Cornwall, or about the Lancefields, and they don't understand why Jason hasn't been in touch with them or responded to any of their attempts to contact him. Andy's tried to spare their feelings by telling them that Jason is still in shock, but he isn't sure that they bought it.' And why the hell should they? 'That young woman's family deserves answers, Tom, and right now I don't have any for them. I need to put something together before they get here. Maybe I can persuade Barbara to lean on Jason. She could bring him over to Penzance this afternoon, to meet with the Needhams.' Price put out a hand to open the car's door. 'I'm going back to the station now, via the bakery, if you're interested.'

'To be honest, sir, I'd rather get the CCTV footage out of the way before I think about having lunch. Although I'm still not sure exactly what I'm looking for.'

'Andy has sent you an email with a photo of Dennis Speed attached, to help you spot him making his way around the station. Apart from that, you're looking at anything that bears a remote resemblance to a member of the Smith family.'

Parkinson spluttered a laugh. 'You can't be serious. I've just told you that they've all got alibis.'

'No, Robin and Zak have got alibis. There are two other brothers, and God alone knows how many cousins.' Price rolled his eyes. 'Just take a really close look at the footage, Tom. Find Dennis Speed, and when you find him, watch him closely. See if he speaks to anyone, whether he looks distressed or unwell, and whether anyone around him is paying too much attention to him. Maybe someone followed him. I know it's the longest of long shots, but there's got to be something on that tape that gives us a clue.'

25

Jason rested his elbows on the dining table. 'I suppose they won't serve lunch until Richard and David join us.'

'They won't be joining us.' Seated beside him in the conservatory, Barbara shivered into her burnt-orange jumper dress, though it wasn't particularly cold in the room. 'Richard is taking his lunch in the Dower House and David has gone into Penzance on an errand.' She turned her eyes out towards the garden, but all she could see through the glass was a persistent Cornish drizzle. 'I wanted to speak to you in private anyway. We haven't really had the chance of a proper conversation since I arrived.'

'I didn't know there was anything private to talk about.' There was a sullen edge to Jason's voice. 'We don't have any secrets from the Lancefields, do we?'

Barbara looked down at her fingers and ignored the question. 'You don't seem very pleased to see me, Jason. We seem to have somehow lost our connection.' It would be pointless to ask why he'd set off for Penwithen without telling her, and pointless to ask if it was true that he'd threatened to break up with Emma if she'd broken the news to Barbara herself.

'You're the one who decided to arrive in Penzance unannounced yesterday evening.' Jason bristled as he spoke, an unmistakable ripple of annoyance. 'Anyway, I don't know why you've come.'

'I should have thought that was obvious. I've come to take you home.' He wasn't going to make it easy for her then. 'I've identified Dennis's body for you and I've contacted an undertaker about the funeral. But your father's financial affairs need wrapping up and the house will need clearing. There's still the business to run, and Emma's family will need your help to put her affairs in order.'

Jason growled under his breath. 'It's because of Emma that I need to stay here. DCI Price wants me to stay here while he conducts the investigation into her death.'

'DCI Price has already confirmed to me that we can go back to Liverpool tomorrow morning. Emma's family are on their way down here, and arrangements are going to be made for her body to be returned to them.'

'Not to me?'

'Not unless you agree it with her parents. You're not legally her next of kin, Jason. You weren't married. But I'm sure if you were to speak to them…'

'You seem to have worked it all out.' Jason sounded bitter. 'So what else did you and DCI Price talk about?'

'He asked me if I knew what Emma was doing in the churchyard on her own. He knew that she'd made a call to me yesterday evening, and he thought she might have mentioned that she was planning to go out for a walk.'

'And did she?'

'She mentioned that she needed to get some fresh air.' Another lie. 'Did the inspector ask you, Jason, what Emma was doing in the churchyard on her own?'

'Of course he did. But I don't know the answer to that, do I? She must have left The Lancefield Arms while I was out walking because she wasn't in the room when I got back.'

'So what do *you* think happened to her?'

'Well, it's obvious, isn't it? One of the Smith family got hold of her. They thought she was a Lancefield, like me. But they got that wrong.'

On more than one account. Barbara shivered again. 'We're not Lancefields, though, are we? We're only very, very distant cousins to Richard and David.'

'Distant or not, we're the family they're looking for.'

Jason pushed himself to his feet and walked slowly across the conservatory to the window. 'Just look at that garden, Barbara. That belongs to our family.'

'Our distant family.'

'Dad didn't want me to have any of this, did he?'

The accusation came completely out of the blue, and for a moment Barbara wasn't sure how to reply. She settled on a question. 'What makes you think that?'

'He didn't tell me about the Lancefields.' Jason turned his head to look over his shoulder. 'Did he tell you about them, Barb?'

'Yes, he did.' There was no point in lying about that now. But she could hardly give Jason the same explanation she'd provided to everyone else. 'He'd read about the murders on the internet. He knew that Lucy and her lover had been murdered and that a case was being built against David's stepson. And he didn't want you and me to be caught up in that. I think he was planning to meet with David and Kathryn to tell them that he appreciated the invitation, but he wanted to wait until the outcome of the murder case before agreeing to forge a connection.' It was the lamest of lies, but it was the best excuse she could come up with. 'That's why I think you should come home now. Wait until Marcus Drake's case has come to court, and then we can get in touch with David and Richard again. Start afresh.'

'I don't care about the murders, Barb. I want to be a part of the Lancefield family. Can't you understand that? I don't want to spend the rest of my life as a painter and decorator, scratching to make a living. I want to stay in Cornwall.'

'Have Richard and David invited you to stay?'

Jason's brow furrowed. 'They wrote to my dad to invite us all to Salvation Hall. They want us here.'

'They invited us to visit, not to live here. They want a connection. A connection that we can maintain from Liverpool.' Barbara spoke quietly. 'Jason, our home is in

Liverpool. Our lives are in Liverpool.'

'You sound like Emma.' Jason almost snarled the words under his breath. 'She wanted to go home.'

'I know she did, honey. She only came here for you, didn't she? And when she got here, she just wanted to go home again.'

'She would have come round in the end. She just needed some time to get used to it.'

'That's not what she said to me on the phone. She told me that she wanted to go home. That she'd asked you to go home with her, and you'd refused.'

'And what did you say to that, Auntie Barb?' Jason's eyes suddenly darkened. 'Did you tell her to go home without me? Or did you have some other, more inventive suggestion for her?'

*

'It's a Caribbean soup, Richard. Chicken and sweet potato, with coconut milk and turmeric, and a little hint of ginger.' Becca placed a small tureen down on the table in front of him and lifted the lid. 'Like they make on St Felix.' She placed a soup spoon down beside the tureen. 'I hope you're going to try it?'

Richard stared at the unexpected offering with a suspicious eye. 'And what have I done to deserve such a treat?' It was a far removal from her usual lunchtime delivery to the Dower House. 'Where is my cheese sandwich?'

Becca took a step back. 'I know it's been a difficult week, and I know I don't always make as much effort as I should.' She pointed at the soup. 'It's all fresh stuff. Homemade. I thought it might remind you of Woodlands.' She sniffed. 'I found the recipe in Nancy's cookery book in the kitchen.' Her courage was faltering, her voice beginning to lose its feisty edge. 'Don't you like it?'

The old man lifted the soup spoon, uncertain that

"liking" came into the equation. 'Are you planning to make a habit of this?' He skimmed the spoon across the top of the soup. 'Or is this a one-off because you intend to curry some favour?'

His words hit a nerve. 'Okay, I wanted to talk to you about something. But that's not why I made the soup. I'll make it for you again, if you like it.' She folded her arms across her chest and pouted at him. 'Richard, I know it's none of my business, but do you think you're right to get involved with somebody like Jason Speed? I mean, you don't really know anything about him, do you? How do you know he's a decent person, someone you would be pleased to take into the family?'

Richard bristled and dropped the spoon into the soup. 'What on earth do you think gives *you* the right to ask that question? My relationship with Jason has nothing to do with you.'

'Yes, it does.' She pushed out her lips. 'It has something to do with me if he's going to make threats.'

'Threats? What on earth are you talking about?'

'He thinks he's a member of the Lancefield family already, and he's blaming my brother for murdering his girlfriend. Worse than that, he says that when he comes to live here, he's going to get rid of me.' She stepped forward again and lowered her head. 'Is that true, Richard? Is he going to come and live here?'

Richard scowled at her. 'That, also, is none of your business.' He pushed the bowl of soup away from him. 'Do you still maintain that Emma's death is nothing to do with your brother?'

'Zak is all talk. He likes to talk tough, but he wouldn't hurt a fly.'

'Well, he's hurt me. I've been told that your brother is responsible for all the harassment that's been meted out to myself and David over the last few weeks. And it is no secret that your family is hell-bent on making our lives a misery. It doesn't seem to matter how much I do for you.

Out of respect for Philip, I have kept you on as part of our household. I've given you a pay rise, in spite of your shoddy work, and I've permitted you to stay on in the cottage for a peppercorn rent, despite your appalling attitude. And that's before I talk about the cash you've been given to compensate you for Philip's death.'

'Richard, you know I'm grateful…'

'I know no such thing. You carry out your work here with bad grace, and repeatedly I make allowances for you. Your brother harasses us, and I turn a blind eye. You vent your bitterness upon us as if we haven't suffered losses of our own. And sometimes I can't help wondering…' He drew in a breath before asking the unthinkable question. 'Did your brother go too far, Becca? Was his hatred of us enough to drive him to murder that poor girl?'

Becca cried out. 'No, of course he didn't. He wouldn't. He wouldn't do that. Why would he?'

'Because he makes no secret of his hatred of us.' Richard sighed, and rubbed at his forehead with his fingers. 'I cannot tolerate this situation anymore, Becca. I have tried, and better tried, to play fair by you. I have done it for Philip, and for Frankie. But I cannot do it anymore. I will not have you accusing my cousin, however distant, of threatening you. Notwithstanding that your hypocrisy is breathtaking, you are making accusations without any foundation in truth. Jason will not be coming to live here. But even if he did, he would have no reason to make any threats to you.'

A sullen light made its way into Becca Smith's narrowed eyes. 'Are you accusing me of lying?'

Of course he was. 'I do not intend to prolong this distasteful charade. You can take the rest of the day off.' Richard pushed his chair back, away from the table. 'And do not bother coming back.' He pushed himself to his feet. 'I will pay you a month's wages in lieu of notice.'

'Notice?' She licked her lips. 'You're not giving me notice?'

'I have had as much of your disloyalty as I can take. You will get a month's wages, and I will give you the same amount of time to clear out of the cottage.'

'But what about Frankie?' Becca was beginning to panic now. 'You're Frankie's godfather. You promised to look after her. You made that promise to Philip.'

'And I will keep my promise to Philip. I will never turn my back on my poor boy's child. But I will not be blackmailed or threatened by her mother. You are not respecting Philip's memory.'

Becca jutted out her chin. 'You can't manage here without me. I do everything here.'

'We are not incapable, Becca. And you are not indispensable. I have already given you a month's grace to clear out of the cottage, but you will not set foot in Salvation Hall or the Dower House again. You will surrender your keys to Kathryn immediately. Nancy will be back next week to take care of things. In the meantime, we are quite capable of hiring temporary domestic help to fill the breach.'

Becca lunged towards him and grasped hold of his arm. 'Richard, I was trying to help you. I was trying to tell you what sort of a person Jason Speed is. He's not good for the family. For your family.'

Richard coughed out a laugh. 'Since when did you care about what was good for my family?'

'He's a bully.'

'And you are a hypocrite and a dissembler.' The old man shook himself free of her grasp and pointed towards the door. 'My solicitor will be in touch with you shortly regarding financial assistance for Francesca. In the meantime, I would be grateful if you would remove yourself from my home.'

He put out a hand to steady himself against the table and kept his eyes away from her as she shuffled reluctantly out of the room. *Dear God, that it should have to come to this.* He lifted his eyes up to the ceiling.

Philip, my dear old friend, forgive me. I could see no other alternative.

*

'As I mentioned to you yesterday evening, I'd already established that Thomas Moses Lancefield was my ancestor, and I knew that his father was called Richard and that he was a ship owner. But I had absolutely no idea at all that the Lancefields were a slave-owning family.' Barbara settled herself into the comfortable folds of the library sofa and shivered, an involuntary tremor of revulsion. 'I suppose that makes it all the more remarkable that Thomas signed up for the West Africa Squadron. He must have been a man of very strong principles, to have thwarted his family not once, but twice – first to marry Alice Banks, and then to serve in a squadron whose sole purpose was to police the slave trade.'

'And you didn't know anything about Digory Banks?' Kathryn, seated at the other end of the sofa, ran a finger around the small leather journal resting on her lap. 'Nothing about his voyage?'

'I'd come across the name on the parish registers when I found the details of Thomas and Alice's marriage. But I don't have access to the kind of records that the family hold here at Salvation Hall.' Barbara's gaze travelled to the journal in Kathryn's lap. 'I can't imagine how he coped with the horrors of that voyage. If what you've told me about it is true, then I can hardly comprehend how the Lancefield brothers could have been so inhumane.' She turned her head and cast a glance around the library. 'All this comfort and luxury, all paid for by the suffering of others. It hardly bears thinking about, does it?' She turned back to Kathryn. 'Doesn't it disgust you?'

Now there was a question. 'Truthfully? When I first came to Salvation Hall, it didn't bother me at all. I don't believe that we can judge the present on the sins of the past. Then Richard introduced me to the contents of the storeroom, out in the garden. He has shipped back a fine collection of manacles, chains and branding irons.' Kathryn smiled as a look of disbelief flitted across Barbara's face. 'And before you ask me, yes, I have examined it all and catalogued it. Although what we're going to do with the collection isn't yet clear. I'm still trying to persuade him to donate it to a museum.'

Barbara shook her head and let out a gentle laugh. 'Oh, Kathryn, whatever possesses you to keep on with this?'

'I think you already know the answer to that. You have a curious nature and a love of the past, just as much as I do, otherwise, you wouldn't be researching your family's history.' It was a relief that Barbara was so easy to talk to. 'I will admit that I found the account of the voyage across the Middle Passage to be a challenge though. At the moment, I'm trying not to think about it too much. If I did, I'd probably just pack my bags and head back to Cambridge.'

Barbara thought for a moment and then tilted her head. 'What about Richard and David? Don't they have any shame about how the family made its money?'

'Richard is a law unto himself, as you will discover if you discuss the subject with him at any length. But David has enough shame to make up for them both. He's tried for many years to distance himself from Salvation Hall and Woodlands Park, and the whole issue of slavery. But Lucy's death, and Richard's need to secure the future of the estate, have left him without much of a choice. It's a challenging situation for him, but he's trying to make peace with it on his own terms.' Kathryn hesitated and then asked, 'Do you think Dennis had any idea about the family's connections to slavery? Only, I wondered if that was why he decided not to share Richard's letters with Jason.'

'Good heavens, no. I shouldn't have thought so. He had no interest in the family's history, not even the parts of it that I tried to share with him. And even if he did discover it for himself, I don't think it would have bothered him. He was always more interested in the here and now than what has gone before.' Barbara looked away and blushed. 'I can't tell you the real reason that Dennis didn't want Jason to know. I wish I could, but I can't. His reason was a very, very private matter, and I won't betray his confidence.' She turned her eyes back to Kathryn. 'I hope you can respect that? I can assure you that it was no reflection on the Lancefields, just something private to Dennis, Jason and myself.'

'Something that remains an issue even now that Dennis is gone?'

Barbara shivered again and the colour drained from her cheeks. 'Even though Dennis is gone.' She almost whispered the words. 'When I spoke with Richard earlier today, he was kind enough to remind me that Jason and I are not alone. We have new connections now, in himself and David, and we are very pleased to have met you too, Kathryn. I hope that in time we will get to know each other a little better, and I do hope that I will be able to help David come to terms with his responsibility for Salvation Hall and the Lancefield estates. But for now, I have to take Jason home to Liverpool. We have to deal with Dennis's affairs, and his funeral, and I have to help Jason come to terms with Emma's death.' Barbara's face grew solemn. 'I do hope you understand?'

Kathryn understood the situation only too well. She studied the woman's earnest face for a moment, and then she risked an awkward question. 'Forgive me, Barbara, but this private reason that Dennis had for not revealing Richard's letters to Jason… was Emma aware of the reason too?'

26

'A motorcycle courier has just delivered this. It's addressed to you, from Mayhew and Mayhew.' David dropped the plain brown packet onto the kitchen table as he sat down. 'Is this something to do with your unscheduled trip into Penzance this morning?'

Seated at the other side of the table, Richard acknowledged his son with an almost imperceptible nod of the head. 'Probably.' He was busy adding sugar to a freshly made mug of coffee, his gnarled hand shaking as he lowered the spoon to stir it.

David ventured a smile. 'Couldn't you ask Becca to do that for you? She must be around here somewhere.'

'Becca has gone.' Richard tapped the spoon on the edge of the mug and placed it down on the table. 'I have dismissed her. We will just have to manage until Nancy gets back.'

The news wiped the smile from David's face. 'Now why on earth have you done that? Apart from the obvious domestic inconvenience, I promised Amber that we wouldn't take any punitive action against the Smith family, providing the harassment stopped.'

'This was nothing to do with the harassment. Becca has accused Jason of making threats against her.'

'Threats? What sort of threats?'

'It doesn't matter. I will not tolerate such disloyalty.'

David sighed. 'How do you know it was disloyalty? Have you asked Jason to provide his version of events?'

'I have not.'

'Then how do you know she wasn't telling the truth?'

'Tush. The boy is hardly likely to admit it, even if she

was telling the truth. But even if he did, might he not have justified his actions by accusing the Smith family not just of harassing us, but of murdering Emma?'

'Do you really believe that they murdered Emma?'

'That is for DCI Price to determine.' Richard scowled. 'I have tolerated Becca to the end of my patience, David, and frankly, I do not care if her accusations are true or false. She does not appreciate our efforts to include her in our extended family and she grossly over-estimates her importance in the household. No, she must go. I have given her a month to quit the cottage.'

It was done then. David licked his lips, and slowly pushed the brown packet across the table towards his father. 'Where are Jason and Barbara now?'

'Barbara is in the library with Kathryn, and Jason has gone for a walk around the grounds. He has taken Samson with him.' The old man muttered a laugh. 'My poor old dog, I don't think he was too keen on the idea, but I know he won't tolerate any nonsense. If Jason is foolish enough to manhandle him, Samson will soon set him straight.' Richard stretched out a hand to the packet and picked it up. 'I'm glad that you're here, David, to be with me when I open this.'

'Why? What is it?'

'I'm hoping that it contains the truth. I was troubled to learn that Jason saw fit to lie to us about his mother. According to Jason, his mother died when he was a small boy. But cousin Barbara tells me that the woman is still alive and that Jason has been motherless all these years because his parents' marriage failed. I wanted to know the truth, so I asked old Mayhew to make a few enquiries for me.' Richard looked down at the packet and then cast his eyes across the table to David. 'Was I wrong to reach out to Dennis Speed and set this train of events in motion? Did I make a monumental mistake?'

David let out a sigh. 'If you had asked me that question yesterday, I would have said "yes". But now that I've met

Barbara then no, you were not wrong to reach out to Dennis.'

'Good.' Richard tore at the top of the packet. 'Then we had better open up Pandora's Box and see what falls out.'

*

DS Parkinson leaned back in his seat and folded his arms across his chest. Three times now he had watched the CCTV footage sent through to him by DCI Drummond. And three times he had failed to see anything more than Dennis Speed wandering aimlessly through the busy, commuter-filled concourse of Lime Street station.

Thanks to the photographs sent through by Drummond's sidekick Kate Jenkins, it had been easy enough to identify Dennis among the crowd. The first sighting of him had cropped up on the tape at around ten past seven that morning, when he had alighted from the Huyton commuter train and meandered, hands in pockets, along the concourse to study the overhead departure board. The footage was too grainy for Parkinson to make out the man's facial expressions, but there was a telltale hesitancy about the speed of his movements that suggested Dennis wasn't overly keen to make his journey. He had hovered in front of the departure board, staring straight up at the list of trains for maybe a minute or more, before stepping back and turning on his heel to wander around the main concourse. A few minutes later he had wandered back to the board a second time, pausing for only a few seconds before turning back to lose himself in a nearby newsagents for another three or four minutes.

It was then that the man had made his most decisive move. He had glanced at the departure board for a third time, and then dug his hands deep into his pockets and turned to his left towards the side exit leading from the station into nearby Lord Nelson Street. Parkinson had followed his progress as he disappeared through the doorway and then, thanks to some skilful editing by a member of Drummond's team, the film had cut to a second camera outside on Lord Nelson Street itself. Dennis had been caught on camera picking his way slowly and carefully down the icy pavement and had rounded the corner only to be lost in a blind spot just at the point where he slipped. Edited a second time, the footage now showed the full horror of the accident in which Dennis lost his life, the tragedy picked up by a camera at the front of the station. By this point, the victim had already lost both his footing and his balance, and his body was making its way in almost graphic slow motion under the front of a double-decker bus.

It had taken DS Parkinson almost twenty minutes to recover his equilibrium after watching that harrowing piece of footage, but at least the second viewing had been a little easier. He had concentrated his efforts on following Ennor Price's instructions to look for anything that resembled a member of the Smith family. But despite the best of his efforts, the exercise had proved to be a fruitless one. And the third viewing had been equally unproductive.

He puffed out a breath and leaned forward again in his seat, to stare at the screen of his computer. Was it worth one more attempt? One more scan of the footage before he admitted to his senior officer that there was nothing of note to be seen? He knew how badly Price was going to take the news, but he also knew Price would take him to task if he missed a crucial clue, some unexpected face in the crowd that would lead them away from the assumption that Dennis Speed's death had been accidental. He had watched the film once to monitor Dennis's movements, a second time to look specifically for anyone in the crowd who might have been related to Becca Smith, and a third to cast a broader eye for anything that looked remotely suspicious. How many more viewings would Price expect him to make?

It was a question that he would soon be able to answer

for himself. He put out a hand to click at his keyboard, ready to close down the file and call it a day, and as he did so the mobile phone on his desk skittered into life with an incoming call. His attention diverted, he stretched out a hand to pick up his phone and was surprised to see that the incoming call was from Becca Smith. He swiped at the screen and pressed the phone to his ear. 'Becca? What's up?'

Her voice was breathless at the end of the line. 'I don't know what to do. Richard's told me to clear out of the cottage.' The words became a wail. 'Tom, I don't know what to do. You have to help me. He's given me the sack.'

Tom Parkinson closed his eyes and muttered to himself. It had only been a matter of time. 'Just calm down, and tell me from the beginning.' He spoke gently into the phone. 'Why on earth, after all this time, has the old boy finally given up on you? Have you crossed the line and said something to him that you really shouldn't have said?'

27

The bouquet was exquisite in its simplicity, a breathtaking arrangement of soft deep-pink roses interwoven with vibrant lilac carnations, all arranged against a generous swathe of aromatic foliage. Barbara had carried it carefully down the lane from Salvation Hall and it occurred to her now, as she bent forward to gently place the flowers on top of Lucy Lancefield's grave, that she couldn't have chosen better for herself. 'God bless you, Emma.' She whispered the words under her breath so that Jason couldn't hear them. 'We will miss you so very much.' She straightened her back and glanced across the churchyard to where her nephew was standing. His head was turned away, out towards the main road, as if he couldn't bear to watch. 'Don't you have anything else to say to Emma before we go?'

'No. Not now.' Jason held his gaze away from her. 'I don't know why you wanted to come down here.'

'Because I wanted to pay my respects to Emma before we travel back to Liverpool tomorrow.' Barbara cast a final, wistful glance down at the grave before stepping slowly away towards her reluctant companion. 'It was kind of David to arrange for flowers to be delivered, wasn't it?' She resisted the temptation to ask why Jason hadn't left some flowers of his own. 'Are you sure you don't have anything you want to say to Emma before we go? You must miss her.'

'Of course I miss her.' He had begun to walk slowly down the path towards the lychgate, hands thrust deep into the pockets of his coat. 'What sort of a question is that?'

The sort of question that you ask when you're still struggling to find the courage to ask the only questions that matter. Barbara was only a few feet behind him now, and she drew in a deep breath. 'Did you and Emma argue about anything else on the night she died, Jason?'

'Anything else?'

'Other than the fact that she wanted to go home, and you didn't.'

'It wasn't an argument. It was a disagreement.'

'So are we going to have the same disagreement now? Because I want you to come home to Liverpool with me, and you don't want to go?'

Jason shrugged his shoulders. 'We don't have to disagree about it, Auntie Barbara. You can just go home tomorrow and I can stay here.'

'Do you think that's what your father would have wanted? For you to stay here, to turn your back on your home, your friends, the business… to turn your back on me?'

'I'm not really sure anymore what my dad would have wanted. To be honest, I'm beginning to wonder whether I knew my dad at all. He didn't want me to know about this place, did he? He didn't want me to know about the Lancefields or our connection to them.'

'He didn't want you to be disappointed.'

'Disappointed? With all of this?' Jason threw up his hands to stress the point. 'Salvation Hall, The Lancefield Arms, the estates on St Felix… how could anyone be disappointed by all of that?'

Was he trying to draw her in? Barbara felt suddenly afraid. 'Dennis only ever had your best interests at heart, Jason. Whatever he did, he did it for you.'

'For me? Does that include the lies?' Jason's voice had taken on a bitter edge. 'Do you know, he even confided in Emma? He told Emma things about me that he had never told me to my face. He shared a secret with her. A secret about me.'

Oh dear God, she told him. Barbara's pulse missed a beat, but she said nothing.

Jason had slowed his pace and now Barbara was almost at his shoulder. He turned his head to glance at her. 'What I can't help wondering now is whether you knew the secret too. Dad always confided in you, didn't he?'

Barbara slowed her own pace, keeping her distance. 'I have no idea what you're talking about, Jason.'

'Oh, I think you do. I think he shared that secret with you, and you've all been laughing at me behind my back. But you're not going to laugh at me anymore.' Jason was beside the lychgate now, and he turned to block Barbara's path. 'But you don't need to worry, because I won't tell anybody about it. If you go back to Liverpool tomorrow and promise to forget we ever had this conversation, then no one else need ever know about that secret.'

Did he really think it was going to be that simple? Barbara smiled, a gentle and courageous curve of the lips, and then tilted back her head to look at her nephew. 'Just the one secret, Jason? I thought there were two.'

Jason stiffened, and shrank back. 'What the hell are you talking about? I'm talking about the secret that Dad shared with Emma.'

'I know you are, Jason. But if we're going to bring this situation to a proper conclusion, one that satisfies us both, then surely we'll also need to consider the secret that Emma shared with me?'

*

Tom Parkinson flung the Audi across the junction and the car almost skidded off the A394. 'Was Kathryn shocked when you told her?' He cast a sideways glance at Ennor Price, sitting rigid and tight-lipped in the passenger seat.

Price shook his head and pushed his mobile phone into the top pocket of his jacket. 'It would take more than that to shock Kathryn.' A lot more. 'I think she already had her suspicions.' He put a hand up to his forehead and rubbed at it. 'Tell me again about the call from Becca.'

'She called to tell me that Richard Lancefield had kicked her out of Salvation Hall because she dared to tell him that Jason Speed had threatened her.'

'And even though Richard had supposedly challenged her version of events, you decided that she might be telling the truth. And that prompted you to take another look at the footage of Lime Street station.'

The sergeant winced. 'It was just one of those things, Ennor. One of those ridiculous moments when someone tells you something that you think is completely unrelated, and then the penny drops. I had scoured that footage looking for the Smith family, and not paid real attention to who else was on that station forecourt.'

'And the familiar figure you spotted when you looked at the footage again, it was definitely Jason Speed?'

'I'm sure of it. He was wearing what looked like a black waxed jacket and a black beanie hat pulled down over his forehead. He was leaning against the wall, close to the platform where the train came in from Huyton. He watched the train empty, and just as his father came to the end of the platform and onto the concourse, Jason set off in pursuit. He kept to a distance of about fifty feet behind. I don't think Dennis had any idea that his son was following him.'

'And you saw Jason follow him out of the station and into Lord Nelson Street?'

'Yes. But I couldn't make him out after that because of the way the tapes had been edited.'

Price pursed his lips angrily. 'And Andy Drummond missed it all.' He banged his fist against the car's door. 'He was so bloody insistent that Dennis Speed had had an accident.'

'And that might still be the case, boss.' Parkinson flicked on the car's indicator and began to depress the brake. 'Just because I saw Jason on the footage, it doesn't mean that he murdered his father.'

'At the very least they might have had an argument. What the hell would be the point in Jason following Dennis around the station if he wasn't going to confront him at some point?' Unless he was simply planning to stop his father from making the journey down to Bristol to meet with David Lancefield. 'Jason knows a lot more about those letters to his father than he's letting on.'

The Audi took a right-hand turn into a narrow country lane and Parkinson flicked on the car's headlights, illuminating the hedgerows against the failing afternoon light. 'Where is Jason now?'

'He's gone for a walk with Barbara. She wanted to visit St Felicity's before it got too dark, to leave flowers at the spot where Emma died. Kathryn is going to walk down to the village, to see if she can find them. She's asked David to go with her for support.'

'Is that wise, under the circumstances?'

'It's wise for Barbara.' Price snapped out his frustration. 'Kathryn says she thinks she knows why Dennis Speed had to die. But she won't damn well tell me. She wants to deal with it herself.' He laughed under his breath. 'What the hell does that mean, Tom? Why can't she just spit it out?'

The sergeant cast a sideways glance at his senior officer. 'Kathryn Clifton is one of the most sensible, grounded people I've ever met. If she wants to deal with this her own way, she has that right. Our job right now is to get there before her, and make sure that she's safe while she's doing it.' The Audi was gathering speed now and he guided it skilfully around a sharp left-hand bend. 'Providing we get a clear run through, we should be in Penwithen in about ten minutes. How long will it take Kathryn and David to walk down there?'

'About ten minutes.'

'I'll try to make it nine then.' Parkinson's tone was almost jocular. But only almost. 'You do realise we're going to have to eat a lot of humble pie with Becca and her family if it turns out that your hunch is right?'

'The Smith family deserve everything that they get. They don't exactly go out of their way to be clean-living, upstanding citizens. Anyway, it's not a hunch. It's a gut feeling.' A gut feeling honed by more years of experience than Price would care to remember. 'And it's only about Dennis Speed.'

'Not about Emma Needham?'

Detective Chief Inspector Price felt an unbidden stabbing at the back of his eyes, and he ground his teeth to suppress the emotion. 'I haven't got around to thinking about Emma yet, Tom.' If pressed, he would have to admit that he simply couldn't bring himself to think about it. 'Right now, my sole concern is to make sure that we don't have another death on our hands. I just want to make sure that Barbara Gee's name isn't added to the list of this week's innocent victims.'

*

It seemed unthinkable to Barbara now, that she had never asked Jason the obvious question. Even more ludicrous that neither DCI Drummond nor DCI Price had thought to ask it. 'Where were you, Jason, when Dennis met his death?'

'I'd gone to the Cash and Carry. Dad had taken the day off, but I was planning to make a start on the next job, so I went to buy the paints.'

'At six thirty in the morning?'

'I couldn't sleep. Emma knew that I'd had a restless night, and she knew what time I went out, and what time I came back.'

'But she didn't know where you went.'

Jason leaned against the frame of the lychgate. 'I've just told you where I went. I went to the Cash and Carry.'

'I'm sorry, but I don't believe you. I think you went to Lime Street. I think that you went to the station to stop

Dennis from travelling to Bristol. You wanted to stop him from meeting David Lancefield.'

'I'd never heard of David Lancefield until the police gave me those letters.'

'And I don't believe that either. I think you found out about those letters, and that Dennis had kept them from you.'

'He had no business doing that.' Jason's face suddenly clouded. 'We were all invited – you and me, not just Dad.'

'He was thinking of you, Jason. He would have done anything for you.'

'Now who's lying?' Jason spat the words out, and then let out a hollow laugh. 'You know the truth, don't you, Auntie Barb?'

'I know that if we go home to Liverpool now, we can forget all about it. We can pretend that none of this ever happened. We can bury Dennis and say goodbye to Emma, and pick up our lives and start again.'

'We don't have to go home to Liverpool for that to happen. You could just keep quiet, and we could make a new life down here with Richard and David. The Lancefields need us.' His lower lip began to tremble. 'Please, Auntie Barb, I don't want to have to hurt you.'

'Hurting Barbara wouldn't do you any good now, Jason. We already know the truth.' Kathryn Clifton's voice rang out suddenly from behind him. 'We've seen a copy of your birth certificate. I have it here.' She stepped through the lychgate, the brown paper packet in her hand. 'There's no father named on it.'

Jason Speed stepped back, shocked by her sudden appearance. And then he frowned, a surly, dismissive curve of the brow. 'So what? My dad didn't have to be named on the birth certificate. It's not a legal requirement. He was married to my mother when I was born.'

'He didn't have to be named to be your legal father.' Kathryn took another step forward. 'Is that why you lied to Richard about your mother being dead? Because she was the only person who could confirm irrefutably that Dennis wasn't your *biological* father?'

Kathryn's words hung in the air for a moment, and then Jason spun on his heel to face his aunt. 'You knew, didn't you? He told you the truth.'

'Yes, I knew.' Barbara's shoulders sank under the weight of her confession. 'I knew that Jean had been unfaithful to Dennis, that she'd been having an affair for almost a year before you were born. But the man ended the affair when she told him she was pregnant.' A solitary tear rolled down Barbara's cheek. 'Dennis still loved your mother and he promised to bring you up as his son. But he wouldn't be named on the birth certificate. He said it would be a lie, and lying was a boundary that he wouldn't cross, but he would settle for ambiguity. And that's why we hid the letters from you and turned down Richard's invitation to Salvation Hall. He wouldn't lie to Richard and David. He couldn't let them believe you were a blood relation to the Lancefield family when you weren't.'

Jason's eyes went blank. 'He'd lied to me all those years, pretended that he was my father, but then he wouldn't lie to the Lancefields. Not even for me.' Jason sniffed back a tear. 'I couldn't let him make that trip to Bristol. I couldn't let him spoil my chances of having a better life.'

'Dennis would never do anything to hurt you, Jason. When Jean finally left him, he just carried on bringing you up as his son. And he didn't turn his back on the Lancefields to spite you. He did it to protect you. And I agreed with him. We both wanted to connect with Richard and David, but we agreed to give that up for you. Because Dennis never wanted you to know that you weren't his son. He didn't want to hurt you like that.' Barbara lifted a hand to her face and wiped away a tear. 'And neither did Emma. Until she realised that you might have been responsible for Dennis's death.' Barbara took a step closer to her nephew. 'And that's why you killed her, isn't it?

Because after speaking to me on the phone that evening, Emma put two and two together and came up with the truth?'

28

It was peaceful in the kitchen at Salvation Hall.

David had lit the room with nothing more than the downlighters beneath the upper run of kitchen cupboards, and the pair of glass art deco wall lights that hung at either side of the window bay. It was a soothing, restful glow and he hoped that Barbara would find it comforting. But, sitting silently at the kitchen table, she still cut a sad and lonely figure. Her head was turned towards the window but the night was black and nothing could be seen of the garden. 'I suppose you heard everything that was said in the churchyard?'

David lowered himself onto a seat and pushed a mug of freshly-brewed cocoa towards her. 'Yes, I did. But you mustn't blame yourself, Barbara. None of this was your fault.'

'Then how come I still feel responsible?' She wrapped a hand around the mug for comfort. 'When Emma called me, she admitted that she was afraid of Jason. That she wondered if she'd always been a little afraid of him. All through their relationship, she'd been convincing herself that Jason was just highly strung, but he wasn't. He was more than that. He was selfish.' Barbara turned to look at David. 'Emma said she had realised that her feelings didn't matter to him. She was so upset that my heart went out to her, and I made a dreadful mistake. I told her that I was sure that wasn't true and that I could make Jason come home and forget all about the Lancefields because in truth he wasn't a Lancefield. I made the mistake of telling her that Dennis wasn't his father.'

'And I suppose that after the call, she realised that

Jason had a motive for getting rid of Dennis before Dennis had the opportunity to break the news to us.'

'It never occurred to me for one minute that she would go ahead and challenge him about it. But if Jason is telling the truth this time, she went out into the village to look for him, and she found him in the churchyard, looking at Lucy's grave.' Barbara turned her eyes down, to stare into the cocoa. 'She confronted him with the truth and he didn't deny it. But he wasn't going to run the risk of her telling you or Richard. He cold-bloodedly murdered the girl he'd been planning to share his life with. And then, to add insult to injury, he took the card from those flowers that the Smith family had left on Lucy's grave and placed it in Emma's mouth.'

'He was trying to pass the blame.'

'And he very nearly succeeded. If I hadn't shared that secret with Emma, she might still be alive. She even let Jason think that Dennis had told her, so that it wouldn't rebound on me. And she paid with her life.'

'If my father hadn't invited you all to Salvation Hall, then both Dennis and Emma might still be alive.' David stretched out a hand and placed it on Barbara's arm. 'But we will never know. So we must make the very best of what is.' He couldn't quite bring himself to say that there might so very easily have been three deaths, that if he and Kathryn hadn't arrived at the churchyard in time, then Barbara might also have been lost.

His cousin lifted her eyes to look at him again. 'What will happen to Jason now?'

'I should think he will be charged with both murders. He pretty much confessed to you, after all. DCI Price will see that he gets a fair hearing.' David squeezed the arm beneath his hand. 'Let's not talk about this anymore this evening. It's all a bit too much.' He took back his hand. 'Leave your cocoa for a moment and come with me, onto the landing. There's something I want to show you. I don't know why I didn't mention it to you before.' He pushed himself to his feet and gestured for her to follow.

Outside in the hallway, with Barbara following in his wake, he made his way up the central staircase. 'There, look.' He halted on the landing and pointed up at the wall. 'Can you guess what the subject of this painting is?'

Barbara paused on the step behind him and lifted her eyes to look at the picture. It was small and rather understated, barely two feet in width, a study in oils of a ship in full sail making its way into a beautiful, tropical bay. 'It's a sailing ship. Dating from perhaps the early nineteenth century?'

'Indeed. And until this week, we didn't understand its significance. The painting has hung here since long before my father was born. We know that the bay is Quintard Bay. It's part of the Woodlands Park estate on St Felix, and it was named after one of our early ancestors. But there has never been a nameplate on the painting, and we always just assumed that the ship was one of many that made its way in and out of the bay. It was how supplies were delivered to the estate, and where rum and sugar were collected for transportation back to England.' He turned his head to look down at Barbara, standing on the lower step behind him. 'And now, thanks to Kathryn's sterling work, we believe this to be The Redemption. Barbara, we believe this to be the ship that was captained by your ancestor, Digory Banks, from Liverpool to Africa, and then across the Atlantic to the Caribbean and St Felix. This is the ship that undertook that dreadful voyage.'

Barbara drew in a sharp breath. 'The slave ship? Are you sure?'

'Well, Kathryn is convinced, based on the documents she has seen. But we are going to take further steps to validate her assumption.' David's voice softened. 'I would like you to take the picture, Barbara. As a gift. You have far more right to it than we do.'

Barbara smiled. 'Oh no, David. It would look far too silly hanging on the wall of my Liverpool semi.' She reached up and patted his arm. 'And if it stays here at Salvation Hall, then I can enjoy it whenever I come to visit.'

So she would come again then. David nodded to himself. 'I had hoped that, as a direct descendant of Captain Digory Banks, you would find it in yourself to forgive us for the transgressions of our distant ancestors. You will always be most welcome here. And perhaps when things have settled down you might consider joining me on a trip to St Felix, to visit Woodlands Park?'

'Would you consider visiting me, David? Would you come to Liverpool to see for yourself where The Redemption started her journey? Perhaps we might do something together to make a tribute to all the poor souls who suffered on that voyage.'

'My dear Barbara, I would be absolutely delighted.'

*

Ennor Price pressed the mobile phone to his ear. 'I'm still at the station. I just wanted to let you know that Jason has formally confessed to both murders and agreed to make a statement. We're just waiting for a duty solicitor to represent him.' The inspector picked up a pen and tapped it softly on the desk. 'I wondered if you'd broken the news to Richard yet.'

Kathryn sounded tired at the end of the line. 'I'm at Salvation Hall now. Barbara asked to be the one to tell Richard. I thought that was very brave of her.'

'I suppose now the old man will cut him adrift.'

'Then you obviously still don't know Richard very well at all. He's back at the Dower House already, on the phone to a solicitor.' Kathryn paused, and then added, 'He's talking to Oliver Redmond.'

'But Oliver Redmond has already been engaged to represent Marcus Drake.'

'Well, you know how Richard likes to keep things in the

family. Redmond is already familiar with the Lancefields, with Marcus, with the Smiths…' She let out a sigh. 'We're never going to hear the end of this from Becca, are we? That was rather a neat twist by Jason, putting the card from the flowers in Emma's mouth so that it threw suspicion on whoever was harassing the family. Do you think now that the method of killing was just a coincidence?'

The question hit a nerve and Price winced. 'I don't know. Jason has admitted that he'd seen a report of the case on the internet, so he knew that Lucy had been strangled with her scarf. But I don't believe that he set out to commit a copycat killing. I don't think that he intended to murder Emma at all until she accused him of killing his father.'

'I take it he's also confessed to pushing Dennis under the bus?'

'I'm afraid so. You know, he almost got away with that. It's hard to believe that neither Andy nor Kate asked him for an alibi.' Price flinched, aware that he had also dropped the ball in that department. At a push, he could justify the oversight. After all, Parkinson had continually reminded him that Dennis Speed's death wasn't their affair to investigate. But it wouldn't stop Price from feeling guilty for missing the obvious. 'Still, fair play to Kate Jenkins. She knew there was something fishy about that death. It was Andy who didn't want to read too much into it.' The policeman smiled to himself. 'I suppose this is the point at which you say you feel sorry for Jason.' Just as she had for Marcus Drake.

'Of course I feel sorry for him. His mother walked out on him, and he lost the only father he'd ever known from the moment that Dennis admitted the truth. Then he lost that father a second time when he decided to take his life.'

'He murdered the man who raised him like a son.'

'I know he did. And there can be no excuse for that. But there is such a thing as forgiveness, Ennor. Wounds can be healed, can't they? Don't you think that Jason was provoked? That maybe he acted out of anger and grief? Now that Dennis is dead there can be no second chance, no opportunity to ask for forgiveness, or to make amends, or to build bridges and try again.'

'You seem to be forgetting the other side of Jason's personality. Barbara wasn't lying when she said that Jason was impressionable and entitled and that he wanted that connection with the Lancefields because he thought he could screw something material out of it. He'd admitted to Emma that he'd searched for the Lancefield family on the internet, and discovered just how wealthy they are. The murders of Lucy and Philip didn't bother him at all. His interest was in Salvation Hall and the Woodlands Park estate.'

Kathryn laughed softly under her breath. 'I suppose it would be disloyal of me to suggest that he sounds like a chip off the old Lancefield block. At least when it comes to the Liverpool, ship-owning side of the family. But I couldn't say that about Barbara. She's a sweetheart.' Kathryn fell silent for a moment and then said, 'I don't think he would have hurt her, you know. He had plenty of opportunity to do so before we turned up.'

'We couldn't take that risk.' In truth, Price didn't share Kathryn's optimism. 'Did Barbara know that Jason had already seen the letters the night before Dennis died?'

'I think she might have guessed. But I don't understand how he could have seen them.'

'Jason told us that he went to visit Dennis, to discuss a piece of work they were planning to do for a customer later in the week. Dennis had popped out to the corner shop and left Jason alone in the house. And while he was there, he noticed that the bureau in the living room had been closed up and locked. That set him thinking because the bureau was never locked unless Dennis had something to hide. But what his father didn't know was that as a child Jason used to play with the lock, and practise opening it with a penknife. Curiosity got the better of him and he couldn't resist having another go.'

'And so he found Richard's letters locked inside?'

'The letters and the train tickets. When Dennis got back from the shop he confronted him and they argued, and the truth about his parentage came out. So he asked Dennis to lie for him, and Dennis refused. But he did offer to cancel the meeting.'

'Does Barbara know about that? She hasn't mentioned it.'

'I don't know. It's possible that Dennis Speed slept on it, and decided in the morning just to make the journey anyway. Either way, Jason didn't trust him. That's why he made his own way to Lime Street station, to see if Dennis turned up to catch the train. And when he did, Jason decided to stop him.' Price drew in a breath. 'I suppose now that Richard will think twice before trying to track down any more of his distant relatives.' He heaved out a sigh. 'And that you'll be going back to Cambridge in the not-too-distant future.'

'Then you still don't know me any better than you know Richard. I still have documents and artefacts to curate for two other lines of the family, one that settled in London and the other in Edinburgh. I have a fancy to tackle the Edinburgh one first. After all, I lived there myself for many years.'

Lived there, married there, and had her heart broken there. 'What about the bad memories?'

'Perhaps it's time to put those to rest. I can't run away from the past forever.'

Price leaned back in his seat. 'I can see why London might have more than its fair share of Lancefields, but Edinburgh? I can't imagine such a sophisticated and egalitarian city having much to do with slavery.'

'And you have the nerve to call me an innocent?' At the other end of the line, Kathryn Clifton let out an almost-girlish giggle. 'How are you fixed for tomorrow evening? It sounds to me as though we're going to have to meet for another history lesson…'

ABOUT THE AUTHOR

Mariah Kingdom was born in Hull and grew up in the East Riding of Yorkshire. After taking a degree in History at Edinburgh University she wandered into a career in information technology and business change, and worked for almost thirty years as a consultant in the British retail and banking sectors.

She began writing crime fiction during the banking crisis of 2008, drawing on past experience to create Rose Bennett, a private investigator engaged by a fictional British bank.

The Redemption is the second Lancefield Mystery.

www.mariahkingdom.co.uk

Printed in Great Britain
by Amazon

42246838R00148